A GRAND ADVENTURE
INTERPLANETARY

The moon was an inhospitable place. It had virulently hot days and the nights saw the temperature fall well below zero. There were also strange, often-dangerous creatures found on the lunar surface, not the least of which was a race of hostile elephantine creatures that roamed the craters after sunset. Yet in spite of these many dangers, man had conquered the moon and colonized its surface. The moon was rich in precious metals and for rugged, pioneering individuals, the opportunities were endless. So mankind came to the moon in droves, its human inhabitants safe in their glass-domed cities. But just as in the American Revolution, there came a day when the moon's inhabitants tired of the unfair policies of mother Earth and strove to break free. However, this time the oppressive forces came not from across the ocean but from across space itself. It was the dawn of the first interplanetary war! This then, is the fantastic tale of that conflict and of the men and women who fought back against the technologically weaponized space invaders who sought to suppress them.

CAST OF CHARACTERS:

JOHN ADAMS JR.
An adventurous soul, he never imagined the journey he would embark upon when his family migrated to the moon.

JOHN ADAMS SR.
A wise and optimistic man who knew the opportunities on the moon would be far greater than those on Earth.

GEORGE WARRINGTON
The top General of the lunar revolution, whose spirit of liberty propelled his troops forward even in the most trying times.

BENJAMIN GARDINER
The charismatic linchpin of the uprising, and whose inventive ideas and skilled diplomacy proved vital to the war efforts.

LAFOLLETTE
He had a healthy hatred of the Metals Corporation, and was gladly willing to help fund the moon's fight for independence.

PAUL DOANE
If he stayed alive long enough, he could become the admiral of a new fleet of spaceships that might turn the tide of the war.

LERODA VARDOM
She was hunted for her father's achievements and carried the secret of his brilliance for years to come.

JENKINS
A true wanderer who served as the consequential interlunar messenger with his great mooncalf M'Ob.

THE BIRTH OF A NEW REPUBLIC
Illustrated Edition

By
JACK WILLIAMSON &
MILES J. BREUER

ARMCHAIR FICTION
PO Box 4369, Medford, Oregon 97504

*The original text of this novel was first
published by Radio Science Publications*

Armchair Edition, Copyright 2021 by Gregory J. Luce
All Rights Reserved

*For more information about Armchair Books and products, visit our
website at…*

www.armchairfiction.com

Or email us at…

armchairfiction@yahoo.com

CHAPTER ONE
The New Frontier

NOW, in the last year of the twenty-fourth century, I am setting out to devote the final years of a long and active life to the writing of a narrative of my small part in the historic period just closing, which was perhaps the most important in human history. During my lifetime, the human colonies on the moon have grown from weak, scattered cities to the powerful and prosperous Lunar Corporation. I was in the midst of the terrible struggle in which the autonomy of that corporation was won; and it is my purpose to write what I saw of that greatest of wars as simply and justly as I can.

My story must begin with my father.

He was born in Pittsburgh in the year 2276. Even at that time, now over a century past, the United States of America, in common with the other political organizations that once had ruled the world, had ceased to have any real power over the people within its ancient boundaries. Pittsburgh was a stronghold of the Metals Corporation, one of the most powerful of the half-dozen huge trusts that now ruled the world.

It was typical of my father that he should decide, to migrate to the colonies on the moon. His pioneering spirit rebelled at the complex, well-ordered life of Earth. He was a deep thinker, in an original way; he had spent much of his youth roaming Earth in quest of an outlet for his restless energies of spirit. He was far too much of a philosopher to get any satisfaction out of the mockeries, and superficialities of life in the great cities of Earth.

Father was not the man to shut himself up behind a desk in a little glass cage for eight hours of every day, to provide himself with a golden fringe to his tunic and take his wife out to fashionable gatherings, where they would chatter of the latest risqué shows and bet on the rocket races, squander a working man's fortune at cards and dance themselves ragged to blaring jazz, to go home tipsy with "2,200 port." My parents were not that kind of people at all.

It is natural that they thought of emigration to the moon.

THE BIRTH OF A NEW REPUBLIC

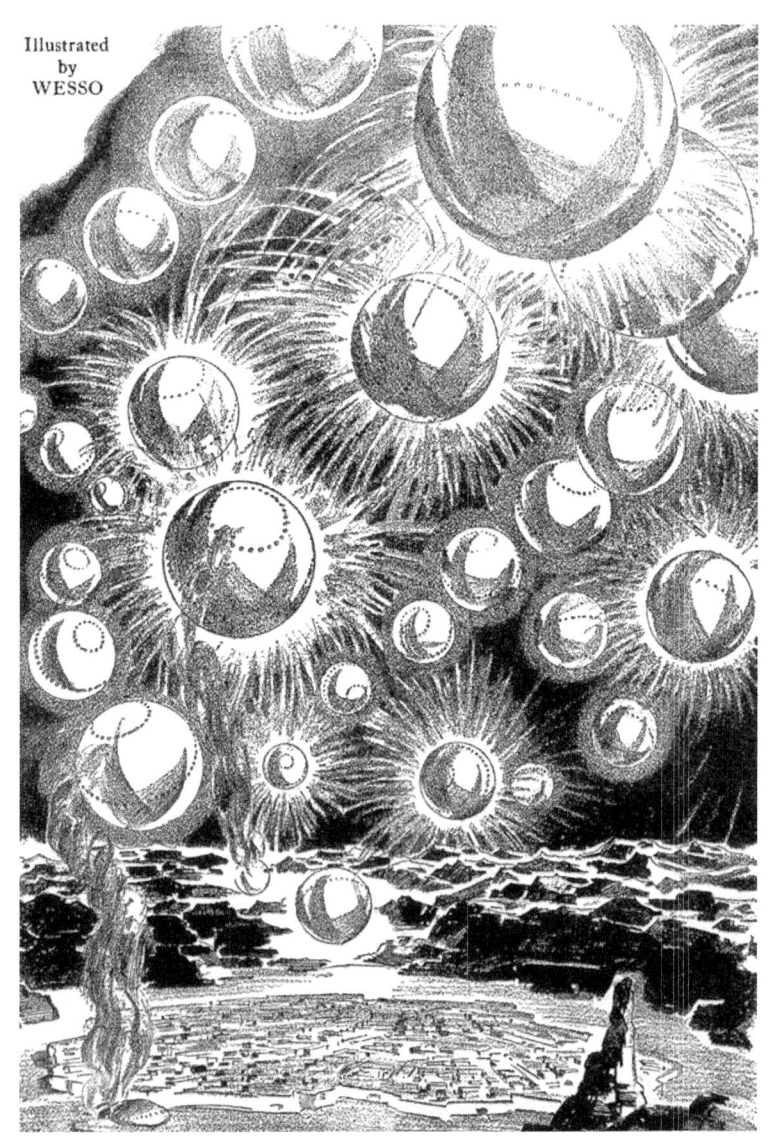

Illustrated by WESSO

"Only some twenty-odd of Van Thoren's globes came out."

There was a new world waiting. There, beyond a quarter of a million miles of space, hardy pioneers had opened up a new frontier, two centuries after the last frontier had vanished on Earth. Life was simple there and hard. Men were free from convention and artificial restraint. They lived close to nature. They fought for what life gave them, depending upon their hands instead of their purses. On the Earth's satellite was a new field for men with initiative and independence, men who could live and work beyond the protection of the machine. On the moon, a man was not a mere cog in the vast, clumsy wheels of society. When he had fought for a home and had won it, he could feel that it was truly his own.

Father was a trained engineer as well as a skilled workman with his hands. He was employed in the great laboratories of the Metals Corporation in Pittsburgh, in which were designed the automatons that each year did more of the routine work of Earth, leaving men more time for vicious idleness and inane recreation. His position was an enviable one in the eyes of his fellows. There was opportunity for advancement, for a salary that would enable his family to take a high place in the artificial society life of the corporation's capital, perhaps even an opportunity, if he showed executive and financial ability, for him to win a place on the Board of Directors.

I remember a fat, pompous, red-faced gentleman named Kieling, who was several times at our rooms—I think he was interested in some fantastic scheme for smuggling drugs from India by submarine and wanted Father to help design his apparatus. However that may have been, he had an excellent standing in Pittsburgh society. He displayed remarkable persistence in coming to see Father about his plan, in the face of every discouragement save actual breach of manners, of which my parent would never have been guilty.

He seemed incredulous when he heard that we were to emigrate to the moon. Young as I was—then hardly five—I remember sitting and looking up at the gross fellow as he sat twisting the blazing rings on his fat fingers and expressed his opinions of such an adventure.

"John, you mean to tell me you're goin' to throw over your job for a fool thing like that. The moon's just a desert—you've seen the movies of it. Hot as hell in the day and freezes the air at night.

Wild mountains, full of the damned Selenites, looking for a chance to kill and eat you.

"No comforts there—not a beach or a pleasure-palace on the whole damned planet. You're not even your own boss. Stay here and you may get to be a director of the corporation. On the moon you can't turn around without a confounded Colonial Secretary of the corporation to give you leave.

"But go ahead, for all of me. I'll wager Mrs. Adams can find another man." He grinned at my mother, who was sitting, primly composed in a rocking chair; then suddenly burst out into an uproarious laugh as if he considered that a joke.

Father said nothing. Kieling pulled out a huge black cigar, lit it, and puffed out a cloud of choking blue smoke before he went on.

"And think of the voyage. I wouldn't make it for a case of Bourbon! Not me! Cold, cramped little rooms, passengers crammed in like sardines. Keep you half suffocated. And the space sickness—one in a dozen dies, you know. The company doesn't give a damn, just so they get the passage money.

"You know Carlton—the Communications Fifth Vice President—he had the fool idea of taking his wife to the moon for a trip when they were married. She took space sickness and died—lack of vitamin J, the medics said. And Hamlin—he was a friend of mine—went on a collection trip to Colon and came back with his lungs wrecked. And Smith—he had been a Colonial Secretary on the moon for fourteen years—he was coming back with his family and a meteorite smashed the ship. Gone, just like that!" Kieling snapped his fat fingers.

My father straightened. "I know all about that," he said in his low, courteous voice. "But nearly two million people have gone to the moon and made a go of things there."

"Yeah! A hell of a 'go!' You've got to get out in the hills with the wild mooncalves and work like the devil for half what you'd get in an office right here. Out in the craters all day, living on a little canned stuff and roasting in the sun—then racing back to one of the shabby little towns to keep from freezing in those endless nights. John, you better think that proposition over again."

"That's settled, Kieling," father said briefly. "I'm having nothing whatever to do with it, no matter how safe your lawyers say it is."

"Dammit, John, I hope Boss Varney gets you—or I would if it weren't for your wife."

Then the conversation turned to Varney and those other famous pirates of space. Tales of them always enthralled me. They were bloody and desperate men, no doubt. But the peril and romance of their calling cast a peculiar lure upon it, and I think most boys of the time dreamed of the day when they might run away to space.

Varney was perhaps the most noted of them all. The tales of his exploits were legion. He had robbed a dozen rich ships. Once he had fought and destroyed a fleet of three space patrol cruisers in full view of New York City. A few years later he had captured the President of the Chemicals Corporation and his daughter, taking them from a liner he had run down on the space-lanes to the moon. He had treated them very hospitably until he could land them at a little village on the California coast. He was variously reported to have had his base of operations in the interior of Greenland, in the jungles of Brazil, in the Himalayas, and behind the moon. In the past thirty years a score of expeditions have been fitted out to search for his buried treasures. But, so far as I know, Varney's gold still lies wherever he may have hidden it; though I suspect that his lawless crews must have gambled and drunk a good deal of it away in the cities in Mexico, in the Orient and on the moon, in any place that was wild enough to tolerate them.

Kieling's remarks about conditions on the space fliers had some justification. They might have been better, but the Metals Corporation maintained a monopoly on trade with the moon and its warships of space ruthlessly rammed every other vessel caught in the lunar space-lanes. The construction and operation of space fliers were expensive, and the ships were crowded with those who could barely afford to pay the passage. Their comfort occasioned the officials of the line little concern.

As the fellow had said, meteorites were dangerous. During the hundred and fifty years of communication with the moon, a thousand ships had been destroyed by collision with these iron wanderers in space. No system of telescopes, searchlights, or radio beam detectors proved a complete safeguard against them. And again and again ships reached the spaceports wrecked and leaking the vital air, with the crews forced to wear oxygen helmets and the passengers dying in their quarters.

Even when the emigrant had been landed in one of the three great cities on the moon, his troubles were far from over. There was the pain and hardship of the physiological changes necessary to fit one for the lighter air and lesser gravity of the satellite. Long days in bed in a compression chamber, with the air pressure gradually lowered, torturing pains in the lungs, and a dull ache in the head for many weeks as the brain became accustomed to less pressure of gravity.

When Colon reached the moon there had been only a trace of air detectable. Since the mass of the satellite is only about one-eightieth that of the Earth and its diameter about one-fourth, the force of gravity at its surface is only about one-sixth of the terrestrial value.

Owing to that, the velocity of escape for the moon is only about one and a half miles per second, as compared to seven miles for Earth. Consequently, the satellite had lost most of her air in ages past; the kinetic theory demonstrates that molecules of air even attain the velocity of seven miles per second required to carry them free of the Earth's pull.

Colon and the other early explorers had relied on air pressure suits, with heating pads and oxygen helmets; and the first mining operations had been in shafts capped with airtight domes, in which could be maintained a normal atmosphere of artificial air. But as the mining industry increased, such methods were hardly satisfactory, and the officials of Metals sought for something better.

Cardigan, one of the first trained mining engineers to go to the moon, encountered and solved the question of artificial atmosphere. The native rocks of the Earth (and of the moon) are composed nearly to the extent of 50 per cent of the vital element, oxygen, held in combination. Cardigan developed a rapid process of liberating it from silicon dioxide and other abundant compounds; and with the limitless sources of atomic power available, his plants were soon turning out huge volumes of the gas.

Nitrogen, the other chief constituent of terrestrial air, is much less abundant in nature; but helium, which is one of the natural products of disintegrating atoms, was plentifully available, along with limited amounts of the other inert gases of its group, and was known to be vastly superior to nitrogen for diluting oxygen for breathing purposes, having been used for many centuries in preparing artificial air for divers in the oceans of Earth. It is less soluble in the blood than nitrogen and does not give the trouble called "the bends."

Cardigan also developed an efficient process for the synthesis of water from hydrogen and oxygen, to provide the requisite humidity for his new atmosphere. His great plants were kept going a quarter of a century before a sufficient atmosphere had been provided, and even now the artificial humidity freezes in the two weeks of the lunar night, though men go abroad during the long day, breathing comfortably.

Even after the emigrant became accustomed to the new conditions of gravitation and barometric pressure, there was a pioneer's rough life to face in the mines or the crater farms. One must start at the beginning, with an iron will to learn the ways of a new planet and fit himself to them. There was no place for the coward or the shirker.

Discomforts and perils were many. During the two weeks of the lunar day, the sunlight is intensely hot and blindingly bright. One swelters in white garments, sun helmets, and tinted glasses. And during the long night it is bitterly cold—so cold that the air grows solid, and falls in a crystal snow upon the rugged lunar mountains. During that terrible period of cold and darkness, the colonists were shut up in their sealed cities, and in the cheerless underground passages of the mines.

Outlawry was flourishing. Bandits had hidden retreats in the wild lunar deserts; smugglers of space regularly matched their wits against those of the commanders of the Metals warships; pirates of space—like Varney—relied for their livelihood upon their daring and their skill in the use of stolen disintegrator tubes.

The Selenites were another peril. Those native inhabitants of the moon were intelligent, savage beings, whose budding civilization had been ruthlessly crushed by the first adventurers on the moon. The more highly civilized and better-natured tribes had been worked to death in the mines. Those that had escaped slavery were, for the most part, bloodthirsty beings, roaming the lunar craters and deserts beyond the outlying human settlements, sometimes descending in bloody raids upon the miners and farmers, massacring whole settlements. There was constant bitter warfare between the settlers and these savage tribes of Selenites.

Such was life on the moon, as it appeared to the friends and associates of my father. His superior in the laboratories talked to him of his plans, outlined these disadvantages, and offered him a better position and higher pay immediately, if he would remain.

There were other things to think of. Mother was a slight, frail woman, for all the iron strength of spirit that shone in her deep blue eyes. She was willing enough to try life on the new planet, but father was afraid that the hardships of it would be too much for her health. Certainly she would be without the thousand luxuries that a mechanical civilization had given the world, until they seemed necessities.

The children were considered. I was five years old; my older sister, Valence, was twelve; and there was a baby girl, little Fay, aged two. Our parents feared that we would not survive the hardships of the voyage. And if we did, what of our education, our future? As we grew up, would we be willing to go without the opportunities of Earth, to be pioneers?

Father and mother talked to us of their plans, though of course I was too young to take much part in the discussion. The matter of emigration was under consideration for some time, and I believe an adventure of my own had a good deal to do with the final decision.

I had a little helicopter flier that father had given me on the Christmas before. Its propellers were operated, I think, from a compact storage battery. The talk of emigration had turned my mind to thoughts of travel, and one day I left the great community—a hotel in Pittsburgh—in which we lived, and flew out over the country. I had been told not to leave the park about the building, but that mattered little against the call of adventure. And the little machine had a safety device that was supposed to bring it down after a flight of two minutes; but I have always had a mechanical turn of mind, and I had been able to incapacitate that with a screwdriver.

With the urge for adventure strong in me, I flew out into the hills for a score of miles or so, before the battery ran down. Even at this period modern methods of communication and the Zaner processes for the artificial manufacture of crude carbohydrates, proteins, and fats, had largely ended the day of farming. Then, as now, the population was concentrated in the cities, and the countryside was a lonely and deserted waste.

I do not remember all the details of the incident, but it was two days before father found me. Fortunately, it was summer. I had found a briar patch, and made several meals on blackberries. My handkerchief was hung up on a pole to guide the searchers I expected. When father came, I had just managed, after a score of fruitless attempts, to kill a cottontail rabbit with a rock. I was industriously rubbing two sticks together with the idea of making a fire to cook it, having heard that savages used such a method. I was taken home, spanked, and cried over by my mother.

I believe that incident, with its display of self-reliance and hardihood, is what determined my father to undertake the emigration. At any rate, the next thing I knew, it was agreed that we were to start—much to my delight.

I remember a trip out to the great spaceport with mother. I can still see the great landing platforms before the hangars, with the cradles on their tracks in front of them. With childish eagerness, I looked forward to the time, when one of those great silver globes would carry me into the mystery of the sky.

It was agreed that we should emigrate to the moon. But before we got off, a very serious difficulty arose—a difficulty connected with the complex and highly artificial social organization of the world, with the relations of the great corporations that ruled the Earth. Not only were our plans disarranged, but father very nearly lost his life.

CHAPTER TWO
A Lecture on Lunar History

ONE evening, when he came home from the laboratory, father called Valence and me to him, and took brown-haired little Fay on his knee.

"I have a new record for the magnetic phonograph," he said, slipping a little spool of thin steel wire out of its case. "It tells about the moon, who found it, and how men are able to live there. Do you want to hear about the world we are going to in the big space flier, Johnnie?"

"Yes, Father. I'll try hard to understand."

Valence ran to get the little instrument, and adjust the spool in place. She pressed the switch, and set it on the table. A few bars of swift music came from the diaphragm, and then the suave voice of the announcer:

"An address on the history of the moon, covering events from the first attempts at interplanetary navigation to the present time, delivered by Professor Avery Smithton, of the Pan-American University."

A moment later the professor's words began, in a rich, lively voice, well in harmony with the mysterious appeal of his subject. I listened in rapt attention, to learn more of the wonderful world to which we were going.

"Crossing the gulf of space has always been one of the great dreams of man. In the great age of scientific progress, which began about five hundred years ago, a great deal of thought was given to the question. A French romancer, Jules Verne, brought considerable attention to the subject with a plausible tale of a voyage around the moon in a great projectile fired from an immense gun. A few years later, an English novelist, Wells, wrote his great classic, 'The First Men in the Moon.' Like an older writer, Jonathan Swift, with his 'Gulliver's Travels,' Wells was satirizing humanity; and, like Swift's, his satire has been forgotten for the interest of his story. Though science has never duplicated his compartments inside its rim, being rotated at sufficient speed for centrifugal force to replace partially the pull of gravity. At one end of the axis of the great wheel was the bridge room, at the other, the battery of atomic blast projectors.

"The departure was made at midnight. The literature of the age is full of descriptions of the scene. The men had gone aboard, and the air locks had been sealed after the last farewells. As the hour drew near, the field about the cradles of the ships was cleared of the vast crowd that had gathered to witness the first act of the great adventure. The ships lay there, huge silver balls, gleaming in the light of the full moon, strange and still.

"The propeller rays were turned on. Vast jets of intense white flame burst from beneath the globes, outlined them in blinding light. Clouds of luminous, weird-colored vapor whirled up about the globes—air bombarded by the radioactive particles became luminous of itself. Veiled in screens of shifting scarlet and green and amber fire, the silver globes stirred, lifted, shot upward.

"On our own day, the sailing of a space flier is hardly so spectacular. That was before the modern refinements in the atomic blast that have eliminated the secondary heat and light effects, with their vast loss of energy.

"In a few moments, the ships were out of sight, gone to mark an epoch in human history. For many minutes, vague mists of shining violet drifted about the field.

"Until radio communication was cut off by the Heaviside layer, the world was in touch with Colon. In fact, the ships were within telescopic view for several hours, during which time a few brief messages were sent from the heliograph on Colon's ship.

"Then long weeks and months went by, and nothing was heard from the explorers of space. In vain, astronomers studied the face of the moon for any sign of human arrival.

"It was four months later that the world was electrified by that famous laconic radiogram, 'Space is conquered and the moon is ours. Jean Colon.'

"That message awoke America at midnight. It meant that Colon was back inside the Heaviside layer. Within an hour, the blazing atomic blast of a space flier was visible over the great southwestern plantations of the Food Corporation; and by dawn, the world knew that Jean Colon, a hero overnight, had landed safely on the New Mexico deserts.

"Only one ship returned. One of the others had turned back, against the orders of the intrepid admiral. Crew and commander must have paid for the mutiny with their lives, for no trace of the ship has ever been found. Like a thousand others since, it must have been wrecked by meteoric collision. The other vessel, too badly wrecked in landing on the moon to be repaired, had been left as a sort of fortress, in which a few men stayed to garrison this new territory of the Metals Corporation.

"It was a strange and rich cargo that the single vessel carried. There were huge masses of yellow gold, and great nuggets of the three heavy metals that were now doubly precious, since they were the source of the power of the Earth. There was over a pound of radium, and specimens of a thousand minerals, some precious, some new to science. The moon, so stated the enthusiastic Colon, and truly, was a treasure house of minerals, a golden mine for the Earth.

"The ship carried strange plants and stranger moving things from the moon. Colon brought proof that the ancient astronomer, Pickering, had been correct in interpreting his observations as showing life in the craters of the moon. Some of the plants and the grotesque insect-like creatures were still alive, but none survived terrestrial conditions for more than a few days.

"The weirdest part of the astounding cargo was a dead, monstrous creature from the moon—one of the Selenites, a member of the ruling race of the moon, a being so huge and so formidable that the explorer had not attempted to bring it alive. But Colon had mounted his specimen, in a pose that suggested alien life. It had a huge, flimsy body, with long, slender legs, four in number. From its head depended a single, long tentacular appendage. There was something elephantine in the bulk of the thing; even in shape it vaguely suggested an elephant on stilts."

"A thing like what we saw in the museum, when we went to see the horse," I broke in again. But the professor's lively account went on relentlessly.

"The stories that Colon told of those creatures seemed incredible to the people of the time. They were intelligent, he said, far more intelligent than the elephants they remotely resembled. Their mentality must have approximated that of the Australian aborigine, called blackboy. The most of their kind were wild rovers of the lunar mountains, but one tribe, isolated in the crater of Archimedes, near which Colon had landed, were developing an elementary civilization, learning the use of simple tools, and building rude shelters. Most of the gold and platinum on the ship Colon had taken from them, giving them a few bits of food in return—the terrestrial foods, especially the carbohydrates, being foreign to the chemical nature of the Selenites, produced in them a curious state of intoxication.

"Those mooncalves, or Selenites, as they came to be called, are far different from the life of Earth, even based upon compounds differing radically from the protoplasm of terrestrial life. The scaly red skin composed largely of silicon compounds, that covered their huge, clumsy bodies, was hard and tough, because of the sharp rocks among which they lived—it was proof against the bullets of the primitive firearms with which Colon had attacked them. But that tough, crimson integument was transparent to ultraviolet light—it has since been demonstrated that these beings draw most of their energy from the sun. The jaws were short and terrifically strong, armed with conical teeth hard enough to grind the rock from which these creatures derive the matter from which they are made.

"The four legs, which support the elephantine body, are oddly long, for jumping the wide crevasses of the moon. The huge eyes, three in number and situated above the trunk-like or elephantine member, are remarkable for their size and for the conspicuous green iris diaphragm, which adapts them for vision both in the dark nights and in the blinding light of day.

"Colon made several more voyages in the larger ships that were soon built by the score. The Earthward surface of the moon was explored; science was enriched with countless specimens of minerals, fauna, and flora from the moon. The markets of the world were flooded with huge supplies of precious metals captured from the more civilized tribes of Selenites. The huge revenue that the Metals Corporation drew from its lunar possessions enabled it to throw off the last vestiges of political control, and take its place at the head of the new Union of Corporations.

"What does it matter if moralists say that the conquerors did wrong in destroying the most cultured races of the mooncalves, for the sake of a little precious metal? Corporations have souls no more than nations have them.

"A Moon Company, subsidiary to Metals Corporation, was quickly organized. It ruled and exploited the moon as the British East India Company had governed and fattened upon India for two centuries after the expansion of European power.

"In a dozen years after Colon's landing on the moon, space fliers laden with bands of adventurers had overrun all the Earthward face. Two great nations of Selenites, possessing culture that, according to recent 'lunarcheologists' had developed to a surprisingly high degree, had been conquered, robbed, and enslaved in the mines.

"The most remarkable, perhaps, of these lunar nations, was that of the K'Inva, in the great crater of Tycho. One of the most interesting topographical features of the lunar surface is this annular crater, 150 miles in diameter, situated at 43° South, 12° East. It is surrounded by a perfect ring of cliffs 15,000 feet high, and from it radiate the white 'rays' which so puzzled terrestrial astronomers until it was shown that they were Selenite roads. Protected by the cliffs, the tribe called K'Inva had built up a marvelous culture in this crater. Conquered, despoiled, and enslaved by Count Vauban and his lawless followers, kept in subjection by intoxication with artificial carbohydrates that wrecked their physical and mental powers, and worked to death in the mines, hardly a one of them was left alive in a hundred years, and now hardly a memory of them survives.

"However, bands of the ferocious wild tribes, the K'Larbah and others, still roam the lunar deserts, sometimes doing a little useful work for the human prospectors and miners, who use them as beasts of burden, but more often intoxicated with the synthetic carbohydrates with which they are paid for their labors, they run amuck, committing frightful outrages."

"Oh yes, I read a story about that," Valence's sweet voice chimed in. " *The City Behind the Moon!* A ship was wrecked on the back of the moon. There was a brave man named Charlie. He fought a lot of the wild mooncalves, and saved a girl named Lydia. He carried her and ran. The night was coming, and the mooncalves were running behind him. He came to a city of silver towers, where nobody—"

But the phonographic lecture went steadily on, and father held up his hand to silence her report on the wild romance.

"—years went by. The Moon Company began the importation of human labor. At first the tendency was to send only criminals and undesirables generally. But as civilization became more complex, and the corporations began to encroach more and more on the rights and privileges of the individual, there were many who were willing to pay their own passage to the moon, to win new freedom.

"These hardy settlers found and worked new mines of their own, when the new lunar atmosphere enabled them to live without spacesuits, trading the metal to the Moon Company for food and supplies from the Earth. Farming, on a limited scale, was undertaken in the arable craters; some of the native plants of the moon produce drugs which command a high price in the markets of Earth. Manufacturing, though discouraged by the Metals Corporation, was undertaken; and now vast quantities of simple synthetic foods are manufactured on the moon, as well as a variety of metal commodities.

"The Moon Company, originally a small corporation subsidiary to Metals, is now almost altogether in the hands of the inhabitants of the moon, since the Lunar cities, as well as the more prominent citizens of the moon, have from time to time purchased blocks of stock, with a view to controlling all their own affairs.

"Metals has never made public the secret of Orloff and Smith's atomic blast, and the projecting engines had never been placed on sale; hence the corporation maintains a virtual monopoly on trade with the moon, and the directors feel sure of their ability to control the settlers, even while humoring them by letting them have the stock of the Moon Company.

"There are, however, many crews of pirates and smugglers, operating space fliers, that had been obtained by fraud or capture, with which they carried on a lucrative illegal trade, escaping from

Metals' warships, and sometimes capturing a vessel laden with precious metals or equipment. The trade of piracy seems to have no particular dishonor attached to it, though pirate ships are rammed, when possible, on sight, and captured crews are electrocuted.

"At present, the population of the moon is nearly two and a half million; there are three great cities, Theophilus, Colon, and New Boston, and scores of smaller settlements. The satellite represents an excellent market for terrestrial manufactures; and the value of the metals and chemicals received from the moon is of incalculable value to the Earth's industry.

"Recently there have been hints that the lunar population is becoming discontented with the strict rule of the agents of Metals, and that there is dissatisfaction with the prices paid for metals on the moon, which average less than half their value in Pittsburgh. The speaker cannot recommend too strongly that every means be used to foster the former good feelings between the two planets. It is hard to visualize a greater tragedy for the Earth than the loss of the resources she has been drawing for so long from the moon."

The lively, animated voice stopped abruptly, as the professor had worked his way up to a current political issue. A few brisk bars of music came from the little machine. Then a clear female voice began to speak rapid, persuasive comments upon Cynguff's Synthetic Beverage Tablets. "A pitcher of water and a purple pill! What shall it be, whisky or cognac, bourbon or gin?" Father pushed the switch, and the words stopped in the middle of a sentence.

"Johnnie and Valence, that's the moon, the big world where we're going. We may have a hard life there. But I know that you children will grow to be fine, strong men and women. That's the thing mother and I are living for—"

"Oh, I see it outside the window," I cried.

I pointed my childish arm to the bright, mottled silver disk, floating huge and mysterious above the trees in the park.

CHAPTER THREE
War between Corporations

IT was late in the year 2306 that my father made his decision to emigrate to the moon. He arranged for passage on the great ship *Venus,* of two hundred feet diameter, which was to sail in August, 2307. Father was moderately wealthy. Though the rates of passage to the moon were rather high, his fortune was great enough to pay our fare and leave funds for the purchase of a mining prospect and machinery on the moon.

But, before the time for our departure, a serious difficulty arose.

The Transportation Corporation, or "Tranco," as it is more usually termed, had long been jealous of Metals over the space lines to the moon. Over a hundred years before, when the great trusts had ended a century of warfare by the formation of the Union, it had been agreed that Tranco would have a monopoly of transportation on the Earth. And Tranco had always claimed that the operation of space fliers to the moon, by Metals, was a violation of that ancient agreement. Blood had been shed over the matter a score of times; but since Metals had never revealed the secret of the atomic blast projector, its rival was helpless to build space fliers of its own.

To present the situation clearly, I must outline briefly the decline of political government and the rise of the corporations.

The League of Nations had successfully prevented war among the nations after the first half of the twentieth century, and gradually the great standing armies of the world were done away with. In the meantime, the power of the corporations was growing steadily, and presently, as the old political governments grew too weak to enforce law and order, the armed guards and watchmen of the corporations had taken the places of policemen and soldiers.

By the time of the first successful voyage to the moon, the real power of political government was ended throughout the Earth, although certain of the old national organizations continue to exist in name, and some of them, such as the United States, exert considerable moral influence, even though devoid of any real authority.

For two centuries great confusion existed under the control of the corporations. At times their wars threatened to destroy the age of industry that had ended the old political regime. The development of the disintegrator ray (or the "D-ray")—an offshoot of the discovery of Orloff and Smith—made war so terribly destructive that at last the corporations saw it to their advantage to maintain the peace.

Shortly after 2200, a series of great mergers resulted in the formation of a half dozen huge corporations, each controlling one commodity over the entire Earth. Of these, the greatest was the Metals Corporation, which was already drawing vast revenues from the moon, though the Food, Power, and Transportation Corporations were formidable rivals.

The Food Corporation had come into possession of most of the farming lands of Earth, Metals claimed the mining sections and the great manufacturing cities, Transportation owned seaports and rights-of-way, Power owned cities and transmission lines. Each corporation maintained a vast army of guards to see that its property and trade rights were not encroached upon, and the complexity of the map furnished room for a thousand disputes.

Early in 2307, months before the time set for our departure for the moon, officials of the Metals Corporation were much perturbed by a rumor that the secret of the atomic blast projector had been rediscovered, and that the discoverer was disposing of the long-kept secret to the Transportation Corporation.

At first the report was indignantly denied by Tranco. But Metals possessed, at that time, a system of espionage that is probably the most perfect that has ever been devised. Within a few weeks, the fact was discovered that one of the great floating islands, designed by Tranco engineers centuries ago, to facilitate transoceanic aerial communication, had been moved to a lonely position in the South Pacific, and had some secret activity going on upon it.

Spies succeeded in reaching the island, and brought back the news that eight space fliers were in course of construction there.

When the news was made public, the greatest excitement reigned. Men were loyal to the corporations with a real loyalty. Men loved Metals or Tranco with an affection as deep as that which their ancestors had had for England or America. Soldiers were willing to fight for their corporation not only for pay, but because they believed in it, loved it, because their homes and their lives depended upon its defense.

My father was as patriotic as any man; at the first threat of war, he hastened to volunteer to enter the forces of Metals Corporation, even though it meant indefinite postponement of his plans for emigration.

I remember very clearly the day when he came home, at an unusual hour in the afternoon, with tears in his eyes to tell mother and Valence and me that he had entered the army, that he had to go away that night. For long hours we sat in our little drawing room in the great hotel. Father held me in his lap. They talked of our plans, and how they had failed. Then father kissed us all and went away. I saw the hopefulness and forced cheer of the parting; the fear and the tragedy of it I did not understand until long after.

The next day the great city was oddly still, and a fleet of spaceships floated like silver bubbles in the air above it. Those who had not been called to war gathered in little groups and talked, usually in tones unconsciously lowered, though sometimes there was shouting and hysterical laughter. Metals and Tranco were at each other's throats, in a struggle that had flared up, almost overnight.

We saw none of the fighting in Pittsburgh. But there was much hand-to-hand conflict, with heavy loss of life, in localities where men of both corporations were living side by side. New York, Galveston, London, Tokyo, and Perth—great seaports owned by Tranco—had been swept by "D-rays" from the space fliers of the Metals Corporation, and by way of retaliation, the air fleets of Tranco dealt considerable damage by dropping bombs on the territory of Metals that was not protected by fleets of space fliers.

Before the end of the day, a treaty of peace had been concluded. Such a war was too deadly to last for long without the ruin of Earth. Tranco was compelled to yield the victory, since the floating island, with all the unfinished ships upon it, had been destroyed by a fleet of Metals's space fliers.

The rediscoverer of the atomic blast, one Dr. Vardon, had perished on the island, it became known. It was said that he had a family, a wife, and baby daughter, who had been left in America. But no trace of them was found by agents of Metals.

Tranco had to acknowledge defeat, since it seemed that everyone to whom Vardon had revealed his discovery had died with him.

It was several weeks before we heard from my father. Mother must have been in the most acute anxiety under the fear that he had been killed, but heroic woman that she was, she let Valence and me know nothing of it. It was long years later that she told me of the horror of her days of waiting, of the dreams of her restless nights. To us she was always cheerful and smiling, with the promise that father would soon be back.

At last she heard that he was on a hospital island off Borneo, convalescing from the effects of exposure to the D-ray. This ray, beyond its deadly range, produces severe burns, resembling those of the X-ray or of radium, coupled with temporary blindness and a curious nervous disorder.

Father was among the hundreds of wounded men picked up from the crew of a space flier that had been sent down in the last attack on the fortified floating island. His vessel had carried on after the side of it had been cut away by the disintegrator rays, and been the first to break through the screen-ray defense.

Picked up with his dead and wounded fellows from the floating wreck of the ship, he had lain for many days unconscious and unidentified. At last, he had come to on the hospital island and had been able to give his name. He was immediately put in telephone communication with my mother, and we heard his dear voice coming over the wires. The entire time mother had told us that he was well—I wondered why she laughed and cried so much, by turns, when we heard.

There were more long weeks of waiting, before he was able to leave the island. Mother thought of going to be with him, but he would hear nothing of it, insisting that she stay with us children.

I remember very well the day he came back, a tall, slim young man, his face strangely drawn and pain-furrowed, not smooth and tanned as it had been. But still he could laugh. He brought me a wonderful toy he had found somewhere in the shops of the East; and his return was a splendid holiday.

It was several months before he was able to be up very much—his convalescence was alarmingly slow. As the time for the sailing of the *Venus* drew near, his cheerfulness grew more forced, and even a child as I was, I realized that something was the matter.

But still my parents let me have the pleasure of packing and repacking my toys for the trip to the moon. They did not tell me that the greatest specialists of the day were doubtful of father's complete recovery, that they thought he would never be able to stand the hardships of the long voyage to the satellite.

One splendid evening, he came down from the landing platforms with a triumphant smile on his tired face. He told mother of an examination by a great radiotherapist, who had given him a new treatment, and promised complete recovery. He might even be able to start on the *Venus*, as we had planned.

At last came the month of August, and the week and the day of sailing. I remember very clearly my impatience, my delight when the doctors said father could go, and the thrills of packing my baggage. My dearest possession, the little helicopter, had to be left behind, because it would be too heavy to fly in the thin air of the moon. But in the thrill of setting out, I was reconciled even to that loss.

We left the little bare room, which looked so strange with the familiar articles of furniture taken away, and ascended to the landing platforms. From there we went by air to the great landing place for the spaceships, beyond the city. All the vast, strange spaceport, with its whisper of machines and hum of human voices, its platforms laden with the bright metal ingots and the strangely scented bales of costly drugs from the moon, and stacked with the wooden crates of food and luxuries and machinery consigned to the lunar cities—the picturesque confusion of it all was a little terrifying to me, and I held mother's hand, while father carried little Fay.

Father showed our tickets at the gate and as we went through, I remember worrying about why we didn't carry our baggage along with us. We walked out on the vast, high-walled field, with the colossal, white ships scattered over it like titanic balls of polished silver.

A freighter was just coming in from the moon. The spidery steel framework of the landing platform was extended, a great slender tower in the center of the field, a mile away from us, supporting the great cradle five hundred feet in the air. With the others, I watched the morning sky above. A white speck, tiny and bright, drifted into the blue abyss. For a time it seemed to hang still in the sky, growing larger and brighter. At last I could see it as a tiny white ball, lit on the east by the morning sunshine until it looked like a little crescent moon, and veiled in the weirdly colored mists of the atomic blast which was checking its fall. Amazingly, it grew vast, dropping toward the platform. The two hundred-foot globe struck the cradle, which swung down as the tower folded into its foundation, yielding to the momentum of the mighty ship of space, catching it as a skilled player does a ball.

It takes a skilful pilot, indeed, to bring a space flier down on the ground, or on the rocky surface of the moon, without a wreck. But there is one class of men, the pirates, and smugglers of the space-lanes, who, because they never have the use of elaborate landing towers, are perforce experts at it.

Now the cradle, on its great rollers, was moved off the platform, which had sunk level with the field, carrying the silver ship to the warehouses at the edge of the wide enclosure. And another cradle, with a vast argent sphere upon it, was moved to the platform top.

"That is the *Venus*," father said. "That is the ship that will carry us to the moon."

CHAPTER FOUR
The Voyage to the Moon

ODDLY enough, though it was all the most thrilling experience of my early life, I have no clear memory of our going aboard. I have but one or two pictures. One of the vastnesses was the

"The two-hundred-foot globe struck the cradle, which swung down as the tower folded into its foundation."

*Illustrations by
H. W. Wesso*

mirror-like surface of the ship that bulged out above us as we stood at the base of the steps which reached up to the circular opening. Another, of the inside of the vessel, huge, strange, naked machines of great bare girders, of uncovered metal plates with rows of rivet heads, of sharp, bright lights blazing here and there in a gloomy confusion of exposed metal things. It was somehow like a forbidden glimpse of the vitals of some huge monster. And it all had a curiously topsy-turvy aspect—floors tilted or inverted, hand rails and ladders everywhere.

Then I remember the bare little room in the rim of the great wheel that formed the core of the ship. It was an amazing place to my young mind, with its two floors—one now a wall—with its beds, table, and electric stove fastened in place, yet ingeniously contrived to be tilted over for use when that vertical wall became the floor.

But soon the novelty wore off. We had but the single little room, reached by a sort of ladder from the elevator tube that was the axis of the ship. There were no windows—I could not see beyond the white walls lit by our single light. And it was very still.

I remember sitting there a long time, after we had come aboard, dangling my feet from the edge of one of the bunks, and watching my shadow on the unbroken wall. Father had gone out, and Valence had tagged along behind him. Mother was holding Fay in her arms, crooning to her. The strangeness and the stillness grew terrible.

When father and Valence returned, I learned that we had not left the Earth. They had hardly entered from the ladder when a brisk metallic voice shouted from a little black disk on the wall, "The *Venus* ascends in three minutes. Passengers are advised to prepare for the shock."

Father made us all lie down on the beds. Suddenly I felt immensely heavy, as the folding tower raised the cradle, catapulting the ship into, the air. For many minutes the sensation of excess weight continued, as the atomic blast projectors were building up our speed to the velocity of seven miles per second, necessary to escape the gravitation of the Earth.

Then came again the harsh, metallic voice from the wall, "Warning! Acceleration is about to cease. The centrifugal wheel will be set in rotation. Passengers will prepare for the change."

Strangely, I felt myself grow lighter and lighter, until I almost floated off the bed. The sensation was strangely terrifying—I felt that I was falling headlong, that all about me was falling too. There was a peculiarly unpleasant sensation in my stomach.

Then presently I felt another force that was pulling me out against the side of the room that had seemed a wall a moment before. Now, suddenly, it seemed to be down, and the other floor was vertical. Now I could see the need of the ladder that came down into our room from the center of the ship. The great wheel had begun to turn; centrifugal force was drawing us toward its rim.

In a few moments we were standing on that new floor. The force due to the wheel's rotation was only about one-sixth that of gravity (or about the same as the pull of the moon). It was intended not only to make it possible to walk naturally, to sit or to lie down, to eat and to handle liquids, but to guard against that form of space sickness which is caused by the reduced pull of gravity on the brain and the fluids of the semicircular canals in the ear.

I tried to walk and made an amazing discovery. I sailed half across the little room, and fell sprawling on the floor, yet so softly, that I was not hurt. When I had mastered my balance, I found that I could perform the wildest feats of jumping—I could float to the ceiling and sail down very easily.

But in half an hour, space sickness began to come upon me, hastened perhaps, by my activity. I felt sickness and nausea, a horrible sensation of headlong falling, and a dull, intolerable ache in the head. I was too sick to eat—or even sit up—when a steward brought us food in a great vacuum container.

The ship's doctor came in. He was a fat, kindly man, with crossed eyes and a little red mustache. He laughed and joked with my father, and talked to me while he was taking my temperature. Then he gave me a dose of something bitter that had to be washed down with a glass of water, and told me to go to sleep, which I presently did, feeling utterly miserable because I was too sick to listen to his talk.

When I woke up I felt a little better, though I had a leaden, throbbing ache in the head for many days, until my brain was accustomed to the lessened pressure of gravity. I found father and mother both sitting up, and mother was holding little Fay, who was crying fretfully; and Valence had opened a trunk to get some pictures and bits of bric-a-brac to adorn the bare walls of the little room.

LONG days went by, measured only by father's watch, and by the time we slept, and by the coming of the man with the vacuum tubes of food. In a day or two, our bodies were largely adjusted to the lightened gravity; but another kind of space sickness came upon us.

It was that due to the lack of vitamin J, which is found in natural air, but not in the artificial air of the spaceships. It is thought to be formed by the action of certain unidentified bacteria working in green plants, and all efforts to synthetize it have been in vain.

The symptoms of this form of space sickness are more severe and more alarming than those of the other. They include anemia, rapid breathing, and palpitation of the heart, and a greenish hue of the complexion. Unless oxygen is administered, death is almost certain. And in spite of the best the doctors could do, fully one in twelve of the passengers to the moon at that time died of the malady.

Some have a higher natural resistance to it than others. My parents and Valence and I were only slightly affected, and the kindly old doctor assured us of our safety. But the case of little Fay was more serious. He shook his head doubtfully when we asked him about her.

Several times the good fellow stayed with the sick child and sent the four of us to the deck for exercise. We climbed the ladder to the hollow axle of the great wheel, and then—utterly free of weight—we drew ourselves along it to a great metal floor at the top of the globe. All about the edge were tiny windows.

I remember looking out into space—deepest midnight flecked with flashing stars, an abyss of utter blackness, in which the many-colored stars swam cold and motionless and very bright. Father pointed out the Earth. It was a huge globe of misty green, splotched with patches of startling white. I asked to see the sun, was told that it was so bright that it would blind me to look upon it.

I believe that it was on our fourth day out that a strange ship was sighted. The sunlight, gleaming on the polished shell of a spaceship, makes it visible telescopically for hundreds of miles; and we passed far around the stranger. It seemed to be hanging still, as though waiting; and the officers feared that it was a pirate of space.

It did not pursue us, but our change in course was probably responsible for the accident that did take place. The men at the telescopes were watching the strange ship and a meteorite struck the ship.

I remember the thundering crash of the collision, and the sickening lurch of the ship. Then there was a thin, whistling scream, the sound of our precious air hissing out into space. For a moment, that was the only sound; then I heard a medley of shouts of alarm and screams of terror from the passenger quarters about us in the rim, and the stern commands of the ship's officers.

Fortunately, the inner shell of the ship had not been seriously torn, and soon the break was repaired. Mechanics in spacesuits went out through the air locks and replaced the reflector surface which had been ripped off by the glancing blow of the hurtling stone.

The worst effect of the accident was the psychological one. The blow had been very sudden. No man knew when another iron wanderer of space might come tearing into the ship. The nervous strain grew intolerable. Many of the passengers grew hysterical under the strain, and there were two suicides.

I remember meeting the family in the next compartment. They were poor people—farmers who had left the great Iowa plantations of the Food Corporation. The father, two grown sons, and a daughter had bound themselves to work long periods for the Metals Corporation, to pay for the passage of the family. They were honest, cheerful people, and some degree of friendship sprang up between our families.

But in these long, lonely days in the crowded, uncomfortable compartments, when every passenger was suffering somewhat from space sickness, and from the ever-present fear of meteoric collision, there was little room for social pleasures.

The Earth seemed very remote; one felt almost as if it had ceased to exist. All the world of men, which once had been of such vital concern, was gone. The life that we had known seemed a fading page of half-forgotten history. The cramped ship, with all its discomforts and terrors, was the only real thing. It was almost as if we were dead and in the tomb.

Hope—the Mecca of the Moon—was all that made it endurable.

My little sister, Fay, was still sick. For long weeks we cared for her, hoping that she would last until the end of the voyage would bring a chance for recovery. But on the nineteenth day, when we were but three days from the satellite, she died.

In the two years that she had lived, I had come to love her very dearly, and her death—when at last I understood what it meant—left a dull, restless pain in my heart. All the night after, mother sat crying, and father walked up and down the room, with a strange drawn look on his face. But after that, they showed little outward signs of grief.

There was another funeral—there had been many of them during the voyage. With the few friends we had on board, we gathered about the little wrapped body on the great metal deck above the rotating centrifugal wheel. The captain of the vessel, a lean, hard-faced man, read a short service. Then men in oxygen helmets and spacesuits took up the tiny coffin, and carried it through the air lock, and tossed.

There were three more long, sad days. The nervous strain, the loneliness, the monotony, the sensation of separation from all humanity grew almost intolerable.

Then the broad face of the moon widened out very rapidly before us. It was very welcome, for all the rugged cruelty of its sheer mountain and rocky desert. A strange world of midnight shadow and blazing sunlight. The sun's rays are not diffused by the thin air of the moon; the shadow of a mountain is a world of chill night, even when there is bright, hot daylight all about it.

A great city of the moon was soon in view. It was Theophilus, situated in the crater of that name, before the three great peaks that tower up three miles high in the center of the crater. Here my parents had elected to make their beginning in the new world. Standing on the white rugged plain, that was cut with ragged fissures, pitted with miniature craters, blazing in the white sunshine, the vast city of glass seemed very bright and beautiful—like a great diamond lost in the desert.

We swept lower over it, over the miles of unbroken roof of transparent glass that protected the city from the cold of the night preventing the escape of its vital air, and shielding it, as well, from the heat of the midday sun.

How strange it was to see little white-clad figures moving over that vast roof, or over the swarthy deserts about it, to see the dark specks of machines crawling over the slender white roads that radiated from the city's air locks! Human beings like ourselves!

We neared the landing field that was like a harbor to the city. Our ship dropped into the cradle on the slender tower, and was safely lowered to the surface. The voyage was at an end.

CHAPTER FIVE
Life on the Moon

IN a few hours, we were walking through the strange streets of Theophilus. A vast contrast it was to the gloomy monotony of the space flier! The streets were straight and wide, and bright with the sunlight that streamed through the glass roof supported on the tops of the pyramidal buildings. The wide-spaced structures, of opaque glass and stone and metal, were neat and brightly colored. Below their many-windowed walls were strips of the unfamiliar lunar vegetation—strange shrubs, great fantastic trees, vividly colored of leaf and bloom, lending a breath of sharp fragrance to the cool air.

At every corner was a passage through which one could descend to the endless moving ways, which carried passengers and goods beneath the streets.

How good it was to see the sunlight, the strange exuberant buildings, the vivid, flowering plants! And the people, strolling or hurrying, happy or sober, vivacious or silent! It was wonderful to be near humanity again, to feel in touch with its joys and cares.

After we had breathed the fresh, cleanly fragrant air for a few hours, the weakness and the misery of our space sickness vanished. Soon father had found rooms for us, in a great building similar to the community hotels of Earth, in which we had regular automaton service.

It was early in the fortnight-long lunar day when we arrived, ten Earth days before the sun set. (The twenty-four-hour period of Earth's rotation has continued to be the most convenient measure of time on the moon, for the spinning Earth hangs like a great dial in the lunar sky.) It seemed very strange to me to go to sleep in our pleasant new room with the sun still shining, to wake and find its mellow rays still flooding the bright, weird vegetation of the park below my window.

Valence stayed with mother, while father took me with him on his trips about the city, and out into the mountains. He told me much about the life and organization of the moon, of the two other great cities, Colon and New Boston, of the rule of the Moon Company, formerly a branch of Metals Corporation, and now owned by the incorporated cities of the moon.

During the long voyage, our bodies had become pretty well accustomed to the decreased force of gravity, but now we had to become acclimated to the lighter barometric pressure on the moon. During the two weeks of the lunar night, when the air freezes on the mountains, the barometer falls almost to zero; and even during the day, when the sun has evaporated the frozen air again, the pressure is only a small fraction of that of the Earth's atmosphere. For several weeks we were under medical care, and were compelled to spend several periods in the compression chambers, where, in a synthetic atmosphere of oxygen and helium, with a pressure approximating that of Earth, the distressing symptoms—pain in the lungs, gasping, panting, and also palpitation of the heart—were relieved, and the oxygen in our blood streams was replenished.

The Moon Company had offices in each of the three great cities of Theophilus, New Boston, and Colon, which were the only points on the moon at which landing towers had been constructed for spaceships. At first the agents sent out from Earth had, as a matter of course, enjoyed autocratic power over the moon. But during later years, the increasing number of free colonists who owned their own mines, hired their own labor from human or Selenite, and sold their own metal, had developed a spirit of freedom which had resulted in the local ownership of the Moon Company stock, which resulted in comparative freedom.

The Board of Directors of the Moon Company, composed entirely of lunar citizens, took part in the city governments, in the erection and maintenance of the glass roofs necessary to prevent the escape of the air at night, and bargained with the agents of Metals to keep up the prices paid for the product of the lunar mines and farms.

Owing to the freezing of the air at night, there was no life or travel outside the cities or the mines after the sun went down. Mine owners, farmers, ranchers, and prospectors, gathered in the cities during the long nights, to enjoy the fruits of their toil. The streets were thronged with rough-clad men, and there was much of amusement and glee.

This condition had prevented the spread of humanity evenly over the moon; people were gathered compactly in the three great cities, where they were directly under the eyes of the Metals Corporation's agents, and where their voices might most influence the Directors of the Moon Company.

From the air locks of each great city, smooth highways spread out over the lunar deserts in a network that ran over mountain and crater, connecting all the human settlements on the moon. With the coming of day, these roads were crowded with the atomic-powered "automobiles" of farmer, miner, and prospector; and soon a regular stream of great trucks laden with metals and ores and farm products was flowing back to the city.

The Selenites, the native creatures of the moon, indeed ruled its surface by night. Their cunning had led the warlike tribes—the Ka'Larbah, M'Dawils, and others—to a policy of hiding by day, in the deep caverns and rilles, to come out upon marauding expeditions, when night had driven men to the cities. Many of them, however, were regularly employed to work in mines and crater forms, even to police those at night against their raiding fellows.

I remember very clearly the first one of them I saw. It was on the moon-day of our arrival, while father and I were strolling about the strange streets beneath the glass roof, absorbing the wonders of the odd stepped buildings, the weird vegetation, and the gathering crowds of moon-folk.

The monster came striding down the street. It was oddly like a great red elephant on stilts. The body was huge and flimsy, covered with the rough red skin. The legs were incredibly long and slender, and the trunk-like tentacular limb hung down from the great head, almost to the pavement. Above the trunk, the three huge green eyes, large as plates, were glowing expressionlessly from beneath a horny red carapace.

The thing came on past, swaying awkwardly, yet moving with amazing speed. As it passed, the great flat eyes were turned toward us for a moment, and the trunk swayed up and down in an odd manner—a gesture of greeting, as I afterward learned. The mooncalves have little sense of hearing, and only rudimentary organs of speech; they communicate largely with motions of the long, snake-like trunk. The settlers imitate their sign language with their hands, and so get on with them after a fashion.

Slung over the broad scaly back of the creature was a sort of saddle of some rough fabric, in which I saw a few bags of synthetic flour and sugar—the mooncalves are inordinately fond of all carbohydrates, and invariably demand them as pay for services rendered to the colonists. And these carbohydrates have an intoxicating effect upon them, frequently leading even those ordinarily peaceful to the perpetration of bloody outrage.

WE had been on the moon ten days when night fell. The sun, sinking ever so slowly, crept behind the mountains. At once the world was dark, and swiftly it grew cold. A light fall of frost and snow silvered the desert, and soon the mountains were capped with frozen air.

The air locks of the city had been sealed, and the great atomic lights filled the streets with a soft radiance that shimmered on the glass above. Atomic heaters kept the city warm, and still the streets were jovial with the vivid hues of the strange vegetation, and the warm, pure air fragrant with the exotic odors of it.

From the streets, through the transparent roof, we could see Earth, far to the northeast of the zenith. Four times as far across, it seemed, as the moon had seemed when I saw it from our old home, and of a color that is indescribably beautiful—a soft, liquid green, with the vague outlines of the continents dimly visible

THE BIRTH OF A NEW REPUBLIC

through a film of misty emerald fire. A broad crescent of it was bright with sunlight, the other side dark in shadow, with the region between lit with soft rosy colors of incredible wonder.

There is terror in the fall of a lunar night, though in the warm city I hardly realized it. Awful eternity beckons in the deliberate sinking of the sun. As the blue luminary nears the rugged horizon, it becomes a deep and bloody red. The sapphire infinity of the sky is clouded with gray mists of condensing vapors. Cold, formless fogs obscure the emerging stars, and blue icy mantles shroud the bloody sun. Darkness falls as sere vegetation snaps and crumbles under the weight of drifting snow, swept on a bitter wind. Then the stars burst through, hard and motionless; and the Earthshine shimmers cold and still upon a world of rugged mountains, beneath a crust of snow and frozen air.

Dreadful is the fate of a man caught in the night. For hours, perhaps, he has been walking, careless of the passage of time. Night catches him, and he becomes a strange thing, armored stiff in a crust of ice, struggling pitifully, hopelessly.

The realization of danger is abrupt. It is like a physical blow that dazes, and leaves him stupid and trembling. He feels a sudden great weariness, a weakness in the limbs; and his heart beats high in his throat, with painful pauses. He stares dully at the crimson sun, unable to credit his fate.

Then he perceives the sudden coolness, and the chill of his own perspiration. He starts frantically, runs, with heart beating so high that it chokes his breath. The first snowflakes dance lightly past him, or strike, white and feathery and very chill against his face.

He goes insane with terror. He leaps madly across the empty desert, screams for aid until the loneliness of the mocking echoes appalls him into silence. And suddenly he finds that he is exhausted. He stumbles and cannot rise. And he lies there for the moment, panting and chilled, he tells himself that he must be calm, conserve his strength.

When he rises, the sky is already gray with frozen mist, and the red sun is gone. He hurries on, gauging his leaps to keep his strength. The mists swirl about him, and dull throbbing pains creep up his shivering limbs. His face feels as if set in a frozen mask.

And now his heart pauses with the horror of a new discovery. He is lost! Snow swirls up in the wind about him, hiding the familiar peaks. With a sobbing cry, he stops; but the piercing lances of the cold drive him on.

He runs again, madly, with no sense of direction. His heart pounds, his lungs ache. But his face and hands and feet are becoming mercifully numb; they throb with dull, leaden pains, but feel curiously detached.

He is exhausted again, with the fatal heaviness of fear. His body shrieks out for him to stop. He fights on, in wildly frantic spurts. The wind howls about him, thin, laden with fine, cutting particles of ice, unthinkably cold.

He stumbles on. Darkness deepens. He cannot see. Is it the night? Or his eyes? Vague images—fragments—flash through his mind. His mother's face, white and still. A half-forgotten novel. A yellow dog he once had loved.

He stumbles, falls into a drift of powdery snow. It feels warm, delightful. Dimly, he realizes the peril of it. He tries to rise, feebly, cries out. The relentless wind whips away his voice, drives him down.

Hope is dead. Realization brings dreadful agony. He makes a frightful effort, oblivious to the pain screaming from his body. He cannot move!

In a few hours, the body is frozen hard as metal. There it lies in the hideous horror of that last frenzied convulsion, until the mooncalves come—scarlet, elephantine things, hopping beneath jeweled darkness from crag to snow-capped crater rims, over a world white and still and dead, shimmering in the cold white light of Earth.

More than once, in my life on the moon, I have been near that fate.

During the long night, my father mingled with the miners and farmers who were in Theophilus for a holiday. He took me with him into clubs, restaurants, stock exchanges, offices, and lobbies. And a few times we blundered into secret dens where there was mad music and wild song, with painted women and haggard men, reeling under the influence of drugs smuggled from Earth and the stranger things from the crater forests of the moon.

It was just outside one of the latter resorts, I think, that he stumbled on an old prospector, who claimed to have discovered a wonderful mine in the region to the north, named by the old astronomers Mare Tranquilatis, "Sea of Tranquility." (The colonists and explorers, in the main, have respected the nomenclature of the ancient selenographers.)

The old fellow from the desert—Jenkins was his name—had squandered or gambled away the proceeds of the ore his Selenites had packed back from the mine, and was in dire straits. He was a short, heavy fellow, his skin burned to a fiery red that matched his yellow hair. Father offered to look at his prospect, and advanced the old fellow funds to feed himself until the coming of the sun. I saw him several times, and took quite a liking to him—though mother did not approve of my being with him. He regaled me with tales of weird adventure; and presented me with a curiously carved piece of rock crystal—a really valuable curio—that had been used as a tool in one of the lost cities of Selenite culture.

When day was coming, father took me with him to one of the towers of the city to watch the rising sun. Before and below us spread the vast desert, rugged, rocky, broken with crack and cliff, covered with a blanket of snow and frozen air that shone white in the bright Earthshine. Above the sharp, ragged edge of the desert, the black sky was sprinkled with cold stars, motionless and bright.

In the east was a cone of misty luminescence—the zodiacal light. Suddenly the uppermost pinnacles of the mountain below that vague glow sprang into dazzling white radiance, and the intensely white rim of the sun crept up among the stars in the east. The desert became a plain of shimmering silver flame, crossed with the midnight shadows of the three mighty peaks just east of the city.

All about, as far as my eye could reach (the horizon on the moon is appreciably nearer than on Earth) mountain and plain, all crystal white, stood out with a sharp and motionless distinctness, with a clarity and vividness of outline, that one who had always lived on Earth cannot conceive, with the steady stars still burning in the black sky above.

But soon, as air and moisture began to evaporate in the unchecked rays of the sun, faint veils of blue and purple mist floated up about the distant peaks, and the sun was surrounded with a misty golden halo. The sky faded from utter blackness to a deep ocean blue, with the brightest stars still discernible in it.

In an hour the sparkling blanket of frost was gone, and the blue and yellow rolls of fog that had briefly obscured the moonscape were dissipated by the driving heat of the sun. Stripped of its prismatic mantle, the swarthy desert lay naked before us, revealing the blackness and the grim cruelty of volcanic rock, the fantastic shapes of twisted lava flows, the innumerable tiny craters, and the vast monotonous sweep of cracked and broken plain, which stretched away to the towering crater walls.

The sun had not been up twenty-four hours when father and the prospector, Jenkins, left the city on the road that leads across the Lake of Death toward the Sea of Tranquility in the north. They rode a little metal saddle on a "civilized" mooncalf—a monstrous, scaly red creature called M'Ob, of which Jenkins seemed very fond.

They were gone over a week; it was near sunset when they returned. Father, who was a trained mining engineer, had been pleased with the prospect and had bought it. During the next lunar day, he was very busy, making plans to work it, buying machinery and hiring men. When day came again, he left Theophilus with three great trucks that carried D-ray mining machinery, supplies, and the six men he had hired—he was depending on getting mooncalves for most of the labor. He took several tons of carbohydrates to pay them, and had employed a man with a thorough knowledge of their various dialects.

He had bought a great atomic disintegration ray machine for boring shafts, and a number of the smaller, pistol-like tools for working around bodies of ore, and detaching fragments of it. The disintegrator ray, or "D-ray," is based upon Orloff and Smith's great discovery of four centuries ago. Matter under it suffers atomic disintegration, being converted partly into pure energy, with the liberation of a great amount of heat, though most of it is transformed into the inert gases, helium, neon, argon, krypton, and xenon, which, when the ray is used in mining, escape harmless from the shaft.

When father returned at the close of the day, he reported that the machinery had been installed and that the best of progress was being made in getting the work under way. He had been compelled to build fifty miles of road to reach the nearest highway—cutting through obstructions with the D-ray, and leaving a smooth, glassy pavement of fused rock.

He worked very hard. After he had quarters in the mineshafts which he could inhabit during the night, he stayed on with his task, paying us brief visits during the day. Before the end of the year the trucks were beginning to haul metal from the mine in quantity.

The prospect had originally been for gold alone. Vast quantities of that metal there were, but great deposits of platinum, iridium, and osmium ores were struck at a depth of a few thousand meters. Since the three metals of the platinum group were the only ones that had been successfully used in the atomic blast projector, they commanded the highest prices paid for any metal save radium. Soon the mine was known as one of the most valuable on the moon.

A year after we had landed at Theophilus, Father had been able to construct a glass domed building on the hill above the shafts, in which we might live as comfortably as in the city. Mother and Valence and I were moved out there, and it was there that the happy days of my youth were spent.

CHAPTER SIX
In Which I Grow Up

UNTIL I was ten or twelve years of age, I seldom left the vicinity of the mine. Remotely situated in the great plain of the "Sea of Tranquility," it was much apart from the rest of the moon-world, and as the mine grew, father's buildings became a little city in themselves.

The mineshafts opened into the floor of a low-walled crater, some two miles across. A smooth, white road connected the little metal domes above the shafts with the great smelter and refinery that had been built in the center of the circular valley.

The great buildings in which we lived were located on a little hill just northeast of the crater—a wide, rambling town, enclosed in glass. Always it was the first point lit by the rising sun, when the flat desert about was still shrouded white in snow and frozen air, and lost in the shadows of the night.

Mother christened it "Firecrest," because of the way it glistened in the blaze of sunshine when she first saw it, as we came out in the automobile. Our little city, and the mine itself, came to be known by that name.

Sometimes I went with Valence and my parents on a business or pleasure trip to Theophilus—it took only a few hours to run the three hundred miles in our slender, torpedo-shaped automobile with the Orloff atomic engines. A few times we saw one of the "stereo" pictures from Earth, which, in the wonders of natural color, perfect sound, and life-like depth, gave us children some knowledge of the planet of our birth.

But those trips were rare and great occasions. For the most part we lived at Firecrest, very simply. During the long, hot days, I was free to wander about the wild desert, inside the square of forts my father had erected to guard against the raids of the wild mooncalves. For long hours at a time, I wandered about, climbing hills, exploring craters and rifles and caverns, thrilling over the discovery of strange bits of mineral in the hope that I was finding rare elements. I crept about in the rank, thorny, gray-green vegetation that sprang up in the craters, tasting strange fruits, and stalking the weird little creatures that roamed the spiky forests.

In other words, I was a normal boy, leading on the moon the natural life of childhood that I might have enjoyed on Earth. Sometimes—and quite naturally—I got into difficulties.

My greatest adventure of childhood came one day when I stumbled upon the entrance to one of the great caverns that honeycomb the moon. It had the narrowest of openings, a slender crack between two great boulders, not five miles from "Firecrest." Thrilling with the romance of discovery, common to all youth, I wriggled through, and explored the crack.

As I crept along—nerves a-tingle, trembling with excitement, yet not quite frightened—the fissure led down and down, widening as it went. I stumbled along in darkness, over the coarse sand of a subterranean waterway, ages dry. It must have been a half mile below the entrance that it widened out into a vast space, an amazing, strangely lighted chasm in the moon. A half mile away from me, and far below the bare ledge from where I viewed it, was a lake of black water. And about the lake was a weird forest, of luminous vegetation.

Dense jungle rimmed the lake, a jungle of the strangest plants known to science, the light-emitting flora of the caverns of the moon. Stranger of form than the spiky growth of the craters, the plants glowed with soft steady fire. Great, fleshy trees seeming to burn with dull blue light, huge mushroom-like things shining with a deep green incandescence. Slender, graceful, fern-like fronds glowing with a vivid scarlet radiance. A jungle of flowing flame!

For a long time I stood and watched. I had heard of phosphorescent forests, but this was the first I had ever seen. There was nothing unnatural about it, I knew; the plants merely supported colonies of luminiferous microorganisms similar to those found on Earth. Yet the alien beauty and the weird wonder of it wrapped me in amazement.

For a long time I looked; then, lost in the strange spell of the place, I left my point of vantage, and clambered down over a slope of water-weathered rock, until I reached the edge of the jungle. I broke off thick leaves glowing with cold blue light, and slender stalks burning with violet and green, and a handful of the soft feathery fronds that shone with crimson fire. I wandered about the shore of the black lake, making myself a bouquet of flame.

Then I heard a sound that made me drop the splendorous glowing thing in a panic of sudden fear, a sound that froze me as I stood, with stilled heart and indrawn breath. An animal sound it was, a sort of grunt that ended in a whistling intake of breath. Then there was a rustling in the plants that came toward me.

I saw a single purple eye, large as a man's head, and shining with cold flame, that rose slowly above the glowing plants where the sound had been.

The shock of the sight galvanized my unnerved limbs, and I turned and fled in mad fear. I tore a blind way through the flimsy glowing plants, stumbling over rocks and scrambling desperately to my feet to plunge on again.

At last I stopped, from sheer exhaustion. I was torn, bleeding, stained with black mud and luminous vegetable juices. Hot and panting, I threw myself down on a bare rock. When at last I was able to raise my head and look around, I saw the luminous thickets closing all about the bare boulder on which I lay. In the feeble light, walls and roof were invisible.

I stood up and shouted. There was no echo! The darkness swallowed my voice. Abruptly, I realized the vastness of the cave, and my foolishness in entering it alone. I realized my smallness, my weakness, the futility of my efforts.

I restrained an impulse toward another mad flight, and sat there a while, very soberly considering my chances—and finding them very slight. Then I climbed off the rock, and set out deliberately to find a way out. For a long, long time I wandered, breaking through luminous forests, stumbling over dark, rocky underground plains, running into boulders, falling into pits.

Always afterward, when I look back upon that dreadful time, it has seemed more nightmare than reality. I have no connected memory of it, only vague pictures of endless ages of exhausting effort, of growing hunger and torturing thirst, and of fear that was maddening. I know that sometimes I found black pools and drank, and I must have eaten some fruit of the weird vegetation. And my sleep ever since has been troubled with visions of huge black-winged things, with luminous eyes, circling ominously above me. For hours at a time, I lay trembling in hiding from them.

I slept several times—or at least lay insensible, when I was too exhausted to move again. I had no ideas of direction, no plan save always to follow the passages that seemed to lead upward.

My ultimate escape must be credited rather to chance than to anything else. For the thousandth time, I thought I saw the gleam of daylight, struggled to it with hope and fear struggling in me, and walked into a beam of sunshine that fell athwart the rocky floor.

Above me was a sort of sloping chimney, large enough for a space flier to pass through, with a patch of deep blue sky in sight beyond. I clambered up it, crawled out into a strange little crater, grown up with a forty-foot forest of olive green, spiky scrub, and lit with hot sunlight. The sun was low in the west. It had been morning when I had left Firecrest; I had been underground for a week!

I forced a way through the thorny undergrowth, and clambered out of the little crater. Looking about from a little eminence, I saw the glass-armored buildings of the city, blazing in the splendor of the sunshine, fifteen miles to the west. I was a full dozen miles from the hidden entrance I had found.

Five or six hours later, I stumbled into Firecrest, little better than dead. My parents and Valence received me with unbounded joy. They had scoured the country for me, finally had given me up as a victim of a raiding band of the wild mooncalves.

I told no one but my parents and a few selected friends of the vast cave; and it was a secret that was to prove an important factor in the moon's war for independence.

That near-tragic adventure ended the careless days in which, alone or with a book, I had wandered about the crater, lost in dreams. I suffered a long sickness, induced in part by exhaustion, in part by my reckless meals on the fruits of the luminous plants. It was some months before I had completely recovered my strength; and during a long convalescence, I did a great deal of reading, becoming intensely interested in studies, science especially.

As soon as I felt able, I entered the little school at Firecrest, which father had established for the benefit of his employees' children. After a few years there, I was sent off to the university at Theophilus, where I took a general scientific course, specializing in intra-atomic engineering.

By that time, father was one of the richest men of the moon. Firecrest, inhabited largely by his employees, was a city of some ten thousands in population. He had acquired a sort of fame for justice and honesty, for generosity toward his associates and workers. His wages were the highest paid on the moon; he was one of the few mine owners who had built a glass-covered city for their men.

His character, one of almost puritanic sturdiness and independence, had been of little use to him on Earth; but he was appreciated under the less restrained conditions of the moon. He had become respected and influential throughout the satellite, a leader and adviser when important questions were to be considered.

Several times, in matters of dispute between the colonists and the agents of Metals Corporation, in regard to the interpretation of contracts or prices paid for metal, he had interfered—through his influence the Moon Company had been able to secure more generous treatment for many a poor miner. For several years, he had been a leader in the Board of Directors of the Moon Company.

It was through his influence that permission had been obtained to set up a synthetic food factory on the moon, for the Food Corporation of Earth was jealous of its monopoly—the Corporation had had a small plant at New Boston for years, but the new concern was privately owned, and turned out vast quantities of food, at lower prices. He had also financed other manufacturing concerns that would tend to make the moon less dependent upon Earth, and had encouraged and aided the farmers who were struggling to grow the vitamin-containing fruits and vegetables that cannot be produced in factories.

Entering the university was a great event for me. It was a vast institution, for the moon numbered among its students thousands of young men and women from all the colonies. Located in one of the huge, sunlit, southern towers of Theophilus, with verdant parks about it, it was a delightful place of beauty.

The atmosphere was free and democratic. In my childhood I had been very much alone, self-sufficient and caring little for the society of others. But here I found myself among crowds of happy youngsters, who accepted me as an equal, without thought or inquiry concerning my station in life outside. I felt that their friendship would have been quite as real and genuine, if I had been a common miner's son, instead of the heir of one of the planet's leading citizens.

One of the most pleasant features of my school life was the friendship I formed with the Warrington family. George Warrington, who was a score of years older than myself, came of a family that has been outstanding for generations; and he held an important position in the Board of Directors of the Moon Company. Father had met him and won his friendship; thus it was that I was a frequent guest at his home.

Warrington was a kindly, friendly man, of simple tastes and quiet manners, though those who did not know him intimately, were apt to complain that he was unduly stiff and formal. He was a courteous host; it was delightful to bask in the genial warmth of his great intellect and noble character.

His wife was a simple mannered, cheerful woman, with keen, vivacious wit and a great and tender heart. She was beautiful to my eyes and a second mother to me when I was lonely or homesick. There were no children in the family; perhaps for that reason, I was more welcome to the great, majestic rooms.

It was at dinner there one evening that I first met Benjamin F. Gardiner. His name was well known to me, as to the rest of the two spheres, for his brilliant work in science and philosophy. I was dazzled into diffident silence at meeting one so renowned, though there was nothing overwhelming in the appearance of the stooped, scholarly man, then somewhat past middle age. His quiet, gentle manner inspired only friendship, respect for his deep intellect, and love for his great heart. Several years before he had given up the management of the manufacturing enterprise that had made him wealthy, to devote his time to scientific work for the benefit of mankind.

I had an automobile of my own, a small one, but as speedy as any that had been designed. Frequently I went home to see my sister and parents; and I spent much time traveling about the moon, visiting the other great cities, New Boston and Colon, the one in "The Sea of Clouds," near the crater Herschel and at about the center of the lunar disk as seen from Earth, the other at the base of the Appenines, on the edge of the Mare Serenitatis, or "Sea of Serenity." I toured thousands of miles of smooth highway, visited fantastic and awe-inspiring natural wonders of the moon, and hung about the spaceports, where the great silver globes were landing with food and manufactured goods from Earth, or departing with metal from the mines of the moon.

During one long moon-day, with a band of the more adventurous of my schoolmates, I traveled to the end of the roads in the south. We left our machines and went on afoot, on a prospecting expedition toward the great Doerfel Mountains beyond Tycho. We had minor adventures enough, and once fought for our lives against a band of the wild Ka'Larbah.

But the greatest adventure of my entire college career was one that came within the walls of Theophilus, and during the fourth and last year of my stay there. It was a girl, tall, dark-haired, beautiful. She had not the easy, familiar manners of the ordinary co-ed; she was inclined to be aloof, reserved, and silent.

I went to no end of pains to get an introduction to her. Her name was Mary Jons; I could learn nothing else about her. A few times I met her alone in the corridors or classroom, and on one memorable occasion she consented to go with me to see a "stereo" picture. At first, she seemed inclined to be friendly. I found, during our few meetings, that she had a keen, sparkling wit, a deep and genuine culture, and a wide knowledge of both Earth and moon. But she told me nothing of her past life.

But on the day after we had seen the picture, she was somehow changed toward me. She was reserved, self-contained; a barrier had come between us that I could not break down. When I stopped her in one of the great halls, she left me suddenly, seemed angry and suspicious when I followed. The next day I found that she had left the university.

And do my best, I could not find Mary Jons at all. Whence she had come and where she had gone were equally puzzling. I could not even find anyone who knew her better than myself. Presently, after I had spent a few thousand credit units for private detective work, I began to doubt that her name was Mary Jons at all.

CHAPTER SEVEN
The Fate of the Sandoval

MY college education was done; with a mind filled with impossible dreams of a dark-eyed, wistful girl who had called herself Mary Jons, I went back to the home of my youth—back to lonely Firecrest, standing isolated in that vast tract of grim, forbidding wilderness inappropriately called the "Sea of Tranquility." I was to live with the family, and learn the mining business.

During boyhood, I had been much about the mines, and having the natural inclination toward science that had led me to choose an engineering course at the university. I found nothing difficult about the work. After the careless college years, I really enjoyed the soberer discipline of the long days in the bright, sunlit office, or in the cool, gloomy shafts, with their intricate mazes of conduits for power, for air and water, and for the escaping gases from the D-ray boring machines. I continued my scientific studies too, fitting up a little laboratory in the mine buildings, and having books sent from Earth.

But often at night—and even by day, when I should have been at work—I saw a pair of dear, dark eyes before me, or glimpsed a fading face, with its bright, eager smile. I grew restless, with my dreams of Mary Jons. Perhaps, if I should go to the Earth…I had no idea, really, where she was. But I imagined that she must have flown back across the void, because I had failed to find her on the moon.

The wonders of a trip back across the gulf to the planet of my birth had long appealed to me. I began to ponder it seriously, to imagine that I might meet the dark-haired girl at the spaceport, or in the ways of New York. At last, I resolved to speak to my father about it.

But before I had done so, something happened to turn my attention to affairs nearer home.

For a long time, there had been difficulties between the Moon Company and its terrestrial superior, Metals Corporation. As I have said, the Moon Company had at first been owned outright by Metals. But the thrifty colonists, with a view to profit and to liberty, had bargained for stock in the Moon Company, when they were making a mining contract, or disposing of a cargo of ore. Gradually the incorporated cities—Theophilus, New Boston, and Colon were the leaders, though nine others, including Firecrest, had been admitted to the corporation—secured the ownership of the Moon Company stock, in order to be able to conduct their local affairs without interference from the agents of Metals.

That is, the entire ownership of stock in the Moon Company had passed into the hands of the colonists. When first organized, this company had possessed in fee simple, "the Earth's satellite, known as the Moon, with all mines, manufactories, smelters, refineries, and all other buildings and improvements, of whatsoever kind, that may be hereafter erected thereon."

It was, however, quite evident that the Moon Company did not own such mines as those of my father's, which, in fact, it had never claimed. On the other hand, it did own and operate some of the largest and most productive properties on the moon, and it had built and controlled the great cities and the vast systems of highways about them.

The whole situation was rather complicated and confusing, for Metals Corporation still insisted on tampering with the affairs of the Moon Company. And it ruthlessly enforced its monopoly on trade with the moon, its battleships of space ramming any other vessel found in the lanes.

In this year, when I returned home—it was 2826; I was then twenty-four years old—a great change took place in conditions on the moon. It was due to the growing sense of independence of the moon people. The synthetic food factories and the crater farms seemed a success; it looked as if the satellite might be able to look after herself, with little help from the Metals Corporation.

The Metals officials still apparently considered the moon a valuable property, to be made to yield a good revenue, not a growing nation, to be justly governed. It still insisted upon the purchase of metal on the moon, at prices set by its own official, refusing to permit private trade with the Earth. This trade monopoly, and the dependence of the colonists on imports from Earth, was evidently intended to keep the moon in subjection, even though the colonists controlled the Moon Company.

For years it had been known that the prices of metal on the moon were about a third of those at Pittsburgh. But the colonists had a deep love for the Metals Corporation, an abiding faith in the wisdom and the justice of its Directors. They considered their own debt to the Corporation, for their protection in an alien world, and for means of communication with the planet of their fathers. They thought of the perils faced by the ships that carried the metal to Earth. And the ingots had been regularly sold to Metals, at the price it wished to pay.

But in 2324, prices on all metals were uniformly and arbitrarily lowered by ten per cent, for no stated reason other than that Metals wished to increase the power of her great space-fleets. The corporation insisted that the colonists were bound to sell their products to her, and at whatever price she thought just. And the moon, she said, needed the protection of the fleets.

The result of the reduction of the prices of metal was a protest in unison from the people of the moon, that they were quite willing to build and equip ships of their own, and under the command of the Moon Company, but that they objected to supporting a fleet of vessels maintained largely to keep an unjust monopoly on commerce.

There was, at the time, no hint of rebellion, merely the gravest of petitions from the Directors of the Moon Company. But Metals proceeded to put the reduced rates into effect, and miners who refused to accept them found their warehouses guarded by watchmen with D-rays, on the alert to see that the ingots did not fall into the hands of smugglers.

The important result of all the confusion, with the practical suspension of trade while the boycott went on, was a great amount of discussion, and the revival of keenest public interest in the charter of the Moon Company.

A few patriotic spirits, of whom Warrington was a leader, got in touch with most of the stockholders of the Moon Company, who were scattered all over the moon. Later in the year several score of delegates met in Theophilus to hold an Assembly of Directors, the greatest that had been held since the stock passed out of the hands of the terrestrial holding company.

A small gathering it was, perhaps, but one of earnest and able men, burning with zeal for the cause of liberty and justice on the moon. Warrington was there, lofty, devoted, and brilliant man, who had been in youth an officer in the space fleets, where he had learned the modern art of war. He had more recently won distinction in a long campaign against a rebellious army of the wild M'Dawils—one of the most blood-thirsty tribes of Selenites—defeating them in a brilliant battle near the Hercynian Mountains, on the border of the moon. Gardener was at the meeting, the profound philosopher, clear-headed, practical, far-sighted. Henry Patrick was there, the youthful orator whose later fiery speeches in every lunar city did much to inflame the moon-folk with the spirit of revolution, and my father, John Adams, an able, influential man, skillful financier and sincere statesman.

The great round vessel, rather clumsy at best, and heavily laden with metal, fell an easy victim to the slender, modern, cigar-shaped warship of Metals.

*Illustrations by
H. W. Wesso*

The old charter of the Moon Co. was examined and discussed. Quite explicitly, Metals had granted it the full ownership of the moon, with all mines and cities upon it, as well as the right to protect its territorial rights by force of arras, to build space fliers and to carry on trade with Earth.

These latter provisions must not have seemed important when the charter was drawn up, since the Moon Company was to be only a subsidiary corporation to Metals. But now, even though Metals had never recognized the independence of the moon people, these old charter rights seemed important guarantees of freedom.

After a long and rather stormy session in one of the great auditoriums of Theophilus—there were many so loyal to Metals that they felt it an act of treason to question the wisdom of its government of the moon the Assembly passed the "Assertion of Right."

That famous document merely sets forth in simple language the claims of the moon people to the rights and privileges of self-government, of free ownership of mines and cities, and of freedom of commerce with the Earth, as granted in the charter of the Moon Company.

The document was sent to the Directors of the Metals Corporation, at Pittsburgh, as "an humble petition from your loyal colonists on the moon." The answer was simple and decisive: Under the present system, the moon had prospered for two centuries. Why change it?

And the same ship, that brought back that answer, carried orders that no metal was to be purchased for more than the new low price, and that anyone storing metal about his mine, or attempting to ship it to other points than the great spaceports, was liable for prosecution for smuggling.

With the arrival of the news, an electric wave of excitement ran over the moon. There was much wild talk of war and independence, and below it the awakening of the new ideal of liberty went steadily onward.

In January, 2325, the Assembly of the Directors of the Moon Company met again, in a new session that was to last for six long years, until the end of the greatest war of history.

These men again discussed the Assertion of Right, and in a few days passed the "Assertion of Equality," on January 24, which has since been celebrated as the birthday of the moon's liberty. It stated that the Moon Company was a free and independent corporation, of rank and power equal to those of any, and entitled to her representatives on the United Board of Directors.

At various times in the past, when there had seemed to be need of protection against the pirates of space, the cities of the moon had advanced funds for the construction of spaceships, which had been built in the Metals shops at Pittsburgh, and commissioned in the name of the Moon Company. There were perhaps a half dozen of these vessels with the fleets of the Metals Corporation—it was upon one of them that Warrington had served. They were the property of the Moon Company, and usually manned and officered by men from the moon, though they sailed under commands of the admirals of Earth.

One of the first acts of the Assembly had been to declare these ships to be under its immediate authority, and to command them to land at Theophilus, to await the orders of the directors of a sovereign corporation. Five of them soon appeared above the glass walls of the city. Technically they had mutinied in leaving the fleet; they were refused landing space at the spaceport, though the admiral was too uncertain of the temper of the moon-folk to take more drastic action against them. They came down, with some little damage to equipment, in the desert, a few miles from the walls.

The Assembly, in order to test its claimed rights of commerce with the Earth, announced that one of the ships would sail for New York at once. Thousands of tons of metal were piled up in the warehouses of the city; there was no difficulty in getting a cargo.

On February 6, 2325, when the sun was not four days high at Theophilus, thousands gathered in the streets and on the roofs to watch the departure of the ship, the *Sandoval*. The rest of us had come with father to attend the Assembly meeting; I was among the cheering, madly jovial throngs upon the broad glass roof. It was a motley crowd, of white-clad farmers and grimy miners, of grimy mechanics and brightly attired society folk, haranguing one another, singing patriotic songs—people of many races and of a hundred trades, but all welded into one by the newborn spirit of freedom.

Far too westward lay the silver spaceships upon the swarthy desert, like globes of gleaming white quicksilver scattered upon a dark rock. The sunshine was hot and bright, painting the ships with silver flame, setting them forth very vividly against the black shadows of the hills behind them.

Faint clouds of many-colored mist swirled up about one of the argent spheres, and very, slowly, it seemed, it was lifted into the air.

A great shout—a human cry that rolled over the city's roof like the roar of a breaking sea—arose with the ship into space.

In a few minutes the vessel was out of sight to the naked eye; but still the throng waited, not a mere excited mass of people, but feeling the pulse of awakening nationality, fused into a single unit by an awakening spirit of patriotism.

The *Sandoval* was still within good view of the telescopes that project by the hundred from the towers and domes that rise a little from the city's vast expanse of level roof, when the catastrophe took place. There were a hundred observers; and the whole city knew of the outrage a few minutes after it happened.

The outbound *Sandoval,* fifty miles above the city, was rammed by a warship.

The great round vessel, rather clumsy at best, and heavily laden with metal, fell an easy victim to the slender, modern, cigar-shaped warship of Metals. As a silver arrow might pierce and burst a bright soap bubble, the battleship sped upon the *Sandoval,* ripping it open with an armored prow.

Several hours later, it was reported that a mass of wreckage, laden with dead men and precious metal had fallen beyond the three great peaks in the crater of Theophilus. But before that time, only the moon knew of the deed, and many a man who had thought little or not at all of his relation with the Earth, felt a sudden fierce desire for liberty.

On that day, the independence of the moon was born.

CHAPTER EIGHT
The Radium Raid

THAT cruel and deliberate outrage, the ramming of a ship of the Moon Company's as if it had been a common pirate, set the planet afire with a flame of resentment. For the first time in the history of the moon, its inhabitants began to think of independence, to wonder if they could lead an existence without the commercial relations with Earth, without the protection of Metals Corporation.

Much was written and spoken on the subject in the next few weeks. One anonymous author published a series of eloquent and fiery appeals for liberty, called *The Parting of the Ways,* which were eagerly read and widely quoted. The unknown author—who, I afterward had reason to suspect, was none other than my own father—made a powerful plea for lunar independence.

The moon, he pointed out, had a population as large as the membership of several of the corporations of Earth, and a wealth far greater than that of any, measured in natural resources. Certainly, he said, the moon-folk were as progressive, thrifty, and intelligent as any on Earth; certainly they were capable of self-government.

The moon, he argued, was no longer dependent upon Earth for any necessary articles. The factories in the great artificial caverns below the cities turned out every variety of manufactured article; from clothing, metal goods, and building material, to drugs, medicine, and synthetic food.

The mines of the moon would not only supply all her needs in the way of metals, but their output was so indispensable to the industrial life of Earth that the mother planet would be compelled to resume commerce in the end. Economically, Earth was dependent upon the moon, far more than the moon depended upon the Earth.

The farms, in crater and atomic-lighted cavern, would furnish sufficient quantities of vitamin-containing fruit and vegetables. These, so long the principal importations from Earth, would no longer compel commercial relations with the mother planet.

In one of the last of his papers, the daring author went so far as to suggest the possibility of a successful war with the Metals Corporation. The Earth, he pointed out, would be at the vast disadvantage of maintaining a military force at the distance of nearly a quarter of a million miles from home, while the interruption of commerce would deprive it of the source of metals upon which its military strength is so largely based.

And if the moon people, he concluded, were not trained soldiers, they at least had had considerable military experience in the many bloody wars with the mooncalves; they were used to hardship and danger; they were familiar with the natural features of the moon's topography. And if they were lacking in weapons of war, there were the great D-ray tubes used in boring mine shafts—

powerful enough to bring down a spaceship miles away—and the smaller pistol-like tubes used by individual miners, which would be useful hand weapons.

As might have been expected *The Parting of the Ways* aroused the keenest disapproval of the agents of Metals. The papers were ordered suppressed; such copies as could be gathered up were destroyed; and a reward was offered for the author, dead or alive. But despite the best of their efforts, the writer remained unknown—it was only after the death of my father, years later, that I found among his possessions the plates, from which the outlawed papers had been printed. And all the moon read the tattered little pamphlets that were secretly passed from hand to hand.

Few, who knew my father, might have suspected him of the authorship of those terse, powerful challenges to rise to action, ringing with a brief, emphatic eloquence, simple, throbbing with sincerity and truth. For he was an aging man, an invalid who had relinquished to me much of the management of the business. He had recovered completely from his injuries in the war of 2307. While he was not able to take an active part in the war on the moon, he had more to do with it than was commonly known at the time. His heart was as strong as any patriot's, and he did his part, despite an aged and suffering body.

As the people of the moon read the timely article in *The Parting of the Ways,* and pondered upon the ramming of the *Sandoval,* there slowly crystallized a definite spirit of unity, which grew firmer in the conviction that the moon need no longer lean upon the long arm of the Metals Corporation.

The new spirit was first definitely shown in the "Radium Raid," an incident which took place in New Boston, about the middle of the year.

The Metals Corporation had clung tenaciously to the lowered schedule of prices, despite the boycott of the moon. It was the boast of the new party of independence that not an ounce of metal had been sold to the Metals since the ramming of the *Sandoval.*

That had meant hardship to the moon people, for if no metal had gone to the Earth, Metals had seen to it that no merchandise had been shipped to the moon. The people had accustomed themselves to doing without coffee and a few other luxuries that were not produced on the moon, and large subscriptions had been raised to assist miners who faced ruin for lack of a market.

Nor were the disadvantages all on one side, for on Earth a thousand industries depended on the metal and other products imported from the moon, and the suspension of commerce cut off their raw material. There was a vast pressure upon officials of Metals to raise the prices and resume trade, but they stubbornly held to their point.

As the year went on, it developed that in the warehouses at New Boston, a shipload of radium was consigned to the Metals Corporation at Pittsburgh. The agents of Metals had purchased this radium after the new low rates had gone into effect, but before the boycott had brought an end to trade. Late in June a space flier landed at New Boston, to take on the metal. The situation was a delicate one. Metals had already bought the metal. But according to the terms of the compact among the moon people, no metal was to be permitted to leave the planet until the prices were raised.

Public excitement ran high. The lead chests were carried out of the warehouse, and the loading went on. The Assembly of Directors was still in session, and the question of whether the ship should be allowed to depart was fiercely debated. Its sailing meant the breaking of the boycott; the radium would relieve the present industrial crisis on Earth. Yet the metal had been sold; it seemed the duty of the sellers to let it go.

But public opinion ran high against the sending of the radium. It was argued that the Corporation might at least pay the old price, since the boycott had trebled the price of radium in Pittsburgh. In spite of that, on the last day of June, a messenger came from Theophilus with the news that the Moon Company officially sanctioned the departure of the vessel.

A vast crowd had assembled around the ship, to watch the loading of the lead drums that contained the precious metal. There had been some rather violent demonstrations of popular feeling, and the port authorities had had some difficulty in keeping order. But when the messenger arrived with the news that the ship was to be permitted to depart, and that he had delivered to her commander the clearance papers he had brought from the Assembly, the throngs dispersed and returned to the city.

THE BIRTH OF A NEW REPUBLIC

It was almost sunset. The vessel was scheduled to depart in a few hours. The metal was all on board, the laborers were returning to the city, before the cold would come, and the crew was still busy, getting the cargo in shape for the voyage.

Just as the sun was sinking, and the black shadows of the mountains, chill forerunners of night, were racing across the desert, a band of men suddenly appeared out of a marching shadow and rushed upon the vessel. They were grotesque figures, unrecognizable in the metal armor of spacesuits.

The air locks and hatches of the vessel had been open and unguarded. The vastly outnumbered crew of the flier was taken by surprise, just as the last drums of radium were being stowed in place. In a few minutes, the raiders had overrun the ship. The crew was disarmed, herded into the strong rooms, and locked up.

The cylinders of radium salts were speedily unloaded. Just what became of them is not historic certainty. It seems that outside the vessel they were given to a band of moncalves who vanished with them into the chill mystery of the gathering night.

A few hours later, when the irate commander of the ship had forced a way out of the strong room, radium and raiders alike had vanished. The ship rose at once, and got into communication with the patrol fleets. The surface of the moon about New Boston was combed, but all efforts to recover the lost metal proved in vain.

News of this daring act on the part of a few, determined citizens of New Boston spread like wildfire over the moon. The whole planet waited tense for the reply of Metals.

CHAPTER NINE
The Declaration of Independence

AT the time of the "Radium Raid," father and mother and I were in Theophilus. We had been there, in fact, since the convening of the Assembly early in the year. The mine was shut down, since the boycott had stopped the sale of metal.

Father regularly attended the Assembly meeting in the great hall. To the influence of his great wealth was added men's respect for his sturdy character, lofty honor, and ideals based upon deep human feeling. He was among the leaders of the Assembly.

It was my privilege to go with him daily to the meeting place, as a sort of confidential clerk and stenographer. I shall never forget the long sessions in the dark, cool hall, when its lofty vault rang with impassioned pleas for liberty and right, or whispered an echo to the calm, sober opinions of such men as Warrington and Gardiner.

During my university course, I had done extensive work in science, and a few things I had done during my graduate year had attracted a little attention outside the institution. I was pleased beyond measure to find that Dr. Gardiner had read of my work. Several times I met him to talk over scientific topics—for the brilliant physicist never let such trivial things as politics or wars stop his work. I was among the honored three whom he chose to have present when he first performed his famous experiment with the focusing of the shorter Hertzian waves—from which he later developed such momentous results.

Toward the end of August, disquieting news came from New Boston. A fleet of nine great warships, of the cylindrical type chiefly used in the Earth's atmosphere, had arrived from Pittsburgh, under the command of General McRan. The fliers had landed at the spaceport, and disembarked an army of some ten thousand men, which had taken possession of the city.

The General—a crabbed, autocratic old fellow, according to reports—set up his headquarters in the Diamond Gardens in the middle of the city, shutting the citizens out of that famous museum and amusement place. His men patrolled the streets, rode the ways, and stood guard at the air locks and roof doors. Guards were placed about factories and places of business. New Boston was under martial law, and warnings had been posted that anyone denouncing the administration of Metals, or expressing sympathy with the Assembly of the Moon Company, would be arrested on charge of treason.

The city was compelled to quarter McRan's troops, and to feed them as well as the five thousand men on the spaceships. The protest of citizens and directors only evoked the old general's opinion that martial law was too light a punishment for the city of the Radium Raid.

THE BIRTH OF A NEW REPUBLIC

Yet, McRan had not come to pacify the planet by force. One of his first acts after seizing New Boston was to send messengers to Colon and Theophilus with orders for the agents of the Metals Corporation to raise the schedule of prices to the former level and even to offer premiums to compensate the miners for losses suffered during the boycott.

But these advances were met with scorn. Such methods might have been effectual even a year before, for the cities of the Moon had had little life in common. But the events of the past few months had crystallized a moon-wide spirit of self-dependence that was not to be broken by such an attempt at bribery.

When he learned that this move had failed, McRan's next step was to threaten that if the moon-folk did not yield and resume shipment of metal to the Earth, he would bring enough ships and men to the moon to seize all the cities and starve the inhabitants into working the mines.

The choleric old fellow's threat was a match to powder. Men who had before talked only of just prices and charter rights now talked of liberty and independence. The militia began to repair the old weapons used in the endless wars with the mooncalves, and to devise new machines of destruction. The city governments of Theophilus and Colon ordered the great D-ray boring machines used in the nearby mines brought up and put in position for defense against spaceships.

During that time, the Assembly of Directors was meeting daily at Theophilus. There were many among the members anxious to declare the independence of the moon and begin a war with Metals. But older and wiser men—among them such distinguished statesmen as Gardiner, Warrington, and my father—realizing more clearly the terrible cost in human life and human pain that war would mean, were determined not to take the fateful step until the Earth should force them to do so.

McRan had lost no time in seizing the machinery in the mines under and near New Boston. A part of the ray machines had been brought up and placed in strategic positions about the city, to forestall a possible rising of the citizenry. He also attempted to work the mines with his troop, though their ignorance and clumsiness brought on so many accidents that he gave that up.

He had been on the moon nearly a month before the first battle was fought in the long and terrible war to come. On September 23, 2325, when the sun was near the zenith, five hundred of McRan's men left New Boston to seize the machinery in the Peacedale mine, which is located fifty miles west of the city, near the edge of the crater of Hipparchus. Most of the force was infantry, though there were a dozen great ray tubes, drawn by tractor tanks.

The plan had been known to the citizenry several hours before the troops left the city. Some loyal and fervent patriot, whose name seems not to have been recorded, succeeded in getting out of the city through the ventilator tubes—the air locks being guarded.

He reached the Peacedale mining district a dozen hours ahead of Major Harley and his Tellurian soldiery, with news of their advance. To the miners, long used to being called upon to defend their possessions from mooncalves or space pirates at a moment's notice, there could have appeared but one course of action.

What that course was, Harley found, when his troops met half a hundred grimy miners drawn up in a line, behind a row of atomic boring machines, on the steel bridge that had been erected across the great crack, or rille, three miles from the mines.

Harley tramped out before his men, and ordered the miners to disperse. They refused, stood calm before his threats—his language seems to have been of a rather violent tenor. Fuming with rage, he got back behind his caterpillar tanks, and ordered his troops to fire.

The first burst of flaming rays killed half the miners upon the bridge. Their weapons were not ready; the focusing of a D-ray is rather a delicate process. But the survivors stood calmly adjusting their weapons after their companions had fallen under that pitiless volley. But at last, when the vivid streaks of red and green and yellow leapt from their rude weapons, nearly seventy-five of the close-ranked terrestrials fell. By that time, Harley had his tanks ready for action. They replied with a fiery burst of narrow rays that left hardly a score of the ragged miners on the bridge—and most of them wounded.

Still the little band refused to give way, though they might have found easy shelter in the rocks behind the rille. They kept the great rays flaming from their clumsy machines. Harley was actually forced to fall back a little. Finally his lumbering tanks forced a way across the bridge—but not until the last of those miners had fallen behind his improvised weapon.

The troops had sustained a loss of more than 150 men; and three of the tanks had been wrecked. But Harley pressed on without delay. As he went, he found himself exposed to a continual bombardment of atomic rays. Enraged miners and fanners, hiding in crack and rille and crater-pit, were using their familiar tools to a deadly end in the new trade of war.

The Tellurians marched on to Peacedale, but reached it in a very much-demoralized condition. One of the shafts was taken after a hot and bloody encounter, which convinced Harley that the miners could fight in earnest. A little machinery was destroyed, but the retreat began almost at once.

That retreat ended in becoming a mad flight. Again and again the harried and demoralized troops fell into an ambush or were swept by D-rays from a peak or cliff that rose beside their route. The remaining tanks and the heavy tubes had to be left by the way; and Harley reached the air locks of New Boston with little over a hundred men.

Before the sun had set, an atomobile had arrived in Theophilus with news of the battle. That night, there was a long debate in the Assembly chamber. Before the meeting adjourned, it had taken the most momentous step in the history of the moon.

The assembled Directors of the Moon Company voted that the moon was now, and by right, a free and independent Corporation, to whose liberties the presence of McRan in New Boston was an insult inexcusable. That declaration of independence marked the birth of a new nation. Before, the moon had been merely petitioning justice. Now it demanded it.

On the following day, the Assembly met again, made an appropriation of five million credit units to defray the expenses of the war, and issued a call for volunteers to fight for the freedom of the planet.

By the middle of October, bodies of men were gathering in Colon and Theophilus, as well as in the dozen smaller places, such as Firecrest, where there were permanent populations, to go to the relief of New Boston.

On the first day of November, nearly twenty thousand men were assembled in the vicinity of Peacedale. That horde of raw recruits, without officers, without discipline, without arms and equipment, without military training, even without adequate shelter against the lunar night, was far indeed from an army. But it did have the single vital quality—unfaltering devotion to the cause of liberty.

On that day, the Assembly made Warrington the Commander-in-Chief of the armies of the Moon Company. The day after, my old friend left Theophilus on the lonely road toward Peacedale, confidentially facing a terrific task—the organization of an enthusiastic mob of miners and farmers into an army, with which to face the well armed, battle-seasoned veterans of McRan.

My own fortune was bound up with his. At his request, and with the permission of my aging father, I had become his "engineer attaché"—a sort of confidential private secretary and scientific adviser, rather than a military man.

I wrote a letter of farewell to Valence. Three years before she had married Tom Dowling, a brilliant young fellow who had risen—and before his marriage at that—to be general manager of the Firecrest mines. They had stayed there when I came with my parents to Theophilus; my last view of my sister had been as a young matron, with a redheaded child at her knee.

I pillowed the silver-haired head of my mother upon my shoulder. For the last time, I feared, I held her dear slight form in my arms. Tears were rolling down her faded cheeks; but her eyes were brave and bright as she kissed me farewell.

And I left her—my last memory is of a slight whiff of the faint lilac perfume she had always used, that is associated with so many of my dearest recollections.

Father gave me a crushing handshake, a sincere kiss, and a few heartfelt words of parting.

That night a swift closed atomobile left Theophilus, on the long lonely road to the meeting place of the mountaineers at Peacedale. I was at the wheel. Beside me was Warrington. We were setting out on a great task that was to lead us many times into hardship and peril, into sorrow and pain, into strange adventures and terrible situations.

CHAPTER TEN
The Battle of Meteor Hill

THE sun was low over the black mountains that ring the Theophilus crater, when Warrington and I left the city. It was only a matter of some twelve hours until sunset would bring its killing cold; and we had seven hundred miles to go. Warrington had been urged to pass the lunar night in the comfort and safety of the city, but he wished to be with his army. It was a dangerous choice he took, for we had been able to get no spacesuits; the slightest accident or delay would be fatal; if we did not reach our destination by the time the sun left the sky, we would never reach it.

The atomobile in which we drove somewhat resembled the ancient vehicle propelled, not by efficient and certain atomic power, but by the old clumsy and unreliable internal combustion engine, the motor car called the "automobile."

That is, our machine had four wheels, with flexible tires, supporting a narrow, tapering, cigar-shaped body. The space within the little shell was rather cramped, but luxuriously fitted. There were seats, storage space, and the little white panel with the buttons which controlled the motor. The engines were little devices in the hubs of the wheels, hardly the size of a man's fist. The outside of the shell had been silvered, and it was lined with a non-conductor, making for comfort during a wide range of temperature.

Nevertheless, it would be fatal to be caught out in the lunar night. Not only would the unbelievable cold penetrate the machine, but the freezing of the air would leave one to suffocate, even if he could keep warm.

For that reason, I made the best speed I could down the long white road. Built of fused rock cast in place, it was level and hard. But owing to the extreme irregularity of the moon's surface, it was far from straight. It curved about peaks and craters, zigzagged up mountain slopes, dropped into valleys.

It was a lonely road. We might travel a dozen miles, or a hundred, between the scattered mines. Once we stopped at a little settlement. It stood on a low hill—a serried row of glass-armored towers and domes, with squat metal shaft-houses below. A great D-ray mining machine was being dragged across the plain toward the town—to be set up for defense, I suppose. A motley group of people were assembled about the tractors that were pulling it. And a hundred men or so, in ragged nondescript uniforms, were being drilled below the walls, marching and wheeling enthusiastically.

We got a bit of lunch, and had the waiting mechanic oil and inspect the machine. The genial keeper of the little inn recognized Warrington. He refused any pay, and ran out to spread the news. We departed with a cheering throng of miners speeding us on.

As the silent, racing machine shot swiftly over the winding road, the scenery changed rapidly about us. Cruel slender mountains and grim mysterious craters flashed into view as we topped a ridge or rounded a curve, and grew swiftly, swung and wheeled about us, dwindled, vanished behind. The moonscape changed, yet it was always the same—lofty, ragged mountains, broad, black volcanic deserts of twisted lava streams, burned, cracked and rugged, strange circular craters, walled with sheer grim cliffs—all intensely bright where the sun's rays struck it, or hidden in a startling, rayless obscurity of shadow.

To drive was an exhausting task, to sit there alert, forcing the machine to the limit of speed the road permitted, sometimes, it seemed, escaping disaster only by the narrowest of margins. But I rather enjoyed it—the perfection of the machine, the ease of its answer to the wheel, the intoxication of boundless power at my fingertips. Even the danger added zest.

An hour after we had left the mining town, we had a near catastrophe. At one point, at the foot of a long slope, the road passes through a narrow gorge. As we entered, we came suddenly upon a rough wall of boulders piled across the roadway. Instinctively, I pressed the brake-button. The machine checked its speed, but still maintained momentum enough to pile us in the front end of the car when it struck.

We clambered back to the seat and took stock of the situation. We were both bruised somewhat; Warrington had an ugly contusion on his temple with blood oozing from it, and I had a skinned side. But we were not seriously hurt. The machine refused to respond when I pressed the buttons; it seemed to have been injured the most.

"Look there," cried Warrington, who had been looking out as I tried the controls. "The Mooncalves!"

I looked through the broad round windows. A halfdozen great scarlet monsters were approaching, hopping like colossal fleas through the yellow, spiky scrub that covered the mountainside—moving like red fleas the size of elephants. It was a band of wild mooncalves, whose elementary cunning had led them to try this method of wrecking machines in the hope of spoil—of which human bodies would have been the most attractive item.

Fortunately, we carried pocket D-ray tubes. They were light weapons; their focal range limited to two hundred yards, but serviceable in such a case as this. Warrington covered the Selenites on one side; I covered those on the other. He gave the word, we pressed the contact levers. The narrow red rays reached out, intense and brilliant.

And the great creatures fell as the scarlet fingers touched them.

We must have killed four or five. There were a score in all, or more. The others leapt away into the endless thicket of brown, thorny scrub, now dry and sere in the lunar evening, and were lost to view. We got out. Warrington kept watch and cut the boulders out of the way with his ray, while I tinkered with the injured motors.

In an hour we were on the way again.

DURING the latter course of the war, the roads were hardly passable at all, due to such barricades and ambushes. Military dispatches were carried mostly on friendly Selenites, the lightest tractor tanks being used when the mooncalves were not available, though they were not half so rapid.

We had no more serious accidents. The sun was still half the breadth of its disk above the horizon when we reached Peacedale. An odd scene, it was, to be the camp of twenty thousand men. Only a rugged, cracked crater plain. It was six miles across with a few little shaft-houses of metal and glass standing here and there about it, with the white ribbon of the road running from one to another.

We left the machine and were eagerly welcomed by the guards from the shaft-house by us. The black shadow of the crater walls was leaping across the floor, and already we felt chill in the thin bitter wind that blew out of the shadow toward the bright, sunlit mountain on the eastern side, carrying a few fine flakes of snow upon it.

We were conducted down into the shaft. For all their lack of organized discipline, it seemed that the men had been making wise and energetic preparation for the long cruel night. Heavy metal doors had been arranged, where they were not already in place, to confine the precious air in the passages. There were atomic heaters and lighting systems. Equipment had been provided to purify the air by condensation, and there were tanks of liquid oxygen to replenish the vital element. The greatest difficulty had been in the matter of food supplies, but sufficient rations had been obtained for a month at least.

Within an hour after our arrival, the passages had been sealed, and we had begun the long fortnight of complete isolation from the rest of humanity. Warrington worked for long hard days, organizing the men into companies, and teaching them to use the slender D-ray tubes as skillfully as weapons as they had used them as rock disintegrators.

In my capacity as engineer attaché I was busy enough, superintending the control of the intricate system of machinery that kept our mineshafts habitable, and as well, working on the details of the changes to be made in the great D-ray rock-borers, to adapt them for use in war.

When the sun went down, it had been a mere rabble of men that crowded into the mine passages. When the long night ended and they emerged, it was an army already whipped into a single unit, responsive to the will of a single man, organized and taught the first lesson in discipline.

As soon as the driving rays of the sun had cleared the sullen mists of evaporating air and frost, Warrington moved the new army out of the mines, and marched on New Boston. For the most part, the men who did not carry the standard D-ray pistols bought during the long wars with the Selenites were equipped with the small portable rock-disintegrating D-rays. Most of the men, too, had been provided with white uniforms, pith helmets, and smoked glasses, so that they would be able to march in the open by day. We had a sufficient number of atomobile trucks to carry the commissariat; and there were two hundred of the great ray-machines, drawn by tractors, that I had been able to convert into terrible instruments of war.

We came in sight of New Boston before the sun was a day high. Its glass walls and towers, flung over hill and valley, were a splendid sight in the sunshine, with the naked black mountains behind them. We located our camp perhaps eight miles east of the city, and cut off from it by the elevation known as Meteor Hill, which rose about midway between us and the city with the spaceport beside it. In the little valley where we stopped, the olive-green vegetation was just putting up slender tendrils that in a few hours would grow to the impenetrable spiky thickets of the amazing forests of the lunar day.

Warrington had his plan of siege well worked out. Within a few hours, half his army, with almost a hundred of the great mining tubes, was flung out in a ring, fifteen miles across, that circled city and spaceport. His next move, undertaken while the first was yet uncompleted, was the occupation of Meteor Hill.

From this eminence, his rays could sweep the city and the spaceport at will. With eight thousand men and the remaining hundred of the huge ray-tubes, we marched up the hill. Some opposition had been expected, but only a few surveyors and engineers, who were apparently planning fortifications upon that strategic point, were encountered.

In full view of the city and the ships, our men fell to work with a will. It was only a matter of a few minutes before the pocket D-rays had cut deep trenches in the hilltop, from which the army was not easily to be dislodged.

It seems that the terrestrial commander had intended to occupy the hill "as soon as temperature had moderated sufficiently." It is said that he was thrown into a rage of anger to find that Warrington had marched fifty miles to seize a position before he had thought it safe to leave the city walls. This was the first hint that under lunar conditions, Warrington could best the terrestrial generals, even though they were distinguished veterans.

I was with Warrington when we took the hill. I remember standing by him, after we had cut the pits for the tubes and placed the weapons in position, looking down upon the city. It spread over the vast, uneven plain below us, with the vast, towered glass roof blazing diamond-like in the sunlight, enlivened by colored ornaments and merry pennants that hung above the towers. Just below the city was the spaceport, where the nine great war-fliers lay, gleaming like nine polished cylinders of silver.

Later in the war, fleets of the more efficient globe-shaped vessels appeared on the moon.

It was not long before we saw a good deal of activity on the rocky plain below our point of vantage. Scouts reported that great masses of troops were leaving the city and gathering in canyons and ravines below the cliffs at the foot of Meteor Hill.

Our tubes were hardly more than in position when great tongues of blinding light—scarlet and green and yellow—reached up toward us from the walls of New Boston, and from the ships in the port. The color of the D-ray depends on the one of the three metals, platinum, osmium, and iridium, from which it is derived. Slender, flickering fingers of intense livid flame played up and down our lines. Rocks and creeping vegetation, men and weapons, before them burst into momentary incandescence and faded away, disintegrated, melted into nothingness. McRan had gone into action.

Our own tubes replied at once, with a great curtain of wavering light, firing largely upon the space fliers, for to sweep the city was to kill friend with foe.

In a few minutes, thin lines of white-clad men were seen below, running up the hill with ray-tubes in hand. The Tellurians were storming our position. Warrington ordered the great tubes to be depressed whenever possible, to cover the infantry advance. As soon as the troops were in range, the hand weapons were put into action.

Meanwhile, the dazzling rays played up and down our lines, sweeping down those caught exposed, and slowly cutting away the solid rock before our trenches. The section of the hill we occupied was slightly crescent-shaped. The Tellurians formed in the hollow of the crescent and charged up the hillside in thin, scattered lines, firing flaming rays of red and green and yellow as they came. It was a heroic attempt—those veterans from Earth knew how to advance into certain death, if need be.

In a few minutes the front line of the terrestrials came over the brow of the hill. The fire from our great tube could no longer meet them, and a desperate hand-to-hand conflict raged all along the line.

Our standard—it was merely a blue square of cloth, bearing a white crescent—was cut down by a D-ray. The confidence of our men might have fallen with it, but for a young lieutenant named Andrews. He sprang boldly out of the trench, seized the rude flag, and stood holding it up, exposing himself to the flaming rays, until the tide was turned. As the terrestrials retired to form again, he fell, decapitated. "Remember Andrews" became a rallying cry for the rest of the battle.

Warrington had only a few minutes to reorganize his defense before the attackers had formed their ranks again and returned to the storm. For ten hours the fighting went on. Sometimes the terrestrials won a way even into the trenches, but the cry "Remember Andrews!" seemed to raise even the fallen to drive them back.

At last, a definite retreat was made from the hillside. Exhausted, half our men fell asleep in the trenches. But Warrington went tirelessly about the task of consolidating his position. More trenches were dug, more great D-ray tubes moved up from the camp. And our flaming rays fell in an unbroken storm upon the ships in the spaceport, and the batteries that protected that and the town.

Our position commanded the port and the town. On Nov. 17, 2325, General McRan loaded the remnant of his troops on the six of his war-fliers still able to move, blew up the other three, and left New Boston.

The air locks of the city were opened, and jubilant throngs poured out and up the hillside to welcome the men of the deliverer. The excitement and rejoicing was incredible. In spite of all that Warrington could say, men felt that victory was already won.

THE BIRTH OF A NEW REPUBLIC

*Illustrations by
H. W. Wesso*

It was not long before we saw a good deal of activity on the rocky plain below our point of vantage. Scouts reported that great masses of troops were leaving the city.

And the victory had real value, even if enthusiasts were inclined to over-estimate it. Even skeptics had been shown that the moonfolk could engage the veteran troops from Earth on equal terms; that the chance for liberty was at hand. The prestige of Warrington and of the Assembly grew immensely. Supplies and reinforcements began to flow toward New Boston from all inhabited regions.

But, as Warrington said again and again, war had just begun.

CHAPTER ELEVEN
The Eagle of Space

IT was October 3, 2326. Nearly a year had passed since the battle of Meteor Hill. Van Thoren's fleet had come from the Earth—half a hundred mighty globe-like ships of space; and Humbolt's army had replaced McRan's—fifty thousand seasoned veterans from the guards of the Corporation.

For a year, Warrington has matched his inexperienced and poorly armed recruits against that overwhelmingly larger force. He had marched here and there about the moon, from city to city and from mine to mine.

He had fought half a dozen battles. None of them were victories, yet he had never been decisively defeated. His greatness had been shown by his skill in avoiding overwhelming forces, in striking when he might demoralize the enemy with but little danger.

With a matchless tactical skill, he had evaded Humbolt's and Van Thoren's traps again and again, miraculously contriving to reach a city or a great mining district in which he could find refuge, when they had left him to perish in the night upon a desert.

As a matter of course, the Tellurians controlled the skies; they were the masters of space. That gave them great advantage; they could move their troops easily and at will—and they received a stream of supplies and reinforcements from Earth, without which their campaign must quickly have collapsed.

It was not long before we saw a good deal of activity on the rocky plain below our point of vantage. Scouts reported that great masses of troops were leaving the city.

Yet the moon was not without an arm in space. The four small vessels left before Theophilus after the ramming of the *Sandoval* became the core of the Lunarian navy; and a few former pirate or smuggling vessels had been commissioned as privateers. Small ships they all were, and usually obsolescent. But they were manned by skilled and dauntless men, and commanded by a hero—Paul Doane.

Doane had been able to get his little fleet into space before the arrival of terrestrial ships at Theophilus. He had roamed the lanes of space between Earth and moon, committing daring raids on the transports bringing supplies. His ships had engaged and destroyed a dozen vessels, and had brought four prizes to the moon, laden with priceless cargoes of arms, chemicals, and munitions of war.

The spaceports at the three great cities, were, of course, occupied or blockaded by the Tellurian fleets; and Doane was obliged to make his bases of operations the lonely craters that once had been pirate strongholds. Landing in such a place, without the complicated machinery of the ports, is always hazardous, and requires the utmost skill on the part of the pilot to bring the vessel down gently enough to keep from wrecking it on the rocks. But Doane had in his fleet men of years of experience in piloting; in his rather romantic career, he had doubtless become familiar with such tricks himself.

The Tellurians had learned of such difficulties, to their cost, when they attempted to trap Warrington's army in the crater of Hipparchus by landing the fleet and disembarking soldiers in a circle about him. Several fliers were dashed to pieces on the rocks, because their control was not sufficiently delicate, and before Van Thoren had completed the maneuvers that were to bring Warrington's camp under the rays of his fleet, the general had left the crater by the rock "back door," a narrow ravine which led him into the rear of the enemy, where he had played havoc generally with supplies and reserves, and captured a score of great D-rays.

At this time, in October, 2326, Warrington occupied Theophilus. The spaceport was blockaded; and though the location of Humbolt's army was not certainly known, it was expected that he would be landed near and attempt to invest the city.

New Boston, after Warrington's campaigns had led him away from it, had been reoccupied by the Tellurians, after a siege of a week. Colon had been twice assaulted by combined surface and space forces; but her citizens had put up a heroic defense, and she remained free of the terrestrials.

I was with Warrington, of course, in Theophilus. I had hoped to meet father and mother there, but I found that they had both gone back to Firecrest. Why, I did not know at the time. Certainly there seemed no use in working the mines when the roads were so torn up and blockaded that metal could not be moved in safety.

The Assembly was still in session. There were troubles enough before it. It was becoming difficult to finance the war. Warrington was in sore need of men and supplies. The moon had both in plenty, but the terrestrial control of space had so far disorganized industry and communication that they could not be got to him.

It looked to many as if the war might drag on indefinitely until the moon was ruined. In the difficulty, the Assembly resolved to call on outside assistance. A few years before, as the reader will recall, the Transportation Corporation had been at the throat of Metals. If it could only be induced to return to the attack, lunar independence might easily be won.

After long debate, the Assembly voted to send a representative to Earth to call upon Tranco for assistance in the war. As to who the delegate would be, there was little question. Benjamin Gardiner was known throughout the Earth as well as the moon for his additions to scientific knowledge and scientific literature, and for the writings on philosophic subjects that had established him as possessing one of the most brilliant minds the human race has produced.

I have never known just why I was selected to be his private secretary on the trip. Certainly I wanted to go badly enough, and did everything I could to get the appointment; but there must have been a score of other applicants. Perhaps it was my old friendship with both Warrington and Gardiner that won me the place.

Gardiner was a man of above average height, massively built, with a firm, powerfully chiseled face, and keen, penetrating blue eyes beneath shaggy brows. Even the stranger was impressed by the vast, restless power of the man; he carried an aura of dynamic and resistless energy, both of body and mind. At this time, he was well past middle age, but the casual eye saw nothing of senility in his erect, vigorous frame.

On October 3—it was yet in the forenoon of the lunar day—Gardiner and I left Theophilus on our momentous mission.

Before we left there had been a dinner at Warrington's headquarters. In the huge bright room, among massive pieces of furniture scattered with reports and maps and plans, we had eaten a sober meal, talking quietly of what the war had brought and of what it might yet bring. Then, with a smile and a genial handshake, the General had wished us good fortune in our hazardous mission.

Clad in light, white garments and pith helmets, we had left one of the small valves in the city wall. Save for a briefcase of Gardiner's, that I carried, and our hand weapons, we had no luggage. In the dazzling blinding glare of a sun that blistered and stung, we crept cautiously away from the city, through the rapidly growing brownish-green spiky vegetation on the great crater floor, keeping hidden in the thorny growth, or in ravines and canyons, out of sight of the five great sphere-ships that hung above the city, to keep the port blockaded.

Our way led us beyond a shining summit and over the grim, gray, and disordered desert plain, wrinkled into hills and ridges, thickly pocked with craterlets. Soon we were beyond the sight of the city's gleaming towers, though the three slender, black peaks still rose behind us. We forced a way through prickly thickets of the olive-green herbage, and clambered over loose mossy rocks, weirdly splotched with green and purple and scarlet lichens. An inconspicuous sign here and there sufficed to keep us on the regular path of Warrington's intelligence service.

Steadily the sheer, threatening barrier of the crater wall rose before us, ranging up thousands of feet in a rugged wall of naked, black rock. Several times we stopped to rest at one of the little hidden stations, where food and bottles of water were cached. Even after it seemed that the grim dark wall was almost over us, we struggled on for many weary hours. But at last we reached it, crept through the narrow defile that had been cleared with the D-rays. And we walked out of chill shadow into the hot blaze of the sun.

We stopped in a little bare open space, where the very rocks seemed quivering in the sun's unbroken glare. Out of his pocket Gardiner drew a little flag of yellow and scarlet, which he waved above his head.

In a moment, a white-clad man appeared from a mass of thorny, bayonet scrub on the hillside behind us, below the frowning barrier of the black crater-wall and the ragged line of summits that lay in a broken line against the dark blue of the sky. The fellow stood half hidden in the dull-green scrub for a moment, cautiously peering through tinted glasses, with D-ray in his hand. Then suddenly his manner changed, and he came leaping down:

"Gardiner! The great Gardiner! We use your atomic heater, to warm our little post here! But I never thought— We are at your command."

The old scientist smiled genially. "We are going to station K, to meet Paul Doane," he said. "I need mooncalves to carry myself and my companion, and a guide."

"Sure," the fellow grinned behind his green goggles. "Just a minute and I'll leave the post to my partner and guide you myself."

He left us, and ran back through the scrub to the boulder from which he had appeared. He vanished behind it and for a few moments we stood alone on the edge of the desert.

"Wild and lonely, isn't it?" Gardiner remarked. "I lived on Earth for years in my youth and I can never get used to this again."

"Harsh and cruel enough," I assented. "And yet there is something alluring about it; the mystery, the romance, the unknown."

"Yes, I have felt it—have even wished I had time to go prospecting myself. The moon is rather inhospitable to man, and yet the very difficulty of this life has made the moon people what they are."

Suddenly a great mass of coralline cactus-like growth on the hillside above us was bent aside, to reveal the mouth of a cleverly hidden tunnel or cavern. From the black opening three bulky mooncalves emerged, with shining metal saddles strapped on their broad backs.

On the foremost was mounted the man to whom we had spoken; the two others were for us. The guide flung out his arms in a curious gesture. It was caught by the great flat green eyes of the creatures, for simultaneously, their long spidery legs bent, they crouched, and then their colossal, scaly red bodies were catapulted into the air. Down they came toward us, vast scarlet elephantine creatures, hopping like grasshoppers.

Obedient to the gestures of the white-robed rider, who seemed a mere midge upon his gigantic mount, the three Selenites came down toward us, at the end of the last leap landing so near that I had a momentary fear of being crushed beneath them. One of them fell right before me, landing agilely on slender, spidery limbs. Its broad green eyes with the tiny black pupils stared at me inscrutably. Those eyes were very strange, very alien—with no trace of feeling in them.

The huge red thing bent its spindling legs, bringing its glistening, scale-armored, scarlet belly to the rocks. A leap carried me to the metal saddle. Gardiner permitted the third monster to lift him to his seat with its trunk-like appendage. In a moment the guide had signaled with his hand, and we were off.

"Hoo-Ayae! Hoo-Ayae! M'Ob!" his deep voice rang out in the ringing command. The vast bodies beneath us were catapulted smoothly and swiftly forward. We swept through the air on a high, swift flight, for a hundred yards or more. Then down to the rocks, a sudden rocking of the saddles and another great bound.

Again the guide called out his chanting cry, "Hoo-Ayae," and repeated, in an affectionate voice, the name of his mount, "M'Ob." And suddenly I recognized both beast and man. The fellow was Jenkins, the curious man of the desert, who had discovered the Firecrest mine, and sold it to my father. As a boy, I had rather liked the short, sunburned fellow, in spite of his roughness. But it was many years since I had seen him.

As we swept through the air, the three great beasts leaping abreast, I called out to Jenkins and told him who I was. He seemed oddly pleased, and professed to think that he would soon have recognized me. He made eager inquiries about father and the rest of the family, and seemed delighted at the news that Valence was happily married to Tom Dowling—it seemed that Jenkins had been with the young fellow on a prospecting trip a few years before; he told me, "Tom's a real man. He's got guts!"

Presently the old scout began a long-winded account of how he had come upon the Firecrest prospect, but my experience was so novel and exciting that I soon lost interest in his words.

There are few more thrilling ways to travel than upon the back of a Selenite. One sits in the little boxlike metal saddle, with the bright-colored sunshade above him. He gives the signal with his hand. The slender legs of his vast mount bend and the armored red body sinks almost alarmingly. Then the spring—a long, deliberate surging sweep that sends one on a lofty flight of a hundred yards or more. One mounts swiftly, plunges delightfully forward through the cool air, and settles easily to the surface again, ready for the next rocking leap. It is a splendid means of travel, affording marvelous sensation and superb views of the moonscape. And it is surprisingly rapid.

Like great, barrel-bodied insects hopping, our Selenites carried us swiftly into the wild regions west of Theophilus.

The vast slender mountains, baked and blazing in the sunlight; cracked, stony deserts, wild ravines, and ebon-shadowed craters. A pitiless contrast of blinding illumination and mysterious shadow. Here and there, a splash of violent color—scarlet lichen, purple scrub, rich-blue mosses, patches of emerald green. And above all, the sky was a bluish black, set with many stars even by day.

Leap... Leap... Leap.

Hour after hour. The weird panorama of harsh and startling contrast in form and color, in blazing light and profoundest blackness, dropped, slid beneath us, rose to meet us again.

I gazed about, ever enchanted. I was lost in awe at a vast majestic peak, crowned in solar splendor. I exclaimed at sight of some strange shrub, bright with a foliage of vivid green or startling magenta. I was startled at some quick, slender leaping thing that sprang up like a flash of living color before us, to vanish in a mass of bayonet scrub.

Hour after hour. The weird panorama of harsh and startling contrast, in form and color, in blazing light and profoundest blackness, dropped and slid beneath us, then rose to meet us again.

I gazed about, ever enchanted. I was lost in awe at a vast majestic peak, crowned in solar splendor. I exclaimed at sight of some strange shrub, bright with a foliage of vivid green or startling magenta. I was startled at some quick, slender, leaping thing that sprang up like a flash of living color before us, to vanish in a mass of bayonet scrub.

Gardiner had his notebook out, and was recording observations or speculations of some kind, I suppose. Jenkins was muttering low words that I did not understand, to M'Ob, the love of his life.

THE BIRTH OF A NEW REPUBLIC

Illustrations by H. W. Wesso

One mounts swiftly, plunges delightfully forward through cool air, settles easily to the surface again, ready for the next rocking leap.

Leap... Leap... Leap.

I grew sleepy in the unbroken heat of the sun, and dozed as we swept through the air, jarred into wakefulness at each rocking landing. The air was hot and still near the rocks, and laden with sharp, strange odors. But high on the long arc of our flights, it was cool and pure.

At last, my mount failed to rise again, and I sat up sleepily to see what the matter might be. My companions had come down beside me. Before us, a quarter of a mile away, rose a ragged mountain wall. Below it, and extending to our feet, was a dense forest, perhaps the thickest I had ever seen, of the dull-green spiky plants, dotted with purple and scarlet trees, and festooned with coralline creeping vines.

I turned my head. The towering walls rose unbroken all about us. We had entered a crater through some concealed passage. The high-rimmed cup was not a mile across. The whole floor was densely covered with the thorny lunar forest.

And in a little rocky glade beside us was a space flier.

The great sphere, nearly a hundred feet in diameter, lay on a bed of rocks, where it must have taken unusual skill to land her without disaster. The upper part of her gleaming silver surface was covered with brown-splotched canvas, to conceal her from the eyes of the terrestrial fleet. Below the edge of the cloth was the name, stenciled in gold letters, *Eagle*.

A few yards from it was a circular opening in the rocks, closed with a low metal door—the mouth of a shaft. And a little distance away was a tiny cleared patch, covered with rows of red and green plants, the garden, I suppose, of the ship's crew.

No one was in sight when I sat up. But suddenly a sentry sprang up out of the tangle of yellow scrub a few yards away, with a D-ray projector in his hand. He swept a keen eye over us, shouted a familiar greeting to Jenkins, and turning, sang out something in the direction of the ship.

In a moment, a man sprang out of the open air lock of the vessel, a dozen feet above the ground. He landed with cat-like grace, and came bounding toward us. A striking figure, truly. Face thin with blue eyes eagle-keen and stray wisps of bright red hair sticking from beneath a white topi helmet. Body tall and spare, clothed in clean white ducks, and girdled with a sash of brilliant red—a memento of what the hero's earlier adventures had been.

"Paul Doane!" Gardiner cried.

"Gardiner! My old school master! Welcome to the *Eagle!*"

A smile of real pleasure lit the great space-captain's lean brown face. Instinctively I paid my homage to this great hero of the void.

In a few minutes we were in the bridge room at the top of the ship—a wide space, covered with a low metal dome in which were a hundred little windows. In the center was a circular table, built about the axis of the rotation wheel. It was covered with tubes and levers, signal lights and buttons, and with periscope screens that gave the view in all directions. There were the telegraph dials for communication with the engine room, and the telephones to the D-ray decks, the winking lights of the meteor detection devices, and the keys of the complex calculating machines used in plotting courses. Quite a complicated set of instruments, all told.

Doane's second officer, a lean young chap named Bris, stood by the table. He saluted respectfully as we entered. Doane presented us warmly, and rang a little gong. In a moment a white-clad steward entered, with glasses, siphon, and a great flagon of Doane's favorite beverage.

"Doane," Gardiner said briefly, as he set down his glass, "we must go to New York."

"To New York?"

"Exactly."

"You know there are certain risks?"

"The danger is inevitable."

"It is my trade, of course; but you are a statesman, a valuable citizen—"

"The cause of the revolution demands that we treat with the Directors of Tranco."

"I will get you there if it can be done."

"Good. When can we start?"

"In an hour."

The interview was over.

CHAPTER TWELVE
A Trip to Earth

AN hour later, as Doane had promised, the crew of two hundred men was aboard the *Eagle*, the canvas cover had been removed, and we were rising swiftly out of the fantastic yellow forest.

Swiftly the blue-black sky grew blacker, and tracks of nebulous stardust crept out among the brightening stars. The sun, driving intense shafts of fire slanting across the control room, became a great and incredible wonder of livid, winged, white flame. I donned my tinted glasses and viewed it—a great sphere of white light, marked with the redder sunspots, with the serpentine prominences of the corona writhing about it.

Doane had crowded on all our power, in the hope of getting away without being observed by the patrol. Great trails of fire were flaring moonward behind us, and the acceleration drew me so forcefully against the deck that, as used to as I was only to the feeble gravity of the moon, I was very uncomfortable.

Gardiner and I were alone on the bridge with Doane and his first officer—the men were below, at the machines, or in their quarters. Doane and Gardiner stood over the great round instrument board, Bris, our mate, was making entries in a log book, and I occupied myself in nervously pacing the deck, stopping to gaze out first at one window, then at another.

Doane suddenly muttered a low exclamation, and began to manipulate the telegraph dials before him. He called Bris, gave him a quick command, and the officer fell to pecking swiftly at the keys of the machines which plotted the course. I felt the ship swerve, and our speed seemed increasing more rapidly than ever.

Gardiner beckoned to me.

"Look," he said.

I peered into a ground-glass disk that was evidently the objective of one of the telescopic periscopes. In it, against a field of utter black, were two bright points of fire, far apart and apparently motionless.

"Those are two war fliers," Gardiner told me. "We see the sunlight reflected from their hulls. They were picked up by the automatic radio-beam detector that enables us to avoid meteorites."

"The indicator shows that they are approaching us at almost a thousand miles per hour," Doane added casually. He seemed undisturbed, bending over the bewildering array of instruments as calmly as though no peril were in the offing.

"How far off?" I questioned.

"Three hundred fifty-one miles," Doane said. "And if they are Van Thoren's cruisers, as they must be, their maximum acceleration will be somewhat above our own. We have several hours, though."

Presently I went away from the table, where Doane and Bris bent so intently over the instruments, and fell to walking up and down the floor again. The bridge room was a strange place, dark despite the shaded lamps above the great round instrument board. The narrow blazing shafts of sunlight glanced blindingly on the floor, hardly seeming to light the rest of the room.

The nervous tension and the inactivity preyed on my mind.

Doane had showed me the little dials that indicated the distance of the pursuing ships, and sometimes I went to look at them. Always the distance was a little less. In two hours we lost only a hundred miles, though the moon had shrunk from a weird, rugged plain to a bright mottled sphere that seemed to hang very near in the night of space.

Presently, as I was pacing up and down, Bris, the mate, touched my arm.

"I'm going down to see the men. Care to go along?"

I did care. Anything to relieve the strain of monotonous inactivity was welcome. We climbed down through a round manhole to the D-ray deck just below the bridge. A great circular space, rimmed by the wall of the ship. All about the edge, in a ring, were the huge ray projectors, twenty-four in number. They seemed in readiness, polished and gleaming, with the crews of three men each, near them.

It was curious to note the occupations of the men in the present proximity of peril. A few were busily polishing their weapons, as if those were their greatest loves. A few were standing about, whistling, chatting or smoking, as if they had no care in the world. Two or three were reading in secluded corners under their pieces, and one young fellow seemed to be writing a letter. But the great attraction seemed to be a game of chance; fully half the white-uniformed crew were gathered in a ring in the center of the deck about the ivory cubes.

Bris called them to attention, delivered a few words of cheer. He told them that Gardiner was aboard and that his fate, as well as the probable fate of the moon, depended on their bravery and obedience. They responded with a cheer and then fell to singing a rough ballad of one "Boss Varney, free rover of space." Their rich, mellow voices, swelling up in that old pirate song, carried an infectious spirit of youth and courageous enthusiasm.

We left them, as the minor officers were getting them to their pieces, three men to each great, gleaming tube. On down we went into the bowels of the ship. We passed the power plant, a vast, gloomy space in the center of the sphere, crowded with huge and complicated masses of throbbing, whirring machinery. The revolving wheel that carries the quarters of the crew was like a great ring about us. Here and there were grimy engineers, standing beside the vast humming generators or intently watching dials. Greasy oilers swung like black spiders here and there in the web of black metal. Even they seemed to take the coming action with a good enough spirit, for many of them were singing or humming at their work.

Through this, we clambered down the long ladder to the lower D-ray deck, where there were twenty-four more great tubes, and seventy-five-waiting men. Below this deck, at the pole of the sphere opposite the control room above was the projectors of the atomic blast that hurled us through space. Bris repeated his speech, the men moved to their stations, and we returned to the bridge.

The pursuing fliers had gained seventy miles in our absence.

Another hour went by, with our ship plunging Earthward at the limit of its speed. Now the other war-fliers were but forty miles away. One hour more, I thought, and their vastly superior armament will have swept us out of existence.

But I did not know Paul Doane.

I was standing by the little round disk of the periscope, watching the two points of fire that were the ships. They were very bright now. Suddenly Doane leaned forward to a bank of keys, depressed a group of them in a certain complex pattern.

I felt the *Eagle* lurch a little, heard a sound like the firing of an old-fashioned cannon. A few minutes later, the projectiles he had fired exploded behind us. White luminous clouds spread from the quick bursts of flame, grew until they were vast masses of mist, hiding the other fliers and filling the sky with an opalescent curtain.

(These projectiles were the Ziker space-screen bombs, which form vast clouds of electrically charged particles in space, lit in part by the sun, in part by the radioactivity of the constituent matter. They are an important item in the strategy of space fighting.)

When the forming clouds had grown large enough to protect us from the searching telescopes of the other ships, Doane cut off our acceleration; and we floated a few miles back of the cloud, waiting.

With the blast projectors shut off, our sensations were the most unusual. Gravity seemed suddenly gone. We floated in the air, pulling ourselves about by handrails, or walking only with the aid of magnetic shoes.

We waited for the war-fliers.

Suddenly, at the same time, they burst through the luminous mist screen, plunging Earthward so fast that they passed beyond us, one on each side. The *Eagle* was ready, with a pole turned toward the path of each. A broadside of rays from our upper D-ray deck caught one of them, and the other found itself the target for the tubes of the lower deck.

The Tellurians must have been taken somewhat by surprise, supposing Doane to be seeking flight beyond his mist-screen, for their fire was delayed and ineffectual. It was evident that our rays had done serious damage, for the silvered reflector screen was cut in great streaks from the ships, and the naked plates beneath were heated to incandescence; and the propulsion machinery of both seemed crippled.

I have no doubt that Paul Doane would have won a complete victory if he had stayed to fight, but he was intent not on victory but on escape. Before the crippled vessels could turn, he had driven our ship into the vast luminous cloud. And a moment later, we were out of it, on the other side and sweeping toward Earth again.

Either the other ships were too badly crippled to follow, or they searched for us in the cloud until we were beyond the range of their detectors. They did not follow.

A day went by, and our beams showed no sign of pursuit.

In the long days that followed, as we were hurtled through the fantastic, lonely desolation of infinite space, I spent much time in clambering about the ladders and catwalks of the ship, from bridge room to blast projector. I learned something of its mechanism, and made friends of several members of the crew—who were mostly cheerful, happy fellows, with the oddest childlike faith in little talismans they carried to ward off the thousand terrors of space.

One man had a mooncalf's scarlet scale polished to a ruby disk. He wore it on a platinum chain, and swore that no harm could come to him until it was lost. Another pinned his faith on a fragment of a meteorite that had somehow found its way into his bunk when the stone had struck the ship upon which he was then serving. And there was a tall young Canadian who had a red wool sweater of marvelous properties—he had had a miraculous escape, after a collision in space, while wearing it. He had unraveled so much of it to give away as charms to his comrades that little more than the collar was left. And all swore devoutly that not a man had been injured in the thousand perils of their trade, who had had a thread of that sweater about his person.

Gardiner was utilizing his spare time to write a monograph on his latest work in electromagnetic vibration, and I helped with that, taking dictation and revising his notes. He was one of the few men of great intellect, whose genial good nature and unfailing cheerfulness makes it a pleasure to be near.

And, as we sped through space, I thought more of the girl I had met at Theophilus, who had called herself Mary Jons. I wondered who she really was, where she had gone. I wondered if she could be actually as beautiful as I recalled her, wondered if I would find that I loved her as much as I felt that I did, if I should ever see her again.

There seemed small chance indeed that I would meet her on Earth. But I had always imagined that she had gone back there. And I had a lover's optimism.

In spite of our delay during the battle with the war-fliers, our passage was unusually short. It was just nineteen days after Gardiner and I had left Theophilus when we entered the Earth's atmosphere. On the night of October 22, 2325, we entered the air, over the North Atlantic Ocean.

Landing had seemed to me quite a problem, in secrecy, at night, and on a strange planet. But Paul Doane did not seem at a loss.

He took us westward, at an altitude of some fifty miles, until the lights of New York City were visible like a great flake of silver fire in the darkness below.

Then he slanted down, reaching the ocean a few miles off Long Island. Landing on water, of course, is a far simpler matter than coming down on the cruel rocks of the moon, though the vastly greater gravitational pull of the Earth complicates the matter somewhat.

And the gravity of Earth, six times that of the moon, was a very serious inconvenience to our own movements. Even with the *Eagle* resting still on the water, I felt the same unnatural affinity for the deck as when we had been accelerating with all our power, in space. Seats had been provided in the bridge room, and feeling heavy and uncomfortable, we all made use of them.

Our voices sounded increasingly loud, as air was slowly admitted to the flier to raise the barometric pressure to that of the new planet. Not only does the heavier air of Earth carry sound better than the atmosphere of the moon; but our auditory and vocal organs were adapted to the rarer air. After the landing, I found my hearing almost preternaturally acute; and I had considerable difficulty to keep my voice low enough not to sound conspicuous among the terrestrials.

The great shell drifted landward under the merest impulse of the blast, until the dark line of the land was visible through the murky air of Earth, a half mile away. Then the men produced and launched a small, sheet metal rowboat, which, I suppose, had been built during the voyage for just this emergency.

Gardiner and I stepped into it, after the oarsman was aboard, shaking hands with Doane. In five minutes, we were landed on the sand and the man took the boat back to the dark mass of the space flier. Watching, we saw the merest wisp of iridescent mist swirl toward us from where it had been, and it was lost in the night.

"Where is he going?" I asked Gardiner, my voice unexpectedly loud in the dense air.

"He intends to hide the ship in the north of Greenland. He will be back here three weeks from tonight and will send the boat to take us up."

My sensations were the strangest imaginable. My memories of the Earth were but scattered and vague, and when I had been taken to the moon, I was too young to appreciate the strangeness of a trip between worlds.

The gravity of the Earth gave my body a leaden weight. Accustomed to travel by great strides, or by bounds of many yards, I found it difficult to pick up my feet. The air felt oppressive, close, and moist. It was a squeezing pressure on my chest. And my sense of equilibrium was affected, for I reeled and stumbled, and had to sit down on the sand. Gardiner seemed to be suffering as much as myself.

"It's just the gravity," he said. "It will pass. We will be acclimated by daytime."

For long hours we sat there.

All my sensations were strange, but I think the strangest thing was to be out of doors at night. I could not remember having been out at night before, for on the moon the touch of night is death. As we sat there, I looked at the stars. They were not motionless and bright like those of the moon; the thick, murky air gives them an odd wavering motion, the sky is never really black, and most of the stars are always screened in the air. Odors, too, were strange. There was a curious smell of growing things, of unfamiliar flowers, and the salty tang of the sea.

Then came sunrise. Not a sudden burst of blinding fire, but a symphony of changing, multitudinous shafting shades of liquid light, wonders of pale dawn-cloud, tinted with softest gold, miracles of crimson and purple, splendors of deepest azure of gorgeous gold. A ruddy sun was born from a sea of molten glory.

And we rose from our seats on the sand, two strangers on an unknown sphere—with a vast and perilous mission before us.

CHAPTER THIRTEEN
The New York Negotiations

THE beach on which we had landed had seemed very lonely by night, but it was not so by day. A half mile above the water rose the colossal pile of a building, enclosed in a glittering armor of glass, somewhat like my familiar cities on the moon. But this edifice was slender, and two hundred stories tall, with a flat landing stage upon its summit.

All about it the grounds were beautifully landscaped; hedges, lawns, and clumps of flowering trees, scattered with fountains, golf links, and promenades, extended down to the beach where we stood.

A mile farther on was another vast building, and to the right of that were two more slender, towering structures. And there were more beyond, the farther ones dwarfed by distance, and blue-like, far-off hills. Long Island was scattered with them, and the land beyond the Sound.

The carefully tended pleasure-gardens were incredibly beautiful to one from the drear wastes of the moon, bright with the luxuriant emerald vegetation of eternal spring. With climatic control, which boundless atomic power had made simple on Earth, though it is impossible under the vastly different conditions of the moon, winter has not come to New York for a hundred years, and orange trees bloom in its parks.

As we strolled up the silvery beach, under an oddly mild and genial sun, lost in the wonders of this unfamiliar world beneath a blue sky so bright that the stars could not be seen by day, the place awoke. The gleaming wings of airplanes flashed across from landing stage to landing stage; and the gardens were soon dotted with the dull-gray uniforms of the caretakers, and flecked with the brighter garments of a few young idlers bent on morning exercise.

Our sun-helmets and tattered white garments must have made us rather conspicuous, for I remember one blear-eyed old fellow, who was running a whirring automatic mowing machine, who stopped and stared at us a full minute as we walked past him. A bit farther on, strolling over a soft rich lawn bordered with a blaze of orchid bloom, we met a brightly dressed young man and girl, with tennis rackets in their hands. "Hello, there my men. What's your idea?"

Taken rather aback at this uncalled-for question, I looked at Gardiner.

"Tranco. N3D. 136 kn 9." The old scientist answered glibly.

"Yes?" There was a note of suspicion in the youngster's voice. "Then what's the matter? How'd you come to be in a rig like that?"

"We've been in the Sahara. Prospecting. Aero dropped us on the beach at daylight." He fished in his pocket, drew out a little disk of stamped aluminum, and extended it to the fellow. "See?"

"Yes. Iden, all right. 'Tranco. N3D. 136 kn 9.'" He handed it back. "Looks all right. But you had better watch out for the information gang."

He turned to the girl, threw his arm about her familiarly. They strolled on over the bright garden, turning once or twice to stare back at us as if suspicious of our garb.

Gardiner turned to me. "Idle pleasure seekers!" he muttered, a little contemptuous. "What would they do, set down to farm a crater on the moon?"

He handed me a little disk of that metal. "Identification tag. What he called an iden. Everybody has to have one. It tells what corporation you belong to, and how much pay you get. Also has your identification number on it. A man is ranked socially by the amount of pay shown on his tag.

"And as the young man hinted, we must be careful. Metals has spies everywhere, and we Lunarians are fair game for them, to be treated as traitors if caught. We will be safer after we get under the protection of Tranco, but we must get to town at once and change into different clothes."

We walked on across the bright, unfamiliar gardens to the vast pile of glass and steel. We passed beyond the emerald lawns and masses of bright shrubbery, and entered the great building through revolving doors. An elevator shot us down to the business levels, a few hundred feet below the surface, where we found a dry goods shop. Gardiner was well supplied with Tranco credit vouchers; and soon we were attired in the fashion of the city. I chose a crimson tunic, with blue robe and sash, while Gardiner contented himself with a dark green suit, with black mantle.

Then, at a higher level, we found the dining rooms and had a breakfast of synthetic food mixture, served with orange juice. Having eaten, we purchased a news strip, upon which the happenings of the last few hours were recorded in the modern printing shorthand, and took the elevator to the roof.

On the landing stage there, we engaged passage to the building on Manhattan Island which houses the executive offices of Tranco. Gardiner, reading the paper as the swift atomotored flier cut silently through the air, assured me that nothing was said to indicate that anyone had seen the arrival of the *Eagle* in the Earth's atmosphere.

In a few minutes we had landed on the great, three-decked stages of the Tranco Building, one of the largest in the world. Two hundred and seventy stories high, it covers sixty acres, and is the capitol of one of the largest corporations in existence.

We dropped by elevator to the floor given over to the Board of Directors. This proved a veritable palace of beautiful architecture, finished with a splendor that was amazing to me. Here we interviewed a few secretaries in the little glass cells before the offices of the dignitaries whom they guarded. Gardiner did not wish to disclose our identity until he had learned something of the attitude of the corporation toward the war on the moon; but it seemed impossible to see anyone in authority so long as we were unknown.

But at last, in one of the long, bright-lit, splendid halls, which had moving ways like the streets of the moon cities, we met a little wrinkled man, who sprang to greet Gardiner with an eager exclamation.

He was, it seemed, one Robert Bakr, himself a Director of Tranco. A man of scientific interests and aspirations, he had long known of Gardiner and his brilliant work, had even met him at scientific gatherings in New York, years before.

He seemed delighted to meet the old scientist. He hurried us into his sumptuously furnished office, and inquired about our business on the Earth. Gardiner lost no time in telling him the object of our visit. He could give us no assurance that Tranco would be willing to break the peace with Metals, but he assured us of the cordial friendship of the corporation.

After a time, he conducted us up to the offices of the President, in a suite of such splendor as would make a Lunarian gasp with wonder. We were most warmly received by that dignitary, a tall man with iron-gray hair, named Frank Lewis. He inquired about conditions on the moon, commented on Gardiner's scientific achievements, and invited us to come again.

He gave orders that we were to be treated as honored guests of Tranco. From his office Bakr took us to another where we were given passports that would insure our personal safety. Then he carried us off to his palatial suite in a building above the Palisades, and made us stop with him. We stayed at his splendid establishment as long as we were in New York. He and Gardiner had long discussions over my friend's latest work in space-radio. The monograph was read, and I think Gardiner and Bakr worked out one or two new experiments together.

We saw Lewis again. He was certainly friendly enough; and I knew that his best wishes were with the insurgents on the moon, for the revolt threatened to break the power of his greatest enemy. But his memory of the war of 2307 was so strong that he hardly dared to take any open action.

One day a meeting of the Directors was called in the spacious and magnificent auditorium in the Tranco building. Gardiner spoke before it, making a powerful appeal for the cause of the moon, stressing not only the cause of right and human liberty, but the advantage to Tranco in having a free corporation on the moon, with which it could trade on equality with Metals.

The Directors were doubtful, some of them frankly afraid. The meeting presently broke up without having come to any definite conclusion; but the case, we understood, was almost hopeless.

But Gardiner was not one to give up easily. He kept at work on the project. He saw Lewis often, and was most cordially received. And sometimes I warmed the cushions in an outer office for long hours while he was closed up with some other official. Now that his identity was known, his popularity became immense. He was a lion at the great social affairs, a guest eagerly sought for by the most exclusive circles. His simple manners and quiet taste in clothing even caused a fad of imitation in the fickle fashions of the time. But he did not forget his purpose; he used wit and intellectual attainment to work steadily toward his end.

That men were willing to listen to his brilliant talk or to invite him to their select social functions, did not mean that they were willing to go to war for the cause of the moon. After we had been on Earth ten days, the Directors held another meeting, influenced, perhaps, by diplomatic complications with Metals that had risen from our efforts, and solemnly resolved to let no cause "dissolve the ties of peace and friendship" that bound them to Metals.

But even then, Gardiner did not despair. Bakr was still warmly friendly; he was still an admired and welcome guest in social circles, and at the offices of Lewis. He had met a wealthy young man, Lafollette, the head of the Chicago offices of Tranco, who held a deep devotion to lunar liberty. It seemed that Tranco might help us secretly, if she dared not do so openly.

One day, after he had been to some sort of secret conclave in the offices of Lewis, Gardiner returned to Bakr's suite, where I was waiting, with his smile of encouragement on his lean face. In reply to my eager inquiry, he said:

"Nothing definite. But a chance for something that will be worth a great deal to the moon."

"You remember the war of twenty years ago?"

"I should. Father was almost killed in it."

"Then you know that Tranco had been building space-fliers. One Doctor Vardon had sold them an invention of his, a process for using gold to generate the atomic blast for propelling spaceships. The experimental ships were discovered by Metals, wiped out. Vardon and all the men working with him were killed. The secret of the discovery was thought to have died with them.

"But Vardon left a widow and an orphan child—a girl. A few days after his death, they vanished. The information service of Metals hunted them for years, and Tranco officials, suspecting something, joined the search.

"Until a few years ago, it was not known why Metals wished to locate the mother and the girl. But last year Lewis received a communication from one Leroda Vardon, who claims to be the daughter of the dead scientist. She stated that she had in her possession the secret of the gold atomic blast, and offered to sell it. Lewis had her come to his offices for an interview, and had an investigation made of her claims. He is satisfied that they are genuine.

"It seems that the matter was brought up before the Board of Directors in secret session. Remembering their previous experience with the invention, they were afraid to make any attempt to use it. They endeavored to get possession of it; but the girl wanted a million units—the secret is worth a thousand times that, of course—and the penurious Assembly, not daring to use the secret after they had bought it, would offer no more than a half million. Nothing came of it except that the young woman was granted a pension to keep her from trying to dispose of the secret elsewhere.

"And, John, Leroda Vardon is now in New York. Lewis has arranged for Bakr and me to call on her tomorrow. It is possible that we can make some arrangement to get the discovery, if she really has the plans. And if we get it, it might be possible to build a fleet on the moon, in which the blast-projectors can be installed.

"And once we have a fleet, so we can communicate with Earth, I think we can get help."

The next afternoon we flew out to one of the great buildings on Long Island—the very one at which Gardiner and I had landed. With Bakr as our guide, we descended elevator shafts, and glided down moving ways, and at last stopped before a door at the end of a hall, where there was a huge window looking out upon the green expanse of the ocean of Earth.

Bakr pressed a button, and presently the great door swung open. We stepped into the vestibule, where Bakr left us seated for a moment, while he walked on into the next room. In a few minutes he came back and called Gardiner, and they were both gone for a time. I was not included in his gesture; and I remained seated, though I had a rather strong curiosity to see Leroda Vardon.

At last the door swung open again, and Bakr came into the little room, with Gardiner at his heels. Gardiner was speaking back over his shoulder in a hopeless tone:

"No, the moon could not possibly pay a million units." Then I heard a woman's voice, trembling with emotion and determination:

"But it cost me my father and my mother. Because of it, I have been a fugitive, a homeless wanderer, hounded by the spies. And I must be paid—"

That voice was familiar.

The sound of it brought me a curious, eager thrill. For a moment I stood there, heart thumping madly. Then I brushed Gardiner and Bakr aside, and rushed through the door.

Before me stood the girl I had known on the moon as Mary Jons—the mystery girl, who had vanished so suddenly. Beautiful as ever she was, tall and slender. Her oval face was flushed with feeling now, and there was a gleam of moisture in her eyes. There was something about her that suggested the fresh, clean wind of the seas of Earth.

I seized her white forearms, looked into her dark, shining eyes.

First she jerked back, in surprise. Then a sudden light of incredulous gladness flashed over her face, and she whispered in an odd tone:

"You!"

Her arms trembled in my hands. She closed her eyes, swayed a little toward me. Then suddenly she stepped back, pulled free of my grasp. I stood there, speechless, overcome with a peculiar, tingling delight.

"Mr. Adams," the girl began, trying to be formal, "I am glad—"

Then she seemed to choke, and stood with tears brimming in her glorious dark eyes. I stepped to her awkwardly, held out my hands. She thrust out her own slim white hands, uncertainly, as though groping through a cloud of tears.

I grasped them, drew her to me. She trembled, yielded. Another moment and she was in my arms.

A few minutes later we were sitting together on a divan at the end of the bright little drawing room. I do not know how long Gardiner and Bakr waited outside, before they ventured to come in and interrupt us.

Then Leroda Vardon proved herself a charming hostess. She went to a panel on the wall, pressed the buttons that brought a great tray of delicious refreshments up the service tube. I confess, however, that I have little idea of what those delicacies were; I do not remember whether I did full justice to them or not.

Presently we left, but not until she had promised to go with me to one of the pleasure-palaces.

We had, as I remember it, a gorgeous time that evening. The details, perhaps, are a little vague in my mind. I have no definite memory of just what we did. There was a theater, with a silly play, no doubt, and a supper afterward, and probably we went the round of the fashionable amusement places. But the important thing was Leroda. I was intoxicated with her charm, her beauty, her vivacious wit. How I treasure the memory of those last moments in the flier, as it brought us back to her building!

I bade her goodnight at the lift, but not until she had promised to play tennis with me next morning in the bright, fragrant beach gardens.

I planned to make the most of the eight days until Paul Doane was to come back for us.

That night, when I had flown back to Bakr's apartments, where Gardiner and I were staying, I found waiting for me a sealed note, addressed in Gardiner's flowing hand. I opened it to find a brief message in his shorthand, fine and clear as if printed.

"Dear John," it read, "I am flying to Chicago tonight, with a friend. Will return in time. Enjoy yourself. B. G."

I wondered who the friend might be, but I did not let worry interfere with following his last injunction.

CHAPTER FOURTEEN
The Secret of the Cylinder

THE days that followed slipped by in a sort of golden mist. Leroda and I were together most of the time. Walking together, we explored the entire green fairyland about the great building, discovered a dozen little nooks in the fragrant, flowering shrubbery where we felt delightfully alone. We lunched and dined together, and danced afterward; from a private box we witnessed the changing wonders of Earth, on the "stereo" picture screen—when our eyes were not upon each other.

And one day we hired a little flying boat—a tiny machine of bright aluminum, with wings painted red; it was driven by atomotor. We had a cruise of delightful adventure down the Atlantic seaboard; and spent the night on a great floating pleasure island, in the warm waters of the Gulf Stream, off the Florida Keys.

Perhaps the recreations there were artificial and mechanical, but we had a most delightful time. The magic of our association turned the world into a joyous paradise.

After a day there, we returned to New York. The gleaming little machine, with airfoils folded and atomotors driving whining propellers, was cutting through the air at nearly a thousand miles per hour. Leroda sat beside me in the little enclosed cockpit, her slight, warm body in thrilling contact with mine, managing the controls of the little machine with unconscious skill.

Suddenly she cut off the motor. We dropped in a long arc toward the blue, sun-bright Atlantic. Swiftly, the air-speed indicator and the altimeter dropped toward zero. She watched the instruments alertly, presently switched on the landing helicopters. The little vessel struck the warm, glassy surface lightly as a bird, floated buoyantly, rising and falling a little on the swell.

We were utterly alone. The white flat desert of water stretched about us, glittering in the evening sun, broken only by a thin green line of land in the west, with a gray smudge of cloud above it, which was flame-tipped by the sun.

I turned expectantly to Leroda, to find her blue eyes serious and thoughtful.

"John," she began slowly, "I have something to tell you."

"Let me kiss you first," I demanded cheerfully.

She submitted gracefully, but without the loss of her sober manner.

"I have a secret, John. It cost my father's life, and then my mother's. It has made me a hunted woman. It is father's invention—a new source of atomic power. It is worth billions to the Earth, for it would make over all industry. I have tried to sell it for a mere million units. It is worth a million times that; but after the terrible war when father was killed, men have been afraid to buy it. They are afraid of Metals Corporation."

"Then you have Dr. Varden's formulas and plans?"

"Exactly. The invention that Gardiner was trying to buy—when you came to me. Of course I can't carry such a thing with me. The spies of Metals have been on my trail for years—they would murder me cheerfully for the secret, if that would get it.

THE BIRTH OF A NEW REPUBLIC

"Father gave his papers to mother when he went away to build the ships for Tranco. I was a baby, then. Father knew that he was doing a dangerous thing; he had warned my mother. She slipped away, when—when—it happened. She hid the records.

"Spies hunted us. Metals knew that if they could get the secret it would make them the most powerful corporation in the world. We were poor. We had to go from city to city, with the spies always after us. We had to take false names, to live in miserable tenements, to work for our food. When I was old enough to understand, mother told me all about it, told me where the plans were hidden. And she said it would be safer if we were not together. She put me in a school, and went away. She sent me money regularly—she must have slaved for it.

"I was twelve years old when they caught her. She managed to send me a farewell message, and her savings. She told me to go to a school on the moon—it would be safer there. I don't know what they did to her; she died in prison.

"And on the moon, at Theophilus—" She smiled through the tears brimming in her earnest eyes.

"I found you," I supplied.

"And because you followed me home, I imagined that you were a spy. I could not trust my heart. That is why I left. And then, a few days ago, you came with Gardiner, and I knew—"

Blue eyes were laughing now, through her tears. It seemed the psychological moment, and I took her in my arms. It was somewhat later when she spoke again: "But the secret. I must tell you where to find father's records."

"But the moon cannot pay—"

"I'm giving them—to you, John."

"Oh! But you mustn't—"

"It has been a curse to my family, anyhow; and it probably would never do me any good. My mother sealed the papers up in an aluminum container, and flew with them to the island of Tobago in the West Indies, just off the South American coast. It is years since she told me where they were hidden, but I can still hear her words:

" 'There is a rock with a pinnacle like the steeple of a church, with a big round boulder beyond it. They lie in the sea, off the end of the northeast promontory. The cylinder is between them, lying on a rock bottom, about a fathom deep at low tide.'

"That's all I remember, but you should be able to find it. Now repeat what I said."

I did. "I'm sure we can find the spot. Doane will have charts. And if we win, you will be paid—"

She stopped me with a kiss.

In a moment she moved the switch that set the helicopters spinning. The little machine rose off the placid sea, and a few minutes later we were skimming northward again, high in a warm blue sky. We talked of many things, but not of what we were thinking of most of all—that in a few days I must go back to the moon.

THAT night, when I arrived at Bakr's apartment, I found Gardiner returned from his Chicago trip. Though it was not early, he had a light going in his room, and was bent over a table scattered with loose sheets of paper.

He stood up as I entered, greeted me with a smile. "And who was the friend you went to see?" I presently inquired.

"He is Lafollette. Head of the Chicago branch of Tranco—"

"I remember. We met him the other day."

"He has been a friend of mine for years. We had a delightful visit. And his heart is with us."

"Will he be able to help the moon?"

"He would like to. He's rich enough. And for that matter, Lewis might advance some funds. But there seems to be no way to get supplies and men to the moon. If we had a few more ships—"

He did not finish, but stood in the light, staring thoughtfully at the litter of papers on the table.

"And it is tomorrow night that Doane is coming," I said, suddenly appalled at the nearness of the time.

"It is. And we're lucky if we get away without a scrap. The whole world knows we're here, by this time, of course. And Metals has spies on us, in spite of Tranco's protection."

"Then we're watched?"

"There were two men in this room when I came in, going through my luggage," he said grimly. "They got out through the window. Nothing for them to find, I suppose."

"Have you notified the officers?"

"I thought it better not to. We are already under the protection of Tranco. To raise a disturbance might precipitate trouble. We must go tomorrow night."

Presently I told him about Leroda's gift of her father's great discovery. He seemed pleased, but much less surprised than I had expected. He soon fell to work again; he was still at it, late in the night, when I went to bed.

On the last day, Leroda and I were together all the time. We tried feverishly to amuse ourselves, to forget. But the hour of parting stared us in the face like a dreadful specter. A great concert and the thrills of a rocket race failed alike to take our minds from the dreadful reality.

At dusk we nervously ate a little lunch, and then walked in the moonlit gardens—looking up at the golden mottled world, on which I must go to war. And for a time we sat on a mossy stone bench, trying to enjoy the cool salty breeze from the sea, and the silver radiance that fell upon us in a mellow flood. But I found it impossible to be still; something made me want to tramp up and down. Leroda seemed to share my restlessness, and we roamed about, hand in hand, silent and clinging to each other in a sort of desperation.

I was to meet Gardiner on the beach, at midnight, just after the half-moon had set. We would wait in the darkness for Doane.

The time for parting came. A slight chill had fallen upon the garden, and the crisp air was lightly scented with the flowers of Earth. A thousand stars twinkled feebly above, and the half-moon was just above the western horizon, red and wavering in the heavy air. Leroda was a slim white figure in the night.

"Good-by, John," she said. "I hope—I hope you can come back."

"I will—" I began, but an unusual tension came in my throat, so that I could not go on.

I put an arm about her white shoulders, drew her to me. Her eyes were shining in the darkness, and warm lips came up and found mine. A fragrant wisp of hair drifted against my cheek. Then she was suddenly sobbing and clinging to me. The tremors of her slight body gave me odd mingled pleasure and pain.

Then she thrust herself fiercely away, stifling her sobs. She put a little object in my hand—a slender package wrapped in scented paper.

"It is time," she whispered. "Go."

A moment I stood there, absently holding the little package in my hand, and staring at her slender form in the darkness. I felt a dangerous desire to stay, to forget the war on the moon. If I did not go down to the beach, the *Eagle* would depart without me. But I knew Leroda would never approve it.

With an odd choking sound, she suddenly turned, and vanished in a dark copse of shrubbery. A few minutes later I found Gardiner, briefcase in hand, waiting on the lawn by the orange trees.

CHAPTER FIFTEEN
The Aluminum Tube

SWIFTLY we walked down the hard white sand of the beach. A fog was rolling up from the sea, and it shrouded the entire dark world about us. But still we could hear the sound of the ocean, a restless, living moan, which seemed very strange to me. And it was strange, too, to be walking in a curtain of fog, feeling its cold breath against ray face, to look back and see the bright lights of the land behind us, with the building we had left rising like a tower of fire, soft and misty and incredibly beautiful in the mantle of the mist.

At last we reached the edge of the lapping waves, and stood still in the night. Unconsciously, I trembled and drew my robe close about me, for my imagination increased the bracing chill of the keen moist wind to the deadening cold of the lunar darkness.

"Do you think Doane will come?" I asked Gardiner through teeth involuntarily chattering. "It is so far. Something must have happened. If he tried to land the ship to hide it, it may have been wrecked. Or the fleet—"

"If any man is worthy of our staking our lives upon him, that man is Paul Doane," Gardiner replied hopefully.

For a long time, it seemed to me, we stood there, staring into the black masses of flowing cloud that eddied, leaden and murky, about us.

"If he doesn't come pretty soon—" I began.

Gardiner looked at the gleaming dial of his watch.

"He is not to come until two. It lacks half an hour of the time."

I drew my cloak closer about my shoulders and waited, thinking of the wondrous girl I had just left, wondering if I should ever see her again. The thought that I probably should not was terrible. Fiercely, I clutched at the tiny object she had given me.

Suddenly a bright flash of white light lit the beach about us, illuminating the fog all about until it looked like drooping curtains of yellow silk. Even as the searchlight burst upon us, I felt a powerful arm behind me, which flung me face down on the sand.

A moment I lay there, mouth flung full of sand and the breath quite knocked out of me. I heard the curious hiss of an object under a D-ray; and the air about, when I jerked my head up, was faintly luminous from the radioactive gases evolved by the atomic rays. Suddenly then darkness was cut through by the narrow, piercing green beam of a disintegrator ray.

Abruptly, a little up the beach, there was a metallic clatter, as if some light object had fallen on the sand, then a great, gasping sob and a choking cry:

"My gawd—stop! You're killing—"

I saw a vivid, crimson spurt of flame from an old-fashioned automatic, heard the sharp crack of it, and the hum of its bullet close by us; then running footsteps that ended with the thudding fall of a human body upon the sand.

Alarmed and astounded, I was fumbling for my pocket D-ray when Gardiner's low calm voice spoke close beside me:

"It's all right, John. The men that were in my room, I suppose. I can hear better than they thought, after all my years in the thin air of the moon. I was ready. There was nothing else to do."

"Then you—"

"I killed them. I had to."

We walked a half-dozen yards up the sand, found two human bodies lying there, dark splotches in the night, bleeding and fearfully mutilated by the action of the rays, smelling pungently of burned hair and flesh. I turned away in horror.

"Too bad," Gardiner muttered. "But I had to do it."

We walked back to the edge of the water.

"Someone will be seeking them soon," Gardiner said.

I looked at my watch. It showed six minutes to two. Hours went by, it seemed; but when I looked again, only four and a half minutes had passed. I felt invisible men slipping up about us; I stepped nearer Gardiner, crowded toward the water. Looking back up toward the long, slender pillars of light in the mist, I fancied that I saw other lights flickering, nearer, just above the ground.

It may have been all imagination, but I felt that our enemies were closing in. Then, out in the dark mists of the sea, I saw a faint swirl of phosphorescent mist—vapor that glowed faintly through the fog, with ghostly red and faintest scarlet and impalpable purple. A play of color almost invisible—the radioactive light of the atomic blast.

"Doane," I rejoiced in a whisper.

It was but a moment later, it seemed, when I heard the sharp grating of a boat on the sand, heard a cautious hail, a few yards to our right.

Half a dozen strides over the sand brought us to the little metal boat. We sprang aboard, and I cried to the two oarsmen, "Quick! I think they're coming on the beach." Gardiner chuckled, but he did nothing to restrain the eager efforts of the men. Nothing untoward happened during our short crossing to the flier. It seemed only a moment until its silver side, ghostly in the foggy night and gleaming slightly in the reflected fire of the lights on shore, was visible above us. It floated on the water like a silver bubble.

We reached a rope ladder, grasped it, and swung ourselves swiftly up to the lower ray-deck. The boat had been fastened to the ladder, for in a moment that was drawn up, with the little metal craft hanging to the end.

We hurried up into the bridge room in the top of the ship. By the time we reached it, the vessel had already risen, and was flying eastward in the black fog, just above the waves. Doane and Bris rushed to shake our hands when we entered the room. They, as we learned, had landed the ship in the snowfields of northern Greenland, and covered it with ice for concealment while they waited.

As soon as I could, I slipped off to the little stateroom that I had occupied in the great centrifugal wheel. Eagerly, I opened the little package that Leroda had given me. There was a tiny black box with a thin strip of crisp white paper by it. Written upon it, in Leroda's neat sloping shorthand, were the words in violet ink: "Play this when you wish to think of me. L."

I opened the little box, from which rose a faint whiff of Leroda's favorite perfume, jasmine. Within was a tiny spool of thin steel wire for a magnetic phonograph. Quickly I adjusted the magnetized coil in the little instrument on the table, and turned it on. Leroda's voice sounded out in the little room, sweet and clear.

"John, before you is a long and dangerous way. I would not have you shirk the thousand dangers of it, just because of me. But I hope you think of me, when you are out in the loneliness of space, amid the perils of meteorites and of enemy ships, and when you are fighting on the cruel deserts of the moon. If it must be—I know that you can die fighting for your cause bravely."

There was a little pause, and an odd tremor of the silver voice. The tones were low; they were husky and vibrant with feeling. Suddenly the room grew dim, as my eyes brimmed with tears.

"I shall always think of you, John. I shall hope—as long as there is hope. If you ever come back, I will be waiting. I must keep hiding. But my radio-recorder will be tuned always on 5.678 meters. If you ever come call that and tell me where I can come to you. "You know that I love you—forever. Leroda."

When I heard Gardiner coming in, fifteen minutes later, I was still sitting, staring at the little phonograph. Desperately I picked up a book and tried to appear reading, to conceal my tears.

He told me that Doane had already located Tobago on our charts, had set our course for it.

When the sun came up we were a thousand miles from New York City, in the direction of the ancient Spanish Main, flying low upon the sea, as Doane thought that safer than venturing up into space. Four hours later we sighted the island, a dull green blur upon the sea.

We neared it swiftly, and Doane, with his unerring hand on the controls, brought our vessel down lightly as a feather in the clear blue water, northeast of the island. Only a few hundred feet away white foam was breaking over the rocks Leroda had described, one with a steeple like an ancient church, the other like a great baldhead.

The little metal boat that had landed us at New York was launched again, and four of us put off for the narrow passage between the rocks, where the cylinder was supposed to lie. Gardiner, Bris and I went, and a young mechanic from the crew. In a few moments we reached the place, and Bris, at the oars, held the boat in position, while the rest of us scanned the hard coral bottom beneath the transparent water.

A half hour went by and I began to think we were going to fail. Then Gardiner caught sight of an object that he said must be what we sought. Certainly it was rather cylindrical in form, but half burned in the gravel and covered with a gray encrustation; I had passed it for a mere stone.

The mechanic sprang out, into water shoulder deep, and bent to raise the object. For a long minute he struggled, with his head under water, but he failed to move it.

"My God!" Bris suddenly cried in a voice that verged on panic. He dropped the oars and the current carried the boat away a little while he stared into the sky.

I looked up, saw what had alarmed him. High in the brilliant azure of the tropical sky were several white specks—tiny silver bubbles glancing in the sunshine. Ships of space—a score of miles high, perhaps, but dropping rapidly toward us.

"The spies on the beach!" Gardiner cried. "Metals knew we were here; they must have sent the ships after us!"

In a moment Bris had collected himself. With a single stroke, he brought the little boat back to where the diver had raised his wet and dripping head, slinging the water out of his eyes and gazing in bewilderment and horror at the silvery ships in the sky.

Without stopping to think, I leapt over the gunwale into the chill water. Gardiner spoke a quick word to the other man as I drew a deep breath and plunged beneath the surface. Together we bent, and the object in the sand stirred under our united efforts. We raised it, dropped it over the side of the boat, and clambered in, nearly swamping the little vessel in our haste.

Bris bent his back to the oars, the dripping mechanic seized a second pair, and we darted toward the vast silver shell of the ship, which floated lightly on the water a hundred yards away.

Wet and chilled as I was and alarmed at the bright ships rushing down upon us, I watched Gardiner in his eager examination of the thing we had retrieved from the sand. It was an irregular, grayish cylinder, perhaps a foot in diameter and three in length. He hammered at it with a pocket D-ray tube, broke away the gray mineral crust. The white gleam of metal was revealed.

In a moment we were below the open air lock of the ship. The mechanic seized the ladder and steadied the boat while the rest of us lifted the encrusted tube to eager hands above. Then, desperately, we scrambled up the ladder ourselves. We did not wait to save the boat; the flier plunged upward when the last of us was upon the ladder and was a hundred yards above the water when I scrambled through the opening. Gardiner and I rolled the metal cylinder over on the floor and presently got the encrustation of rust and salt hammered off with a mallet borrowed from the crew of the great ray-tube behind us. We had left after the pounding a stained and pitted cylinder of aluminum nine inches in diameter and nearly three feet long. There was no visible juncture in its surface, no sign of hinge or lid or cap.

Finding that we could not open it, we clambered up the central ladder, sending the tube up by the little electric elevator used for hoisting supplies. I was eager to know what was happening outside; but Gardiner's chief interest seemed still in the cylinder, in spite of the fleet above.

When we reached the bridge, both Doane and Bris were bent over the great round table in the center of the room, working with lever and dial. Looking out through the tiny thick windows of the room, I saw the gleaming spherical shell of a war flier now two miles away. It was almost directly above us, on our path of escape. And the blazing scarlet and dazzling green and smoky topaz of its D-rays were jetting at us in angry spurts.

Our own ship was plunging at it head on. Every tube on the upper ray-deck was trained upon it. Suddenly I was enclosed in walls of dazzling fire as the ring of tubes all about the bridge went into action. For a little time, they played past the vessel above or

THE BIRTH OF A NEW REPUBLIC

Illustrations by H. W. Wesso

Together we bent, and the object in the sand stirred under our united efforts.

fell ineffectually upon its reflecting armor. Then suddenly they all seemed to focus upon it at once; its silver shell burst into sudden blinding incandescence and seemed to melt and flow like wax.

In another moment the other ship was falling in molten, flaming ruin, and we were plunging up past it, victorious because of the better training of our crew, which had enabled them to focus their rays before we had been injured.

Two other ships remained.

We shot on into the sky. Already its liquid blue had darkened to blackness and a thousand stars were starting out. The two remaining ships hung above us, waiting and ominous. Doane used his space-screen bombs again, adroitly placing the vast spreading clouds of vapor to cover our flight and mislead the enemy as to our position.

I had no conception of the skill of his tactics at the moment. I realized what he had done only when we rose from the screen of gleaming white mist and saw the enemy vessels, each half-concealed in ragged clouds of sulphurous blue, playing their rays upon each other!

Doane had gone between them, had so placed his screens that each terrestrial commander took his fellow for the *Eagle*. If they perceived their error when we came into sight, it was already too late, for both were falling.

Swiftly we sped on moonward.

Our own ship was practically unharmed. A ray from the first ship we had encountered had carried off a few square meters of our reflecting shell and one of the D-ray tubes had been fused in its turret, with the loss of its crew of three. But our speed was not held back, and in a few hours the damage had been repaired and the dead consigned to space.

Then Gardiner and I set about the examination of the metal cylinder, which had so nearly cost us all our lives, and which, we hoped, held a secret that would assure the victory of the moon. Since we could find no way to open it, I carried it into the machine shop. Fastening it in a vise, I attacked it with a hacksaw, cutting off half an inch of one end. At last the top of the tube fell off, revealing the end of a great roll of papers.

CHAPTER SIXTEEN
The Battle of Smith's Crater

IT was indeed a priceless document that we took from that aluminum cylinder. Written in the modern "mentographic" shorthand and compactly phrased, it covered over a thousand pages in the original manuscript. It was, in fact, the laboratory journal of Dr. Vardon, covering over twenty years of exhaustive research. Gardiner was expert in the reading of this shorthand system, and I had studied it enough so that I quickly obtained a reading knowledge. All our waking hours, during the first week of the long voyage to the moon, were spent in study of its thousands of entries, which alluded to hundreds of related topics as well as to the principal object of Vardon's work—the rediscovery of the atomic blast.

Vardon, it appeared from a study of his records, had been a genius whom the world had failed to recognize, until Tranco had engaged with him on that disastrous venture that had cost his life. His ideas and theories were engrossing to us; much of his work has subsequently been published.

I think it was on the third day of our study that we came across the tattered sheet upon which were stated the fundamental equations upon which the disintegration of the gold atom is based. Gardiner fairly went into paroxysms of delight at the simplicity and beauty of Vardon's mathematical demonstration. In a few days more we had followed out completely the theoretical side of the matter and had turned to his notes on the practical application of the principle.

I am a fair draftsman and, working with Gardiner's aid, I devoted the last week of our voyage to drawing complete plans for a war-flier to utilize Vardon's discovery of the gold atomic blast projector. It was rather an ambitious project. I had never attempted such a thing before; in fact, a space flier had never been built outside the great yards of Metals at Pittsburgh. I kept a dozen men going over the *Eagle* with tape and rule to furnish me her dimensions. The new ships were to be far larger and more powerful, however, than the *Eagle*, which had begun her checkered career on Earth before I was born.

According to our calculations, it seemed that the available power should be at least thirty-five per cent greater than that of the Orloff generators using the platinum group, and this, we felt, would give our new ships a vast advantage over those of Metals.

After some discussion, we settled upon spherical ships of the same general design used since the old vessels of Colon. The sphere has the advantage of the maximum of strength and of cubic content, with the minimum of weight and of exterior surface.

Some of the vessels recently built on Earth are spindle-shaped or cylindrical with tapering ends. Such a design reduces the resistance of the heavy air of Earth; but in the moon's light atmosphere, or in the vacuum of space, it operates against the efficiency of the ship. (McRan's nine ships, which we had driven from New Boston, had been of this cylindrical type.)

I had hoped that we should be able to land near Theophilus, as I was keenly anxious to see father and mother again before the duties of my position called me to the battlefield. But Gardiner informed me that we were to land at the spot where we had left the moon—in the wild crater far west of the city.

He wished to get in touch with Warrington as soon as possible, to consider the matter of building a fleet for the moon. Some secret spot must be found, where thousands of men could be together and supplied with food and materials for many months. It was a titanic undertaking.

The great silver shell landed with hardly a shiver in the dense thickets of yellow, thorny scrub, beneath the towering crater-rim. A few seconds later the men had it covered with the painted tarpaulins that concealed it from eyes in space; the ground crew was trained, ready at rope and pole, to hoist the great canvas as soon as the vessel touched.

There was, in fact, almost a village in the crater. A hundred men stayed there, living in extensive compartments they had cut with D-rays in the crater walls. They had living apartments, storerooms, and machine shops; they cultivated irregular areas scattered over the crater floor, to provide fresh vitamin foods for themselves and the crew of the *Eagle*. And this was only one of a score of the hidden stations of the moon's ship.

I spent a few hours walking about, picking a cautious way through the spiky scrub. Exercise was welcome after the weeks of inactivity on the ship; and the lesser gravity of the moon was a new delight after I had felt my leaden weight on Earth. After a time I made my way through the passage in the crater wall, which was half-natural defile, half-artificial tunnel.

I gazed across the vast burned plain to eastward. Wild and incredibly lonely and desolate it looked, after my weeks on Earth, yet there was something about the somber swarthiness of its mountainous sweep that drew me to it; this stern world was part of me.

Presently I saw leaping red dots far away, on the shoulder of a black mountain ridge. I focused my pocket telescope upon them, and they resolved themselves into a little group of Selenites. As they drew near, I distinguished the redoubtable Jenkins, the scout who had brought Gardiner and me to the ship. He was leaping in the lead, upon the vast crimson thing he called M'Ob. Half a dozen other mooncalves were with him, two of them of the smaller-bodied, more intelligent tribe called the Ossinae, which can be trained to carry D-ray apparatus and to fight with human cleverness.

The short, red-faced fellow had his mount set him down outside the tunnel entrance, and his monstrous creatures fed themselves upon an outcrop of schist, with a few cubes of sugar that he gave them by way of reward. He hurried importantly down the passage, and greeted me with evident pleasure and surprise. I went with him aboard the *Eagle*.

A squat, thick man he was, with a nose large and red. Face and hands were burned brick red by the merciless lunar sun. He wore an unkempt red beard, and when he removed his greasy topi in the ship, I saw that his tousled hair was also red. It seemed very odd, when he removed his goggles in the bridge room, to see that his eyes were blue and very pale. They looked out of place in a man of such fiery red—for Jenkins even sported a tattered cloak of brilliant crimson velvet, which he wore over his dirty white tunic when he was in the shade.

His voice was rusty and thick, for in his lonely life he soliloquized far more to mooncalves than he talked with men. He strode pompously ahead of me into the control-room, with the bright red cloak thrown over his dingy garments, the worn fringe of it dangling against rusty bare shins.

Doane greeted him cordially enough; with a wink at the rest of us, he ordered the steward to fetch siphon, bottle, and glasses. Bris, the steward, served the four of us, and then himself. While the rest of us were barely sipping our drinks, Jenkins drained his glass at a gulp, and proceeded to turn the bottle up to his lips and take the fiery contents straight.

"A fellow don't get much like that in my trade," he grunted. "This rotten stuff they make in the craters—" Abruptly he straightened, saluted, and fumbled inside his red cloak. Presently he drew a grimy leather belt from beneath his tattered tunic. From that he took a sealed envelope, which he handed to Doane with the words impressively spoken:

"A dispatch from Warrington, sir!"

Doane ripped the envelope open, and lost himself in the neat shorthand of Warrington. Jenkins attempted to read over his shoulder, but to judge from the disgusted grimace of the old scout, he did not understand the system.

Watching the face of the young space-captain, I saw keen interest grow to serious concern. He read the message twice through, and looked up soberly at us.

"The situation is getting serious," he said. "On the morning of the moon-day after we sailed, Warrington left Theophilus to march to the relief of New Boston. He was to be followed by supply trains, and by a caravan-load of food and arms which the Assembly was to gather in Colon."

He began reading little excerpts from the dispatch: "The blockade about Theophilus could do little to hinder our departure, as our D-rays covered the line of march; but the supplies which were to follow were mostly destroyed as they left the city, by the fleet which has possession of the spaceport. And the caravan which left Colon was attacked by a horde of mooncalves, which were well armed, and are believed to have been officered by Tellurians. The supplies were lost, and most of the men with the party killed and eaten, though some few escaped on their faithful Selenites.

"Since these minor disasters, though the Assembly is still in session, nothing has been done to forward supplies. The Assembly lacks real authority; it only commands when men wish to obey. And it seems as if a sort of apathy has fallen on the moon. There are men, and food, and arms, in plenty. Armed forces could get them to us in safety. But it seems that hope is dying. In the last month I have been forced to rely upon private subscriptions raised by that noble spirit, John Adams, instead of the former levies of the Assembly. Unless we have a victory, and soon, the war is over.'"

I flushed with pride at such a mention of my father.

Doane read on: "I have been forced by lack of supplies to give up the advance on New Boston. We have spent two lunar nights camped in the mountains about midway between Theophilus and New Boston, quartered in mineshafts and passages cut with the D-rays. We lack sufficient food, as well as munitions and equipment. There are not even enough atomic heaters and liquid air cylinders to make our improvised barracks habitable. Half the men are sick from the malady due to the lack of vitamin J in the synthetic air they have been forced to breathe in the barracks during the nights. Hundreds are dying; and there have been thousands of desertions—men have left in whole companies, after each terrible night, to try to find a way back to the city or to one of the smaller mining communities, some even going toward New Boston to throw themselves upon the mercy of Humbolt. I can hardly blame them.

"Those still able to answer the roll-call are starved, ragged, poorly equipped. Humbolt's army would not hold together an hour under such conditions; I must praise the loyalty and devotion of these poor fellows.

"The matter is coming to a climax soon. Humbolt has left New Boston, and is marching upon us. He is reported to have nearly forty, thousand men, about four times as many as I can muster. They are mostly Black infantry, who have proven that they can stand the intense heat of the lunar day much better than un-acclimated Caucasians.

"I am preparing to retreat, for we cannot hope to hold this position against such an overwhelming force. Gardiner, and Adams, the engineer, will return with Jenkins and meet me in the vicinity of Smith's Crater. Doane will take to space, collect the other ships, and try to keep our movements from being watched by the Metals fleet."

In his own words, Doane added: "I imagine his plan is merely to evade Humbolt for a few days. It will be impossible, of course, for the Tellurians to spend the night away from New Boston, and if the battle is delayed a week or so, the terrestrial general will be

THE BIRTH OF A NEW REPUBLIC

forced to retreat to the city for protection against the night. But our general may have something more in mind; this is the way he closes the dispatch:

"We must take a decisive step, or soon we can take none at all. We have discouragement to fight—a deadlier enemy than Humbolt's D-rays. Warrington."

An hour later, Gardiner and I had set out with Jenkins for Smith's Crater. Jenkins rode in front, upon his great, green-eyed, scarlet beast, M'Ob. The tremendous leaps of the vast, long-legged creatures were well timed, so that the half dozen of them rose and fell as one, sweeping through the air only a few yards apart on the leaps of a hundred yards or so.

So close together we sped that Jenkins, mellowed perhaps by the long pull at Doane's bottle, grew very talkative. He had to shout in a shrill tone, and even then half of his words were swept away in the wind of our swift flights, or lost in the rattle of stones and the crashing in the brittle yellow scrub as the monsters landed and leapt again.

He began with remarkable accounts of his affairs with women in the cities. But soon he was boasting of his former exploits in the lunar wilderness, of fabulously rich mines he had discovered, of impossible adventures with the Ka'Larbah and other tribes of wild mooncalves. He went even as far as to begin a story of how he had been captured, some years before by the M'Dawils—that half-mythical band of monsters—and carried as a prisoner to the other side of the moon, to a low crater valley of warm and equable climate and marvelous vegetation. In that valley was a tribe of mooncalves having a civilization far above that of the Ton'Kapl Empire in the great crater Tycho, crushed by the first expeditions from Earth.

But while the old scout was in the very middle of his extravagant description of this marvelous place, with its strange inhabitants and its incredible wealth in precious minerals, his tongue became unmanageable. For a time he struggled on manfully, stumbling over the more difficult words.

"Then theysh took me to a palish—pa—palace of purple cryshtal—clistal—"

With a final hiccup, he dropped his head forward on his breast, and presently went to sleep. The intelligent creatures that carried us leapt on as he slept, obedient to his last uncertain gestured orders. Hours later he woke again, grumbling and sullen, and took a great pinch of wiz-wiz—that strange stimulating drug of the lunar forests. Despite my eager questions, he would reveal no more of his adventures back of the moon. I was never really certain whether it was all a flight of imagination, which his headache killed, or whether it had been half-true and he simply did not wish to share his secret.

We had vacuum bottles of hot coffee, and bags of sandwiches; and Gardiner and I ate and drank and slept as we went…leap…leap…leap.

It was thirty-six hours after leaving the ship when we arrived at Warrington's camp. We found it by the rough grim walls of Smith's Crater—a ring of impassable black granite walls, twenty miles across, encircling a torrid, and waste. Warrington had pitched his camp outside those sheer, un-climbable walls, behind a little ridge that offered some protection against the army in the rear.

Humbolt, with his 40,000 infantry, was also camped along the crater wall, four or five miles behind Warrington. He had outdistanced our general in the last march, and caught up. He evidently intended to rest his troops, advance again, and score an easy victory.

The sentries evidently were expecting us; we passed the lines unchallenged, and soon were at Warrington's little tent. He was away, however, visiting the little squad of men who were cutting trenches on the hill behind us, a white cloud of dust rising from their D-rays to mark their location.

We dismounted and waited under the fly of the little white tent, out of the driving heat of the sun. In a few minutes Warrington was back, heavy-eyed, with the face beneath his white topi drawn with fatigue and worry. He took scant time to greet us, or to learn of the results of our expedition. Even as he listened to Gardiner's report on the new gold atomic blast, he frequently turned away to give orders to hurrying aides. Evidently something was afoot.

In a few minutes we left the tent. I saw that the exhausted and half-sick men were being roused from the crude shelters where they had sought relief from the cruel sun while they ate their scanty rations and tried to sleep in the furnace-like air.

With a good deal of wonderment, I saw that camp was being broken and that the men were making ready for a march, while the work of fortification was going on busily behind them. Soon the whole army, except for a few score of men at work on the hill, was marching off down the crater wall, away from the enemy.

I could not understand the maneuver—it looked like a mad and precipitate flight, with disaster and annihilation at the hands of the pursuing Humbolt as the inevitable outcome.

The men were hardly able to march. Half of them had white rags bound around their heads, in place of the pith helmets that were needed to protect them from the scorching, blistering radiation of the sun. Uniforms were tattered and patched, with red-sun-cooked bodies beneath them. And from sickness and hunger, men staggered as they walked, threw away blankets, canteens, trinkets—everything but arms and pitiful hoards of food.

How wonderful the courage and devotion to their commander that led them on under such conditions!

On and on we went around the rim of the crater. At last we had covered thirty miles; we were half way around, and still Warrington kept by the wall. We stopped for a brief rest; the stumbling men threw themselves down in scraps of shadow offered by boulders and patches of dense spiky scrub, to consume their last treasured bits of food.

After an hour or so, we went on around the crater.

At last I understood. It was late in December and no doubt Humbolt's soldiery, certain of an easy victory over Warrington's ragged troops, was indulging in a Christmas celebration. Warrington meant to come upon them by surprise and in the rear—by a march all the way around the crater!

And that is exactly what he did do. His maneuver was as simple as it was daring and brilliant. Doubtless the Tellurian commander had guarded his other flank; but he could not have expected the war-worn troops of the moon to encircle the crater and take him from behind.

Our desperate, half-starved troops, exhausted as they were by that sixty-mile march about the crater's rim, took the terrestrials completely by surprise. They fought with demoniac, insane energy. There was no forewarning of our attack. The few sentries in the rear were dozing in the shade. The sultry heat of the lunar sun, with the effects of celebrating the Christmas season with the fiery spirits distilled in the craters, had been too much for them.

Our men dashed forward in thin, ragged lines; but they were determined, desperate, intent on victory; they knew that their sole chance of life depended on winning. Humbolt and his officers tried to rouse the soldiers and to rally them; for a few minutes the resistance was spirited.

But they failed to withstand the impetuosity of our onrush. Their ranks collapsed and the blacks fled in a disorganized rout. They distrusted the wild life of the moon—regarding the wild mooncalves with an almost superstitious fear.

Humbolt and his officers escaped; indeed, they got back to New Boston with more than five thousand men, but those five thousand were without morale and without equipment.

The results of the victory were far-reaching.

Warrington took twenty thousand prisoners. He captured a vast amount of stores, arms, equipment of all sorts, including three hundred field D-ray tubes, and twenty-seven thousand hand rays.

When our men slept again, it was with full stomachs and in new uniforms, sheltered from the sun by captured tents. By the time the sun had set, a few days of hard marching had brought us back to Theophilus, with all that vast amount of new equipment, and captives that outnumbered our troops two to one.

I was with father and mother again. It was a gala day when I came home. We had a glorious Christmas dinner in honor of the reunion, and talked for a long time afterward in the little drawing room. I told about my trip to Earth. Finally, I told them of Leroda, and as a climax, played the magnetic record of her voice. My parents were properly delighted—though I believe mother cried a little afterward.

The victory at Smith's Crater sent a wave of new courage over the moon. In every city and in every community, men freshly pledged themselves to the cause; money, food, and recruits began to flow toward the camp of Warrington again, while the Assembly had regained its position of authority.

In the enthusiasm of the hour, even the people of New Boston rose against the soldiers Humbolt had left in the city, and expelled them before the defeated general had found his way back; though of course the fleet remained in possession of the spaceport and the buildings about it.

I had at once resumed my old position as Warrington's engineer attaché. Some two days after the setting of the sun, he called me from my work (I had been designing cradles and equipment that would be needed in the building of the fleet).

"John," he said, "I want you to prepare to leave with me in twelve hours. We are going outside the city. Jenkins will carry us on his mooncalves. Spacesuits have been provided."

"Very good, sir. And where—" I stopped short, abashed, realizing I had no right to ask the question.

He smiled, clapped me warmly on the shoulder. "That's all right, John. It is to be a secret conference," he said. "A meeting of men from all parts of the moon."

CHAPTER SEVENTEEN
The Conference at Kurrukwarruk

FATHER and mother were still in Theophilus; they had been there since the trouble that had brought on the war. The Firecrest mine had been left in the care of Valence and her young husband, Tom Dowling. The settlement was so isolated that it would have been difficult indeed to transport its production of metals from its mines to Theophilus. Since the end of commerce with the Earth, the only demand for metals came from the quickening industries of the moon, which was easily satisfied from works nearer at hand. And father was prominent in the Assembly; he would not have been willing to leave the center of activity even if the mine had been in operation.

After my meeting with Warrington, I went home, to find that father, too, was preparing to attend the secret conclave. He retired early, to rest for the long trip. But mother and I sat late in the tiny but rather luxurious living room of their apartments in the great south wing of the roofed city.

She had me play again the sound record Leroda had given me. My eyes filled with tears as I listened to the vibrant silver tones of the girl who was now a quarter of a million miles away. Mother smiled mistily. "She has the grandest voice," she said.

She had a little "stereo" movie camera with sound recorder that had been a childhood gift to her from my grandfather. Now we darkened the little room, and I hung up the screen while she found the cans of film. For a long hour we sat there, in the warm golden glow of the atom-disrupter heater, talking a little in low tones, as we watched scenes from mother's childhood and youth. I cried out in pleasure when father first came into the scenes, as a cheerful, slender boy at a party. Then there was the wedding, and the scenic story of a trip around the Earth. And presently I saw dimly remembered events of my own childhood, and heard long-forgotten voices ringing fresh and clear from the screen.

The picture followed our voyage to the moon, with its fear, and the sorrow of little Fay's death. It showed the hardship and the adventure of our first years on the moon, and brought vividly back to me the delights of my romantic boyhood about Firecrest.

When we had come to the end of the film—the last few scenes showed the wedding of Valence, and then her bouncing child, and a view of the city of Firecrest taken as mother had last left it—we did not turn on the lights, but sat in the gloom. I had fallen into a curious revery of the past. It was the sleeping period of the city, and everywhere was darkness. (The atomic lights have always been turned off for eight hours of every twenty-four, for the over-stimulation of constant light is as destructive to terrestrial plants as it is to humans.)

Suddenly I heard a suppressed sob from mother's chair. With an odd tightening in my throat, I got up and went over to her and knelt beside her, with my arm about her dear, slight shoulders. I had hardly thought, before, of what it must mean to her for father and me to go away. She took my hand, and patted it, and clung to it for a little time. Then she spoke, in a dry, husky little voice:

"I understand, John. I'm glad you feel it. But I want to do my part. I have faith. And if anything happens, we..." She faltered a little, finished pluckily, "...we have such good times to remember."

And suddenly she stood up, as vigorous as a girl, and turned on the light. "Now John," she said practically, "you must be off to bed. You've a hard trip before you."

I kissed her, and went obediently, leaving her standing in the room, looking after me with a tear, I think, in her eye. But I could not sleep, for thinking of the golden time of peace. If it had lasted, I might have found Leroda, and brought her back to a happy world, to live near father and mother.

More than a dozen men were gathered at the airlock at the appointed time. Warrington was there. Gardiner, and my father, with two or three of the other leaders of the Assembly, a few of the engineers who had been working with Gardiner and me on the problems of the new fleet, and two or three of Warrington's officers.

A score of soldiers were there, in spacesuits, with sets of armor for us. Soon we were all grotesque creatures in the strange suits of metal, quartz glass, and impregnated fabric, shoulders bulging with oxygen tanks. The thick helmets of metal and quartz were screwed down; and we were in communication with one another only through the short-wave radio sets that each suit carried.

When all of us were ready—there were thirty-nine, counting the guard;—the inner door of the lock was opened, and we filed into the great cylinder that extends through the city's wall. It was closed and sealed behind us, and Gardiner opened the valve that let the air about us hiss out into the frigid vacuum of the night.

The air in our suits expanded until we were squat, thick-limbed monstrosities. All the sounds of the city faded, until everything I could hear was the quiet hum of the little motor that kept the air circulating between my double-walled helmet and the coils where it was purified and re-oxygenated, and the occasional ghostly voice in the phones.

At last the pressure was equalized, the outer door was opened, and we walked out into the lunar night. The sky was a void of the most intense blackness, sprinkled with a million cold, many-colored

THE BIRTH OF A NEW REPUBLIC

At last the pressure was equalized, the outer door was opened, and we walked out into the lunar night.... In the bright-flecked darkness of it swung the earth, near the full, a vast globe of liquid emerald, alight with misty splendor.

stars, and richly powdered with the luminous silver dust of nebula and galaxy. In the bright-flecked darkness of it swung the Earth, near the full, a vast globe of liquid emerald, alight with misty splendor. The radiance of the green planet fell in a flood of ghostly argent upon the silent crust of snow and frozen air that blanketed the weird rough wilderness before us, shimmering fantastically upon the three sheer peaks beyond the city.

In all that world of night, everything was white, still, lying in death or frozen sleep until the sun would bring the spark of life— all save the mooncalves, the natural masters of the planet.

Moments later we saw a score of the fantastic beasts leaping swiftly toward us through the Earthlight, vast scarlet bodies a-glitter against the still white mountains, green eyes glowing with pale phosphorescence.

Jenkins was upon their leader, hardly recognizable in his gleaming silver space-armor. But his voice sounded familiar enough in the phones when he spoke.

"Good evening, gintlemen, and the best av wishes to ye!"

He flung out ludicrously thick arms in the gestured command that sent his score of weird beasts to their knees before us. In a few moments we were mounted, two to an animal. Then we were off through the silent, frozen night, upon scarlet monsters that leapt swiftly and surely from snow-covered boulder to peak encrusted in frozen air, beneath the white light of the motionless Earth.

I suppose that Warrington had already given Jenkins his orders. I heard him say nothing to the old scout who was leading us unerringly, however, along a path that carried us into the mountainous region between the three great cities, Theophilus, Colon, and New Boston.

We traveled some ten or twelve hours, in which time we must have covered half that many hundred miles. We were almost upon our destination before I perceived it. We were crossing the floor of a relatively small crater many miles northwest of Hipparchus. Abruptly I saw the outlines of a city's roof and towers and domes above the flat, white expanse about us, clothed in a silver blanket of frozen air.

The oddly shaped towers and the irregular roof had been cunningly designed to appear to the casual eyes as part of the natural peak in the center of the crater. A hidden city was here, surrounded by towering crater walls. Invisible, even when one looked upon it, unless he knew its odd outlines.

Warrington's voice rustled in the phones. "Gentlemen, this is Kurrukwarruk. A hidden city. It was built by a patriot who grew tired of the rule of Metals long before the war. He located a mining prospect here, and built this secret city. He has already aided the cause, and he gives us the free use of his location. We have many secret allies."

Another half an hour found us dismounted and inside the air lock of the little city on the mountain, removing our cumbersome armor. It was a good-sized community:—the roof covered a hundred acres and the population was about five thousand, of whom nearly two thousand were men who had been employed in the building of the city, and who now constituted its garrison. The whole mountaintop was a great fortress; every tower of the city carried a battery of D-rays.

Inside the air lock we met the builder of Kurrukwarruk. He was of Teutonic extraction; his name was Meyers. A corpulent fellow, he had an absurdly thin, piping voice. It seemed that he had been born on Earth, and had inherited a hatred for Metals Corporation. He had come to the moon in youth, located the valuable minerals in this crater, and worked the deposits secretly, accumulating a fortune and building his hidden city, against the day when the moon should revolt. He seemed to have a stubborn love of liberty; he had placed the city—and his entire personal fortune as well—at Warrington's disposal.

The secret conferences must have been planned weeks before. Men were there from all over the moon. There were bankers and soldiers from Colon—Crompton, Vendome, Wong Kow, and Olaf—scientists and military authorities from New Boston—Leforge, Handley, and others—miners and scouts who owned no particular home. Starling was there—that romantic poet-adventurer who was one of the few who had visited the terrible hidden side of the moon, and whose life was later sacrificed on the ill-starred Venerian expedition of Captain Cord.

The first action of the conference was to choose Kurrukwarruk as the permanent capitol of the moon. The great statesmen were opposed to having it located in any of the large cities, as it would be the object of Tellurian attack, unduly endangering the city's population. Then Kurrukwarruk was centrally located and rather easily accessible—when one knew its location—from any of the great cities. It was equipped with all the necessities of civilized life. Its fortifications were so carefully planned and so strong that it seemed improbable that it would fall, even if discovered and attacked.

The meeting went on for several days. Important problems were solved, concerning the military organization of the moon's forces, and their support. Plans were made for raising reinforcements and supplies about Colon, as that district had hardly been touched by the war.

Apartments had been assigned to all of us in the most desirable quarters of the city. I shared a suite of rooms with a young officer, Captain Benedict, a secretary to the Financial Director. He was handsome in appearance, rather dashing, and noted for several feats of intrepid courage. Early in the war he had led a daring raid on the spaceport at New Boston, capturing it in the face of considerable odds, though it was soon lost again to Van Thoren's fleet. I think he had secured his transfer to the staff of the Financial Director, because he was not satisfied with his preferment in the regular army.

I had known him at the University; in fact, I had felt almost his friend, until I had once seen him in the company of Leroda. I did not like his manner toward her, and I had dropped him. However, now I began to think that I had let jealousy obscure the character of a brave and noble patriot.

Slowly the conference got around to the important thing, to the question that was the real purpose of the meeting. Early in the course of the discussions, Gardiner had addressed the assembly, giving the results of the trip to Earth, and telling of his meeting with Lafollette in Chicago. He had concluded his talk with what was, for one of his quiet manners, an unusual burst of oratory.

"Gentlemen, Tranco is the hereditary enemy of Metals Corporation. Every man in it, from President Lewis down to the laborers who toil in the factories and ships, feels the strongest antipathy to our oppressors. Openly, publicly, Lewis dares to do nothing.

But this Lafollette is braver than his fellow-directors. He is rich. And he is willing to stake his fortune and his life upon our cause. He is willing to send us money, supplies, and men, if they can be brought to the moon. And while he made his offer as a private man, I know that Lewis is unofficially behind him, with all the vast resources of Tranco.

"It may seem hopeless, gentlemen, to dream of bringing weapons and men from Earth to our aid. But due to the generosity of a friend of young Adams, here, we have a solution to that problem. We have Dr. Vardon's great discovery of twenty years ago—the gold atomic blast. That is the invention with which Tranco vainly tried to throw off the yoke of Metals, failing because her new ships were discovered before they were finished.

"Fellow patriots, we have in our hands the means of building a fleet that can go to Earth to bring back Lafollette and his army. We have the means, even, of building a fleet of war-fliers that can sweep the vessels of Metals from space and make us the equal of the greatest corporation on Earth."

There had been a lot of cheering when he finished, but not much else. Men had to take time to think. But a hundred great minds were playing with the idea. It was some days later that Paul Doane arose and proposed definite plans for the construction of a fleet on the moon, with which we could voyage to Earth to get Lafollette and his men. There were a thousand difficulties in the way of it, but he had gone over each of them with Gardiner and me and some of the other delegates, and his logical arguments convinced the assembly that it might be possible to collect the thousands of skilled mechanics, to find a secret place for them to work, and to provide them with food, with shelter for the lunar nights, and with the vast supplies of raw material that would be needed.

Two or three more days went by, partly devoted to consideration of routine business, though the great project was never far from our minds. Slowly the plan crystallized, until we came to the selection of a secret workshop for the building of the fleet. John Adams, Sr., my father, rose at once to suggest that the ships be built at Firecrest.

He set forth its advantages. The mines would furnish all the metal required for the work. The city would shelter the men. There were farms and synthetic food plants to feed them. The locality was so remote that interference was improbable.

As he was talking, I remembered the great cavern at Firecrest—the vast chasm in which I had lost myself as a boy, escaping by the merest accident. I waited impatiently until father was done, then sprang impulsively to my feet and informed the assembly that I could point out a spot where a thousand vessels might be built without discovery, even if searching fleets cruised over a hundred times. I got a little excited; but with a few questions from Gardiner, I told all I knew about the cavern.

I suggested that it could be lit with atomic lights and that a battery of D-rays would soon clear the jungle off the floor, and that the narrow shaft through which I had entered could be widened and cleared to permit the completed ships to leave. And it was near enough to Firecrest so that metal and supplies could be easily brought from there.

With that addition, the program was unanimously approved, and definite plans were laid to carry it out.

It was agreed that Gardiner, father and I should set out at once for Firecrest, to begin making such preparations as clearing the cavern, widening the entrance, and getting a supply of food and metal as fast as the few men now at Firecrest could provide them.

The delegates from other parts of the moon promised us engineers and men as soon as they could be gathered. Warrington was returning to his army at Theophilus, and Doane to his embryonic fleet. It was yet several days to sunrise—there was time in abundance for us to reach our several destinations before the coming of the luminary signaled the resumption of hostilities.

It was the sleeping period before we were to start. As I returned, after the last meeting of the assembly, to the apartment that I shared with Benedict, the dashing secretary to the Director of Finance, I heard something through the closed door that made me burst into the room in sudden fury.

"...I shall always think of you, John..."

Those dear words, in the rich, vibrant voice of Leroda, husky with the depth of her feeling, came ringing sweet and clear from the moon. Someone was playing the record she had given me!

I found Benedict, my handsome fellow lodger, bending over the little phonograph—through some accident, I had left it on the reading table.

"If you can come back, I will be waiting..." The secretary was intent on that wondrous voice. Startled out of his usual rather haughty dignity, he now jumped up, reddening. I jerked the little instrument out of his hands and stopped it, then reached for his collar. I was almost beside myself; it seemed a sacrilege that he had heard those treasured words.

"Why, what's the matter, Adams?" he sputtered. "I beg your pardon. I don't see— What the devil! I thought it was a standard record—a song or something."

"A standard record with that on the case?"

I pointed fiercely to the words.

"To John Adams. Play this when you wish to think of me," written on the case in Leroda's neat characters.

Benedict's flush of confusion changed to a red flood of anger.

"Adams, if you let word of this out, I'll slaughter you like a dog!"

"You may name a meeting place—" I had begun, when I recovered myself. "No, as officers, we cannot do that. But on the day that peace is made—"

He turned and strode from the moon.

CHAPTER EIGHTEEN
In the Firecrest Cavern

A FEW hours later we were in our spacesuits. Most of the delegates were returning to their cities, though enough remained to constitute a permanent corps for the new executive government. Greenville, the Financial Director, was remaining, with Benedict, the strange young man who had become his secretary—I realized, after cooling of my feelings, that the fellow had committed no worse crime than to satisfy a natural curiosity. I should not have left the machine where he could get his hands on it. Before I left, I apologized for my hasty words; and he, smiling, begged my own pardon. We parted on good terms.

Jenkins, with his Selenites, was to convey Gardiner, father, and myself to Firecrest, and would return immediately to take Warrington back to Theophilus. The General had further business connected with the organization of the permanent government, which prevented his leaving Kurrukwarruk for a day yet.

The four of us, with a toast to the liberty of the moon still ringing in our ears, stepped into the great cylindrical air lock, shut the inner door, and opened the valve. Warrington, Meyers, and Greenville beyond the great transparent door of quartz, waved us a last farewell and hurried away.

The last of the air hissed out with a dying moan. Jenkins opened the outer door, and once again we were in the fantastic ghostliness of the frozen lunar night. The old scout, squat and silvery in his space armor, signaled to his mooncalves. The scarlet, glistening elephantine monsters came hopping toward us on their enormous grasshopper legs, across the glistening plain of frozen air.

Our guide selected four of the fleetest, which, with only a single passenger, can easily make fifty miles an hour at a time. I leapt into my saddle—for I have always had a curious horror of the feel of a scaly tentacle about my waist—Jenkins and Gardiner and my father allowed the long tentacular limbs to lift them up, and we were off.

Jenkins was in excellent humor, having been well fed and cared for during the week at Kurrukwarruk. He regaled us with an interminable series of droll anecdotes in his rusty voice. His stories related mostly to his childhood. He told us that he had never known his father and that he had been brought up on the moon by a crabbed, old Irish prospector, Tim O'Sullivan.

The old scout's voice rang endlessly in the phones. In the vacuum of the night, no foreign sounds broke in upon his narrative.

O'Sullivan, it seems, did not claim to be Jenkins' parent, but said that, while on an expedition in search of a legendary mountain of radium toward the Rook Mountains on the eastern "rim" of the moon, he had come upon a horde of the Ka'Larbah, the most savage of the wild Selenites, about a space flier fallen and wrecked in the desert far south of Kepler.

O'Sullivan had made his way into the ship—it seems that he was on fairly good terms even with those bloodthirsty monsters. He had rescued two living people from the ravenous mooncalves, one of them Jenkins, "thin, a little yaller-headed shaver," as he said.

The other was a man, who gasped out a brief tale of meteoric collision and of a terrible struggle to save the ship that had ended in that crash on the deserted limb of the moon. The survivors had been there nearly a month, dying of their injuries, of hardship and starvation, and maintaining a hopeless defense against the Selenites. One by one the men had died, but they had saved the life of the boy.

Thus Jenkins knew nothing of his parentage—so far as he was aware, he might have been destined for a life of ease, luxury, and prominence, but for the wrecking of the ship. His fellow survivor had told nothing of the boy's people, he had died before his terrible story was finished.

O'Sullivan, it seems, had been a curious man, hardly known in the cities, and hardly tolerated even among the wild Ka'Larbah. He had taken the three-year-old boy to Colon with him, and placed him in the hands of a woman of uncertain social standing. There Jenkins had lived for five or six years, attending school a little and learning far more by roaming the curiously cosmopolitan underworld of the lunar city.

Then the woman had suddenly departed, in the company of a "tall man with whiskers and a glass eye." The lonely boy, perhaps not much the worse for the loss of his guardian, had roamed the streets for months, earning his bread for a time in one of the secret dens where the forbidden drugs from the lunar forests are sold.

Then O'Sullivan, returning from one of his mad wanderings in the waste places of the moon, had rescued the child, and taken him along on the next trip, which, according to Jenkins' story, took them due south, to the left of the Doerfels, to a point where the motionless Earth set behind him. There they had encountered a new race of mooncalves, who were armed with polished rocks, and who guarded a dead city of white metal. After two years of incredible adventure beyond the pale, they had arrived in Theophilus with, as Jenkins put it, "about a peck of diamonds." For a brief period they had lived in incredible luxury "with a red-headed woman." But soon O'Sullivan had squandered or gambled away his fortune, and they had returned to the desert. Three years later, when Jenkins was fourteen, O'Sullivan was executed with the captured crew of a space-pirate, and the boy had escaped only because of his youth and presumed innocence.

To the accompaniment of such a story, which was probably not wholly true—yet which subsequent discoveries show to have been far from altogether false the nine or ten hours of the trip to Firecrest passed in a few moments, it seemed.

I was astonished when I saw the city of my childhood rise before me—a great thick disk of metal and glass, half a mile across and two hundred feet high, resting on the glistening white crater-pitted desert, close against the rim of the two-mile crater in which the mineshafts are located.

A few more rushing leaps of our red-armored, hurtling mounts brought us to the air lock. There Gardiner, father, and I dismounted. The stocky, silver-armored figure of the old scout waved us a farewell, and leaped away upon old M'Ob among the shimmering ice-clad spires of the lunar desert until he vanished in the feeble light, with his "God be with ye" ringing in our ears.

We had rung the bell, and the air lock was quickly opened for us. It seemed very strange to pass so suddenly from the glimmering ghostliness of the lunar desert in the fantastic Earthshine, seen under the weird spell of Jenkins' narrative, into the warm rich glow of the atomic lights.

The familiar city of my youth seemed unusually deserted. There were thoughtless, happy children, and anxious women. But most of the men were gone, to join Warrington's army or to seek employment elsewhere. Everything was quiet, deserted.

Valence and Tom Dowling greeted us in glad surprise. With motherly love, my sister exhibited little Tom Junior, a plump, pink little fellow, just learning to talk. It gave me an odd feeling to think that I was now an uncle.

Gardiner and father and I soon put a different aspect on the quiet town, with Tom's eager aid. The townsfolk had been enormously glad to see father. They held a great banquet in honor of his return; and they showed themselves willing to perform superhuman feats of toil for him. Soon we were working the mines again. Most of the men were busy there; but even the women showed themselves eager to work in the machine shops and synthetic food plants.

Father took charge of the work in general of seeing that raw metal and food were ready. Gardiner went over my plans for the ships, to determine the best methods of procedure, and to find what tools and technicians would be required. Until Doane came, he was "Admiral" in authority over everyone. I was to undertake some researches to perfect the D-ray; but before beginning that, I asked for and received the job of opening and clearing the great cavern.

Forty hours ahead of the rising of the sun, I left Firecrest with a dozen men in spacesuits. We drove atomotored tractors, which dragged three of the great mining D-ray machines, borrowed from the gold workings. When we arrived at the little crack that was the opening of the great cavern, I fastened the end of a long line about my middle, and ventured with a searchlight, a thousand feet down the fissure, to where it widened into the cavern proper. A few measurements and a simple calculation enabled me to determine the place to begin our vertical shaft.

Twelve hours of herculean toil saw a circular vertical shaft, a hundred and fifty feet in diameter, sunk three hundred feet through the roof of the cave. Then I sent the men back to the city to rest while a fresh crew came out to operate the great boring machines.

Fatigue drove me back to the city for a few hours rest. But I did not sleep until I had sketched plans for the great metal valve, which was to close the top of the shaft. I left a dozen men busy on the blueprints of the valve, its frame and hinges, and the atomotor which was to operate it.

The men worked on at the shaft in my absence. When I got back, the boring was six hundred feet down. I brought back two additional tubes, and the work went on more rapidly than before. It was a splendid sight to see the five red beams, like fingers of fire, driving down into the pit from the vast glistening machines on its rim, the living rock melting beneath them into a flaming inferno of blinding light, with the inert gases of the disintegration rising in a furnace-hot hurricane. A strange contrast—beneath was the pit of flame, with the blistering heat pouring from it, and above about us all was night, where the chilling gases from the pit, cooling, condensed in a sort of fog, and fell, a crystal snow, upon the huge machines and the busy men.

Twelve hours later, when the sun came up, a splendid ball of white flame, we were down thirteen hundred feet. In ten hours more, at twenty-three hundred feet, the Assure we were following opened out into the vast cavern. The incandescent bottom fell out of the shaft, and looking down its straight walls, we saw the purple gleam of phosphorescent vegetation.

I went back to the city to snatch a few hours of sleep, and to exchange my spacesuit for the topi and light cotton uniform worn in the day. I left a crew excavating recesses about the mouth of the shaft for the hoisting machinery and the mechanism of the great valve. When I returned, the machinery had already been hauled out on tractor-drawn vehicles, and the installation was almost complete. The huge sliding lid was already in place, with a thin shell of rock over it for camouflage, and the motors, cages, and cable drums were being set up in the space cut out beneath it.

Four hours later a cage dropped down that great shaft, as the winch unwound the steel cable that supported us. I was in it, with father, Gardiner, Tom Dowling, and sixteen other men, equipped with searchlights and D-rays.

A strange and splendid scene it was that burst upon us at the bottom of that half-mile shaft. We emerged into sheer space. Our brilliant searchlights played on an inverted forest of pendant stalactites—a fantastic, topsy-turvy world of glittering, snowy whiteness, dazzling in our intense lights.

The floor of the vast cave was still seven hundred feet below us. A weird thick jungle covered it—rippling with the eerie light of luminescent vegetation. The growth was thick and dense. Great fleshy, fungoid plants rose half a hundred feet high, glowing with pale, uncanny white. Even above them swayed the feathery fronds of fern-like trees, gleaming with viridescent green. Here and there were thickets of low violet growth. The whole floor of the cave was splotched irregularly with patches of fire—white and green and violet, bloody red and shimmering opal and flaming purple.

Almost directly below us was the long black lake I had seen as a child, shimmering with the green and purple of the shining jungle that overhung its silent shores. From it, the flaming jungle sloped up to forests of glittering stalagmites. Beyond the stalagmites the walls of the cavern rose, winding, cragged, and frosty with crystalline deposits that scintillated wondrously in the many-colored light of the luminous jungle.

Swiftly the cage dropped at the end of the cable, the cavern opening up about us. Three thousand feet wide, perhaps, the penetrating rays of our searchlights showed it to be. Its length seemed infinite. The white dazzling rays traced its rugged walls until they lost themselves westward in infinite distances.

We were entering an empire—within the moon!

That such a great cavity is possible on the planet is due only to the slight force of its gravity; on Earth the rock walls would have become plastic under the enormous weight, "creeping" until the abyss was closed.

As our cage dropped low over a dense forest of entwined, palm-like trees brilliant with soft green flame, a strange winged thing sprang up from the black lakeshore. Black it was, and covered with glistening scales. It had two vast eyes, immense oblong orbs, glowing with intense violet. It bore itself on deliberately flapping, leathery black wings, which must have spread a hundred feet.

One of the men in the cage raised his D-ray tube nervously. Indeed, I felt a momentary thrill of alarm on my own part, for the monstrous creature had come directly toward us. But with a word, Gardiner restrained the man.

And the huge black thing, seemingly dazzled by our battery of blazing searchlights, turned and winged a silent way off down the dark passage to westward, until our thin white rags lost it in a maze of ghostly, glittering passages.

Then, swinging there two hundred feet above the luxuriant luminous jungle, we set to clearing the vegetation away. Fantastic glowing plants melted beneath our vividly brilliant D-rays.

As is well known, the D-ray itself is colorless, since it is a vibration in the ultra-violet spectrum, of a wavelength far shorter than that of visible light. The flaming colors seen in practice are due to secondary radiation, which aids in controlling the ray. The difference in color is due to the variation in atomic structure of the three kindred metals used in generating the ray. The platinum electrode produces a brilliant scarlet beam. When osmium is used, the color is a bright, emerald-green. Iridium generates a vivid orange-yellow ray.

Within two hours we had swept the cave from wall to wall, and for about two miles east and west. Where there had been a weird, luminous jungle, only naked rock and bare black soil was left. Then we landed, and left the cage. Gardiner and I set immediately about surveying the spot on the lakeshore beneath the shaft, for the buildings and yards to be constructed there, while several expeditions were sent up and down the cavern.

The men sent westward reported that the cavern curved about, and stretched back to the east in many tangled passages, wider even than the one in which we were, and all grown up with luminous jungle and swarming with ferocious winged monsters. It was through that region that I must have passed in my escape from the cavern years before, when I had come out in a crater many miles east. I was appalled at the men's description of it.

The men sent in the other direction reported that the cavern extended only a few miles that way. We seemed to be in a relatively small, bottlenecked chamber, with the curved neck of the bottle opening out into vast and unknown space beyond.

As we worked, the cage made repeated trips to the surface for more men and supplies. Soon a dozen flimsy towers had been set up about the lake, with powerful atom-disruptor lights blazing from their tops. The stalactites of the white roof caught the light and reflected it in a brilliant flood.

Father and Tom soon went back to the city, to look after the mines and our supply of raw materials. Gardiner and I stayed in the cavern, to get work started on the new ships as soon as possible. The cage brought us increasing streams of men—engineers and laborers from Theophilus and Colon and from the smaller cities. Quickly we erected barracks in which we slept; and a vast open shed, under which cooking and eating was done. Gardiner and I superintended the work, taking alternate shifts of twelve hours each.

With amazing speed the spidery framework went up, which was to support the keels of the score of new vessels. In a week the cradles along the lakeshore were almost completed, and our quickly erected foundries had patterns for the casting of the first huge plates.

THE BIRTH OF A NEW REPUBLIC

Illustrations by H. W. Wesso

And the huge black thing, seemingly dazzled by our battery of blazing searchlights, turned and winged a silent way off down the dark passage to westward....

A strange industrial city grew up along the cavern wall, above the yards. There were furnaces that sent an endless infernal glow upon the hanging roof above, and thundering hammers and rolling mills, and great power plants that hummed with atomotors totaling millions of horsepower. Part of the equipment had been moved in sections from the shops at Firecrest, much more had been built, and other units were always planned, needing but time, men, and money to make them complete.

We had been at work for two weeks, when Gardiner told me that another engineer—his name was Nordeau—I think he came from Colon—was ready to take my place, to give me the time to work out refined plans for the D-rays, with which to arm the new fleet.

I obtained a short leave of absence, and went to spend a day with father and Valence and her family, up at Firecrest—for father had gone back to the city at once.

Before I left Gardiner, I did my best to persuade him that I should be assigned to the new fleet. I wanted desperately to be with it when it went to Earth, so that I might have a chance to find Leroda. And I was afraid that Gardiner meant to send me back to Warrington, as soon as the work was well under way.

The old scientist grinned quizzically at my request, and reminded me that it would be a year before the fleet could hope to leave the cavern, even if all went well. He refused to give me any definite promise.

I got out of the cage, and climbed up the short footway to the great valve to the surface. Once more I looked upon the city of my youth. The gleaming walls rose perhaps five miles away, westward. The city was circular and compactly built many stories high. It was shaped like a great round disc dropped by the rim of the crater—as it gleamed in the bright sunlight, it looked very much like a vast silver coin.

The rich mines, from which had been drawn all the wealth to make this wondrous city, were in the crater beyond, with its grim circular rim rising behind the glistening walls.

As I stood and looked at Firecrest, a fierce pride in it welled up in me. It was ours. We had made it. When father had come here, this had been bare desert. All this he had built. I had helped; part of it was mine.

In a new topi and white uniform, I hurried across the five miles of bare desert to the city, beneath the blazing noonday sun. I went at once to father's office, found him at work behind a great desk piled with papers. I saw that he was doing more work than he had tried in years; but his thin shoulders were straight and his blue eyes bright with enthusiasm.

He was glad as ever to see me. He told me that Jenkins had come and gone, with his inevitable "dispatches from Warrington." And mother had come with him. It had been a hard and perilous trip. The old scout had not wished to bring her; she had been compelled to get an order from Warrington. But she said that the old fellow had cared for her most devotedly.

When father and I went to the apartments, she was triumphant, happy and smiling, as well as ever now, though the fatigue of the trip had left her in bed for a day or two.

When I jokingly scolded her for her hardihood in making the trip, she said, laughing, "I may look like a faded old lady in lavender, John, but I am a girl—and I mean to stay one! Do you think I wanted to stay in Theophilus when I had a chance to come to be with all of you?"

Jenkins, it seemed, had not brought good news. An army gathered near Colon under General Hall had marched for New Boston at the beginning of the lunar day, with the object of uniting with Warrington in retaking the city. Hall had been met by a combined force of three spaceships and five thousand soldiers under Masonby, and a horde of the Selenites called Ossinae, with whom the Tellurians were allied. Hall had been disastrously defeated, retreating with only a fraction of his men. Four thousand dead were left upon the field—upon which it was said the mooncalves had made a horrible banquet.

Then Masonby's force of war-fliers, soldiers, and mooncalves had marched against the little mining center of Kirby Peak. This had fallen after a short but spirited defense. Of the two thousand inhabitants, only a handful had escaped the general massacre. The mining machinery and the store of metals on hand had been largely carried off, and the buildings and shaft houses wrecked with the D-rays from the ships.

Another and larger force, working out of New Boston as a center, had met Warrington in a battle between that city and Theophilus. While the combat had been indecisive, Warrington had lost several thousand men and a good deal of equipment, and had been forced to retire upon the appearance of six ships of Humbolt's fleet.

After a few happy hours with my parents, I went back to our new laboratories in the cavern, to set about the experimental work on the D-rays. Remarkable progress, I found, had been made even in the day of my absence. Some of the new factories were running, turning out mostly the tools with which the ships were to be built.

Weeks went by, weeks of exhausting toll, of slow and painful toil. Slowly my efforts with the D-ray brought forth a military weapon that promised to equal the improved tubes carried on the new Tellurian ships. Slowly the great spherical hulls of the new ships were rising by the lake—though they were yet but hulls, without engines and without weapons.

Warrington, after his defeat, had retired to Theophilus again. Now another day had come and he had advanced again, as Jenkins—the old scout was a frequent visitor now, with his dispatches—had informed us.

I had kept renewing my request to Gardiner for a position on the new fleet. Always he had refused to commit himself. But on this day Jenkins came with dispatches. He brought the news that Warrington had met Humbolt again and had defeated him in a hot battle, winning all he had lost in the previous engagement, and more. The whole moon was rejoicing for the victory.

After Gardiner had read the dispatches and sent Jenkins back with our reports on the progress of the work, he brought me a yellow envelope, addressed to John Adams, Jr., and marked "General's Orders." He had always bantered with me about my desire to go to Earth, with questions about my motive. Now he gravely informed me that I was ordered to return to Theophilus, to resume my place as engineer attaché.

"Warrington is planning a big coup, in conjunction with Doane's little fleet," he said, solemnly. "He wants you along, to help plan some temporary fortifications."

"Very good, sir," I agreed, saluting and trying to conceal my disappointment. "I had been hoping to be assigned to the fleet."

Thereupon Gardiner broke into roars of laughter. Presently he recovered his composure and whispered in my ear, "As if I didn't know! And I know why you are so anxious! Ha! Ha!"

Dazed and wondering, I opened the envelope for confirmation of his words. I read: "It is my pleasure to inform you that you are assigned to Lafollette as his military secretary. You will make the voyage to Earth with the fleet in order to be able to work with him on the return voyage. You will use your knowledge of conditions on the moon and your engineering skill to aid him in every possible way in his preparations for operations here. B. Gardiner."

As I looked up, too much overcome to speak, and wrung the old scientist's hand in silent thanks, he grinned and said:

"Why not bring her back with you?"

CHAPTER NINETEEN
Treason

ON April 18, 2328, Gardiner and I left the Firecrest cavern for the new capitol of the moon, at Kurrukwarruk. It had been nearly a year since the opening of the great cave. The ships were almost done. On May 1, the sun would rise. That was the time set for departure to Earth. We were to attend a last conference in the hidden city, to perfect the plans for the voyage and for the military operation with which Lafollette might take part on our return.

The cavern was a changed place now. The entire great chamber, five miles long, had been cleared, and brightly lit by atomic lights suspended from the glistening stalactites of the roof. It was cut off from the unexplored wilderness of the lower cavern by an impenetrable yellow curtain—an unbroken wall of fan-rays.

There was a new city, of many thousand people, above the fresh-water lake, with fertile gardens of vitamin plants covering the soil where once the luminous forest had stood. The lakeshores hummed with industry, vibrating to the ceaseless throb of machinery—smelters and furnaces, power plants and rolling mills, foundries and machine shops. The reverberation of the mighty hammers that forged the armor plates for the ships vied with the endless rattling clang of the thousand riveting hammers that were fastening them together. And all the activity of the place was drawn from the boundless energy of the atom.

Twenty great ships lay in their cradles about the lake, like vast balls of silver. Already their atomic blast engines were being installed; and the heavy armaments of D-rays, with all the refinements that I had labored so many months upon, were being mounted on the ray-decks. Ten thousand men, from all over the moon, were being trained to man the mighty fleet of space. Two months before, Doane had left the little *Eagle*, to come and relieve Gardiner of his duties as Admiral.

Jenkins had come for Gardiner and me. We left Doane in charge of the fleet, and set out for Kurrukwarruk upon the mooncalves of the old scout. The night had fallen two days before, but in Gardiner's improved space armor, with comfortable freedom of movement and ease in breathing, travel by night was fully as comfortable as in the stinging heat of the lunar day.

Jenkins, as usual, was garrulous, but on this night his talk was mostly of his varied adventures in the last year. He had been almost always on the move, keeping Warrington in touch with us at Firecrest, and with Hall, who was still campaigning out of Colon. Jenkins' talk was almost a history of the war. The moon's fortunes had risen and fallen; there had been enthusiasm and encouragement. Warrington had fought battles that seemed victories, and battles that appeared to be defeats; Humbolt was still trying persistently to widen his territory outside of New Boston. All in all, conditions stood about as they had a year before, except that the moon was learning to depend more and more upon its own resources.

Without accident, we reached the little crater with the hidden city of Kurrukwarruk perched, all but invisible, upon the central peak that rose from a desert of crystalline brilliance, silent and still in the cold pale light of Earth.

Warrington was there, having come with one of Jenkins' fellow scouts, Mendoza the Spaniard. There was another agent who had paid a secret visit to the patriots in New Boston; and Vendome and Wong Kow were there, from Hall's forces at Colon.

Most of them seemed glad to see me again—Warrington especially so. We had a great banquet, arranged by Meyers, by way of opening the conference; and afterward the General invited me to his apartments. He pushed maps and dispatches aside and we had a pleasant social evening, spent in talking over our old times together, and in viewing a comic "stereo" talking picture from Earth, which had been on the last prize Doane had captured—our intrepid captain of space had brought no less than a dozen of Metals' supply ships back as prizes during the war.

Next morning the conference began. As such things go, it dragged on slowly, with a lot of useless oratory. Warrington and Gardiner, with their years of experience at such things, had rare skill at letting the important delegates gain satisfaction by making dry and high-sounding speeches, and then getting them to do what was needed.

On the second day, the Director of Finance reported that his secretary, Benedict, had vanished mysteriously. He was a little alarmed; he said that certain important papers had been disturbed; he had found an empty film carton in the vault where they were kept, and feared that photographs had been made of them. But in spite of his implications, it was hard for me to upset my faith in the dashing, brilliant young soldier. It seemed incredible that the man who risked his life so nobly in the storming of the spaceport at New Boston could now be engaged in foul play.

But Greenville, the Director of Finance, insisted that Benedict's room be searched at once. It was found in disorder, with all the young secretary's personal belongings gone. It was evident that he had left permanently and hurriedly—and without much care for the traces of departure. A young officer, on going through the wastepaper basket, discovered a crumpled sheet of paper that bore a sketch map of this section of the moon, showing the location of Kurrukwarruk. The many alterations and notes showed that it had been merely a rough sketch for a more accurate map.

Was Benedict a traitor? Was he preparing to betray the location of the capitol?

As much as all was trusted him, it seemed that he was.

Investigation showed that someone had passed through one of the air locks about twelve hours before. No one had seen him; but Jenkins put on his spacesuit and went out to interrogate his Selenites, which had been left at the foot of the hill upon which the city stood.

In an hour the old scout was back. He reported that M'Ob, his favorite young male mooncalf, which, he often boasted, had more sense than a man, had seen a strange Selenite slip into the crater many hours before—the mooncalf's sense of time is so different from that of a human that this point could not be definite. The strange beast, which, according to M'Ob's account, as Jenkins gave it to us, was a huge red female of the tribe of Ossinae, and armed with a long D-ray tube, had entered the crater from the direction of New Boston, crept to within a mile of the city, and lay there hidden. M'Ob, who had been about the foot of the hill below the city's wall, rambling about in search of bits of lime-stone to eat, had thought of going to accost her, had been deterred by fear of her weapon. He had been ordered to warn the city in case of danger, but the mooncalf psychology is a curious one, and a single creature did not seem a danger to the fortified city, in his eyes. The strange monster had been in hiding for several hours when a man in a spacesuit, carrying a dark object that M'Ob could not name, had slipped out of the city and reached her hiding place. He had mounted her at once and had been carried off in the direction of New Boston. Such was the story that Jenkins got from M'Ob, for which he rewarded the beast with a package of sugar cubes—upon his promise to take them slowly, and not get drunk.

A little figuring showed us that Benedict, if he had indeed been carried to New Boston, might have reached there three or four hours before our discovery of his absence. If he were really a traitor, and it now seemed that we must admit it, he was likely to send Van Thoren's fleet upon us at once. An attack was likely at any moment.

Meyers set immediately about organizing the defense of his city. There were two thousand troops stationed there, in addition to the five thousand civilian population. Kurrukwarruk had been built like a fortress, armed with batteries of D-rays, atomic vortex projectors, and protecting fan-rays. These were manned by the troops; the citizens had been well trained in stopping leaks in the roof, to prevent the escape of the vital air during bombardment.

For my part, I hurried up to the roof. It was of heavy quartz, with a roof garden below the most of it. Over streets and open spaces was a lattice of walks, for those who inspected or repaired the endless sheet of glass above.

The city had been darkened, and though the roof was frosted with a film of frozen air, it was still translucent. For perhaps an hour I stood there in the blackness, staring up at the bright greenish disk of the Earth, swung in a mist of stars. Below I heard the clangor of machinery and the hum of voices as the city was mobilized. Men were coming up about me—I passed a few words with them in strained monosyllables.

Then the alarm sounded through the entire city. The firing of signal guns and the ringing of bells! And a great cry—picked up and repeated until it rolled through the city.

"The war-fliers! Van Thoren is coming!"

I scanned the sky through my compact pocket binoculars. Here and there, against the nebulous stardust of space, I picked out a little circle of perfect blackness with a weird trail of flame below it—the circle was a Tellurian ship, and the flame the discharge of the atomic blast.

One ship dropped a little below the others, and a winking red light signaled:

"I demand the immediate surrender of Kurrukwarruk, with all rebels and traitors therein. Refusal will mean annihilation. Van Thoren."

I could not see the historic reply that Warrington sent:

"We defy you."

But I did see the winking point of red above reply:

"Traitors, your doom is on your own heads."

The war-flier floated back up again, until it was with the others that floated in slow ominous circles far above, like the vultures of Earth above their carron-prey. Then the bombardment began.

Bright, narrow piercing rays stabbed from the floating black sphere toward the city. Huge flaming globes of purple and scarlet, fearfully explosive atomic vortexes, dropped swiftly down. Rays of blinding yellow and flaming red and crystal green shone upon us from those menacing spheres.

And the flash and the splintering burst of shells upon the thick quartz above told us the enemy was using explosive projectiles, nonetheless terrible because they were invisible in their coming.

But the city was not without defense.

The fearful danger of night attack had been realized long before. The city's roof was dotted with weapons, and every citizen was a part of the well-drilled organization that now rushed to position. In a few minutes a forest of vari-colored rays was rising toward the fleet from the white glass roof that spread far about me;

and broad fan-rays, spreading out, intercepted the falling bombs and disintegrated them harmlessly before they struck.

There were a few of the vortex projectors, too. From two or three points about the city, high on the gleaming frost-silvered spires, great flaming globes of scarlet and purple flame, vast balloon-clouds of living light, rose up swiftly in unending succession. And when one of those glistening globes of colored flame struck a ship of space, the fearful blast of disintegrating atoms demolished it utterly.

I heard sounds below. Harsh orders, stern commands, mingling sharply with bursts of cheering and patriotic song, broken sometimes by the sharp crack of an old-fashioned pistol, or by a wild scream of terror.

All the vast vistas of the green garden, with the endless rows of white metal towers that supported the flat, silvered blackness of the roof above, were now brightly lit with the thousand soft silver globes of the atomic light. And that entire vast roof was crowded with people, in hurrying little bands.

There were men and women, rich and poor, wearing jewels or clad in rags. All were together now, all equal in the time of terror. I saw fine society women in the motley groups, sometimes under the command of tattered grimy fellows who looked like beggars.

There were a hundred of those hastily organized groups of citizenry upon the roof, with stepladders, and ray-welders, air-shields, beams and braces, and great lumps and sheets of metal and glass. The weapons were manned by regular troops; the part of the civilians was to detect and repair breaks in the quartz roof, for if the air leaked out faster than pumps and generators could replenish it, we were doomed.

I had no more than taken in the scene before me, when there was a sudden blinding flash against the roof fifty yards away. The concussion of the explosion was terrific. Stunned and deafened, I was flung to the floor of the roof garden, into a tangled mass of vegetation, conscious of a shower of shattered quartz falling upon me.

I sat up uncertainly, rubbing my bruises, at first unable to understand what had happened. Then, in horror, I saw a vast yawning spot of blackness in the silver roof, with the stars shining

THE BIRTH OF A NEW REPUBLIC

through it cold and hard. In a moment there was a sighing sound from it that quickly became a mighty rushing. A breath of cool air met my face, growing to a roaring tempest.

I struggled to my feet, dashed toward the spot, almost helpless in the grasp of that hurricane of escaping air. Already it was freezing, from expansion. A white flurry of snowflakes was whipped along upon it, and a blue mist had hidden the stars outside. The roof-guards were rushing up from all about, carrying ladders and equipment.

Stunned and deafened, I was flung to the floor of the roof garden, into a tangled mass of vegetation.

Illustrated by H. W. Wesso

I hardly recall the incidents of the next half minute. It was one of mad terror, of fearful effort, of blind, frenzied haste. I have a vague memory of setting up ladders against the wild force of outrushing air, of clambering up them, leashed and half-frozen by the hurricane, struggling with great sheets of metal and glass, toiling madly to get them in place against the prankish, fiendish force of the air.

Then suddenly the awful wind was stopped as suddenly as it had begun. I was standing on top of a ladder, plying the dazzling beam of a welding-ray that was fusing and joining the edges of the sheets we had set up to stop the hole. My hat and coat were gone, a great painful bruise was rising on the back of my head, a little stream of warm blood was running down my face—in fact I was rather cut and bruised all over.

But the damage of the bomb was repaired—all except for the loss of thousands of cubic feet of air. That, we could never replace.

Then there was a little pause, when we could look out through the frosted roof, to watch the terrible splendor of the battle—the war-fliers of the Tellurians, in the weirdly hued clouds of the atomic blast, sometimes black, sometimes blindingly outlined in the glare of searchlights that played from the towers of the city—the rays, narrow and very bright, like fierce jets of dazzling liquid fire, scarlet and green and yellow, darting sharply and quickly like slender fiery swords of ruby and emerald and topaz, or like striking snakes—and the broad misty spread of the yellow fan-rays that shielded the city or the ships, pale clouds of saffron and orange, like great sheltering wings of a hovering bird—most splendid and terrible of all, the globular atomic vortexes, great balls of liquid flames, blue and purple, crimson and violet, floating up from our weapons like a stream of rising bubbles, or dropping in showers from the ships above, all exploding with fearfully destructive flashes of crashing flame. It was like a display of beautiful pyrotechnics. It was splendid, and terrible beyond expression.

For a little time I watched, as all about me were watching, save for a few who had turned from the fearful glory of the scene to crowd around a dying man—a poor fellow who had been struck down by a fragment of glass from the shattered roof.

Then other projectiles, which somehow had passed the protecting fan-rays, were bursting on the roof. I watched another desperate mob, a few hundred yards away, engaged in such a mad struggle as we had engaged in to repair the roof. Then suddenly a sharply focused D-ray cut a circular hole near us, and again that desperate battle with the angry freezing wind, until the break was repaired. But that time, because we knew how, it was easier.

Again and again, a great yawning opening was torn in the thick quartz roof. We ran from one to another, forgetful of time, person, or place. I was cut with fragments of glass, numbed again and again with the fierce chill of expanding air, battered about by the wind, even blistered by an accidental beam from a welding-ray.

And steadily the roof grew colder, as each loss of air chilled it more, and during the rare moments of rest we clustered about the atomic heaters to warm our trembling limbs. And soon I noticed, with a chill of horror, that I could feel the symptoms of the thinning of the air. I was panting as I stood there, and my heart was pounding wildly. And I felt the sticky, cold moisture of blood upon my lip—my nose was bleeding.

When the next breach was made in the roof, many of my fellows staggered and fell as we ran to make repairs. And when at last, after a fearful struggle that demanded the last ounces of our ebbing energy it was done, I saw that many others were suffering from nosebleed, or lay gasping on the ground. Some, I saw, were already dead.

Again came that familiar glare of yellow flame and that thunderous, splintering crash, which showered sharp-edged, shattered glass. And then the thin howling of escaping air. I staggered up with a few of the others; we tottered toward that yawning black space in the roof—with the splendor of the dancing, sword-like rays and the floating balls of many-colored flame beyond.

The thin chill air sucked up past us, seemed drawn from us with a pump. I gasped, choked. I felt as if a demon were drawing the air from my lungs. The intense cold gripped me. A thin frost formed over my bleeding limbs. I saw that others were falling about me. I tried to shout a plea for air—and a fearful hand crushed my throat! Blood spurted from my mouth, and I fell freezing on the platform.

Vainly I tried to get up to stop the tempest of air that was howling with a shrill note through the black star-shot hole above. A great wave of cold surged over me, and seemed followed by a vague mist of golden fictitious warmth. My consciousness faded into a vague chaos of surging purple clouds. I floated—now freezing, now feeling a tantalizing hint of warmth, always with awful hands grasping at my throat.

It seemed a long time before my mind rose out of that black abyss. Then I felt as if I were in a coffin, being carried along. There was something about me, so that my feeble efforts failed to move my limbs. Perhaps, I thought, they were frozen stiff. And I felt a regular swaying motion, as if I were being carried on the back of a man.

Presently I felt warm pads about my body, and heard the thin sizzling of escaping oxygen, and felt a metal valve in front of my mouth that worked as I breathed. With an agonizing effort, I moved. I sat up, and found myself on a sort of litter, easily borne between two grotesque giants of silver metal, with great round heads. And ahead of me were many more strange metallic figures, toiling about some huge machine, dragging it along.

Then my muddled brain cleared somewhat. These fantastic metal giants were men, in silvered air-pressure spacesuits. I had been put in one. And we were going down a tunnel, probably somewhere below the city, with the men dragging a huge machine ahead of us.

Then a voice rustled in the phones of my helmet. An odd metallic ring it had, yet I recognized it as Gardiner's.

"Glad to see you coming around, Adams," he said. "You missed the order to get in a spacesuit, eh? We had a hundred and fifty, enough for all members of the Assembly, and for nearly a hundred men. But how are you doing?"

"Why—well enough," I articulated with an effort.

"Good! Just take it easy. You were pretty badly off when we found you. I imagined you had gone up on the roof, and sent a couple of men up to look for you when you didn't come for the suit."

"Where are we now?"

"About a thousand feet under Kurrukwarruk. Secret tunnel here. Comes out by the crater rim, about two miles north. Some atomobile there we can get away in. The men are hauling along a big D-ray mining machine. We may get in a shot in the rear."

"Warrington, and Jenkins, are they all right?"

"Thanks, and we sure are," came from just ahead of me in the rusty voice of the old scout. Then I recognized his stocky figure; he was one of those carrying me.

For a few minutes I lay quiescent on the litter, recovering my strength. After a little adjustment of the oxygen feed from the tanks and of one of the atomic heating pads, I felt comfortable enough, though rather weak. Presently the party halted, and I made Jenkins put me on my feet—though I could hardly stand.

We had reached the end of the tunnel. The silver-suited men were hoisting the great D-ray tube to the surface. It was a huge thing, almost unmanageable. The silvered quartz vacuum tube, which held the little disk of platinum which was the actual source of the ray, was twenty feet long and four feet in diameter. Surrounded with coils, secondary tubes, prisms and condensers, it was mounted in gymbals in a heavy metal frame, which also carried the atomotors for energizing and controlling it. It must have weighed twenty tons.

At last it was pushed and hauled up through the tunnel mouth, by the struggling men, sweating and swearing in their silvered armor. Jenkins and Gardiner lent a hand, even Warrington himself. I was still feeling unable to do more than stand up.

But presently I clambered up beside the mouth of the tunnel, where the men were blocking the great machine in place, and adjusting it for use. The scene was lit by an awful light. A fearful flickering glow shone over the weird, white desert of lava plains and crater walls, from the brilliant rays and spinning, infernally flaming vortexes above the doomed city. The silver ships of the enemy were drifting and circling low above the glass-roofed citadel on the mountain, gleaming terribly in the dreadful splendor of the battle.

It seemed that we looked upon a veritable storm of fire. From a dozen points about the white mountain burst brilliant geysers of scarlet and green and orange flame—thin narrow rays, blindingly bright, which played quickly and ceaselessly against the utter blackness of the sky. And broad yellow fan-rays spread out like wings of saffron dawn, to armor the city. And from each of the vast white spheres circling slowly above—there were seven of them now—jetted hard, bright fingers of bloody ruby light, and of living emerald and of smoky topaz, wavering over the city like tentacles of a living monster.

And the fearful balls of fire, blue and purple and white, the madly spinning spheres of destruction that were the atomic vortexes, rose and fell ceaselessly, exploding with awful, blinding bursts of flame.

Presently the men passed word that the tube was ready. The captain stood with his hand on the switch; the engineers fussed over the atomotor, the rangefinders stood with tripods and instruments set up before them, sighting; the gunners waited by the wheels that trained the great machine.

In a few moments a great globular ship, in its slow circles over the city, drifted toward us until it could have been hardly two miles away. No yellow fan-ray screened it from our attack—it was not expecting a shot in the rear.

Warrington gave the order. The rangefinders, at their telescopes, spoke terse directions. The slender, silvered tube of the great machine swung slowly in its trunnions. The engineers nursed whining atomotors, and purple sparks leapt between the coils.

Then the click of a switch. An intense beam of crimson light—intense, bloody, sparkling—leapt silently from the top of the silver tube. Looking as solid as a jet of ruddy, molten metal, it impinged squarely upon the vast globe of silver above.

The white ship blackened; then its side was lit with a red glow that became quickly incandescent white. The war-flier seemed to stagger beneath the beam that was swiftly dissolving her armor, and fusing her with the generated heat of atomic disruption.

Still our vast silent beam of crimson clung to the war-flier, despite her zigzag rolling in an effort to escape. Had the tube been equipped with the refinements I had lately perfected at Firecrest, we should have been victors already.

"Into the tunnel!" Warrington shouted suddenly. "All except the crew!"

Pell-mell, armored men piled into the open mouth of the passage, raced down it. We were not a moment too soon and were hardly there when a shattering blast came from the tunnel, and a sudden flare of wicked flame.

Fifteen minutes later we groped our way back to the surface, over a bank of fallen debris. Where the tunnel-mouth had been was now a vast crater. Of the D-ray machine and its crew was no sign. But the war-flier lay, a crushed and blackened thing, upon the snow-covered desert a half mile away.

The six remaining ships continued their bombardment of the city as if the fate of their sister vessel had not been noticed. I saw that the rays from the city's crystal towers were fewer now.

We lost no time in advancing upon the fallen vessel—a whispered conference of a few seconds decided the matter. There was considerable peril in it, if the other ships should happen to see us. But they were still well engaged—one of them was caught by a swirling atomic vortex and demolished in a fearful explosion almost as we started.

Our brief discussion showed varied motives for investigating the wreck. The men had thoughts of tobacco, money, new weapons, and of plunder generally. Gardiner and I hoped to get a few scraps of useful information by inspecting the armament and engines of the fallen ship. Warrington said that the flier had been the flagship of the attacking fleet; he hoped that we might be fortunate enough to find its papers undestroyed and that they might contain valuable secrets.

After a few minutes of cautious advance over the silvered plain, the vast metal hull towered above us, twisted and bent by the fall, blackened and fused by the action of our ray. Hiding under the edge of the wrecked monster, it took but a few minutes for us to cut an opening in her plates with pocket D-rays.

A blast of air met us as the rays cut through. It froze in a thin blue fog, and settled in silver frost upon us. We stood back a few moments, until the force of its outrush was spent, and then clambered through the opening. We found ourselves in the lower engine compartment. Scattered about it were the bodies of a dozen men in greasy coveralls. Some of them were still limp and warm—they must have survived the crash, have been asphyxiated when we let out the air.

We found the air lock that led to the compartment above, and entered it, emerging in the quarters of the crew. There were a score of living men there, but they were unarmed and offered no resistance. From that we went on up to the D-ray deck. The walls of that had been broken, the vacuum of the night already had entered there; and frozen men stood stiff and grotesque about their weapons.

From the ray deck we passed into the compartments occupied by the officers. The walls had held; the men inside were still alive. They were inclined to resist with pocket rays. We lost four men in the brief encounter, and were compelled to kill two Tellurians. But we took seven prisoners, including Masonby, the admiral of the fleet, King, the captain of the ship, and four minor officers.

And the seventh man was Benedict, the traitor. When the others surrendered, he had fled to a stateroom, locked himself in. When we broke the door in, he defended himself desperately with a pocket ray, killing one man and wounding two more in spite of the protection of their space armor. But we took him alive.

He was sullen and silent. His dark face was flushed, and his black eyes smoldered with hate. He stood stiffly at attention, refusing to speak. Warrington had his person searched. Credit units to the value of nearly half a million were found, and his commission as a Director in the Metals Corporation.

"So that is the price of the moon?" Warrington asked him scornfully, waving the documents.

A look of mingled fierce pride and humiliation crossed the face of the prisoner. He bit through his lips until blood oozed from his mouth. But he made no reply.

"We shall be compelled to court-martial you, on charge of treason," Warrington said sternly.

"Go ahead——damn you!" Benedict cried in a hoarse voice, spitting blood from his mouth.

Warrington presided at the military trial, with Gardiner and the other officers present as judges. The charge was formally read to the prisoner, the case briefly considered. He made no attempt at defense; he refused to speak except for bitter curses. The penalty demanded was death.

The prisoner heard his doom in silent defiance, with scornful hatred flaming from his eyes. He was commanded to stand against the wall of the wrecked control-room, and complied like a man in a dream. Three men, in bright silver armor, equipped with pocket D-rays, took their places before him.

Suddenly he laughed in bitter scorn, his black eyes flaming.

"You can kill me!" he cried. "But you will meet the same fate. Your hidden cave! Your little fleet! Humbolt knows all about them! When you get to Firecrest, you'll find a wreck! Now kill me—and be damned!"

He closed his mouth, folded his arms, and stood there composed, leering in a sort of triumphant hate. I might almost have pitied him if his words had not thrown me into a fever of rage and fear.

"God have mercy on your soul!" intoned the officer. "Fire!"

Three narrow rays—one bloody crimson, one emerald green, one smoky yellow—darted from the pistols of the three silver-armored men. For a brief instant, the dark figure was bathed in blinding incandescence. There was a dull, explosive "plop" and a sudden vivid burst of white flame where he had stood.

And the man who had been false to his world was no more.

CHAPTER TWENTY
Trapped in the Cavern

WE left the ship as soon as our business there was done, and beat a hurried retreat. It seemed that we were not observed—the weird battle above the city was still being hotly fought. Five minutes later we were back in the shadows of the crater's rim.

At the mouth of the tunnel through the crater-wall we stopped to watch. Narrow pencils of jeweled fire were still playing upon the silver ships from the city, and the endless bright streams of atomic vortexes were floating up. But those rays were fewer than they had been; and as we watched, another of the great yellow curtains of the fan-ray vanished as an exploding vortex demolished its projector.

That left half the city exposed to the darting fingers of fire from above. One by one the defending rays snapped out. In a few minutes the city was dark save for the crown of vivid rays that sprang from the highest peak of the mountain. Now all the armament of the five war-fliers was focused upon that one last battery. In another minute, its beams blinked out. Kurrukwarruk was defenseless.

The surviving vessels of Masonby's fleet made sure of their victory. Their D-rays plowed the defenseless town until nothing but the bare top of the hill remained. Carthage of old was no more completely destroyed when Scipio plowed salt into its ashes. Even the Tellurian ships that had fallen were obliterated—the object being, I suppose, to keep them from falling into our hands.

Then the five great ships rose, and proceeded deliberately in the direction of New Boston.

We entered the great tunnel that pierced the crater wall, and emerged upon the white, desolate desert outside. There remained less than a hundred of us, out of the thousands who had inhabited the capitol of the moon. Jenkins' mooncalves had vanished; we had to leave by atomobile. The network of roads over the moon, in such splendid condition at the beginning of the war, had been so torn up and barricaded that they were hardly more passable than the unimproved desert; and the machine was a poor substitute for the great leaping beasts.

In view of Benedict's last words, it seemed certain that the catastrophe at Kurrukwarruk would soon be repeated at Firecrest. I cursed the traitor when I thought of mother and father, and of Valence and her little family, when the ruthless fleet should fall upon Firecrest.

A dozen of the machines were waiting in the chamber cut just inside the tunnel-mouth—slender, gleaming silvered tubes, with elaborate springs and tractor tread, driven by atomotors. We started them, ran them out into the bright light of Earth. Wonderful mechanisms they were—wonderful they had to be to traverse the wild mountains of the moon. But under present conditions, when the roads were wrecked or barricaded, they were not half so dependable as mooncalves would have been.

Warrington had to go back to his troops at Theophilus. Gardiner went with him. Vendome and Wong Kow were returning, with a party of agents and officers of various ranks, to Hall at Colon. Most of the government officials who had escaped, including Greenville and Meyers, went with Warrington to Theophilus. The troops in spacesuits were divided about equally between the two parties, to serve as guards in case of accident. The gleaming, cumbrous machines formed two little trains.

To Jenkins and me was left the task of reaching Firecrest, if possible in time to give warning that the city had been betrayed. We had the lightest and swiftest of the atomobiles—a little vehicle, built mostly of an aluminum alloy, and powered to do two hundred miles per hour on a smooth pavement, though we could expect hardly a tenth that speed over the desert. I carried dispatches to Doane. If possible, we were to get the ships out of the cavern before the coming of a hostile fleet bottled them up, and set out for Earth.

It was yet some twelve hours until day when we separated, and clattered lumberingly away into the stillness of the frozen lunar night. The heavens were a rich fiery canopy above—a soft silver mist of stardust, with the incredible hosts of many-colored diamond points blazing hard and cold within it. In the midst of all was the Earth—a broad bright disk of greenish blue, vague and misty with continental outlines, and gleaming with wonderful brightness. A strange contrast there was indeed, between the liquid beauty of the Earth above us, and the cruelty and suffering its people had brought to the moon. White frost lay over all the cruel wilderness of rocks about us, and upon the dead, crushed vegetation of the day; and the bright Earthlight poured upon it in scintillant splendor.

We were many miles from the lost city of Kurrukwarruk when the rising of the white cone of the zodiacal light foretold the coming of the sun. I was at the wheel of the lumbering atomobile, driving in desperate haste across that frozen white wilderness, beneath the jeweled stars and the radiance of the beautiful Earth. As we went, Jenkins anxiously watched the sky for sight of black circles with plumes of fiery mist below them, which would mean a fleet bound for the city.

What if we should be delayed or lost? What if our machine fell into one of the innumerable abysmal chasms of the moon, and we became a prey to the wild Ka'Larbah?

Such thoughts made me fearful of every black shadow that lay behind the rocks and precipices of that brilliant snowy plain. The sky, all the void above, was marvelously clear. Incredibly black, it was, with thick white stars flaming in it. Far off, to right and left and before us, rose ragged mountains—great, slender, rugged white peaks, far sharper and crueler than any hills on Earth. For all the floods of silver light that fell upon their snow-swept slopes, etching cruel cliffs in black shadow, motionless and distinct, there seemed a singular unreality about them. They were grim, and fearfully cold, and terrible.

The utter loneliness of the night; the knowledge that we were scores of miles from any other human; that no living thing of our own planet could live exposed on the white moonscape about us; the fear of the bottomless chasms masked by the powdery blanket of frozen air and snow; and the terror of wild mooncalves—all these preyed upon my mind.

Desperately I urged onward the throbbing machine, toward the vast cone of misty golden fire, the solar corona, which crept up so slowly in the east. Jenkins sat intent and watchful beside me—silent, for once. Ice and frozen air slipped and crushed beneath the tracks, but in the vacuum of the night, we heard no sound of it. Sometimes the machine toppled over unseen edges, and fell into powdery drifts. At the rate we traveled over the naked rocks, the riding was unmercifully rough, and we were bruised and tossed about on the padded seat.

Day came at last, when we were midway of a great crater floor. The lurid writhing prominences of the solar corona rose over rugged black mountains, and struck the frozen air with a heat that sent it hissing into murky yellow clouds. We drove on into a mist of glorious fire, flame-yellow before us, blue and smoky behind. Vapor rolled up in thick clouds from the rocks, lit with red and purple flame; and the vast ruddy sun burned relentlessly through it like a red, malevolent eye.

An hour later we came unexpectedly to a "mooncalf road" as the saying is—that is, a path with a leap at the end. In vain I slammed on the brakes. The atomobile slid through a snow-bank and toppled over the brink, to fall for a hundred feet. It was hopelessly wrecked. We toiled with it for hours; but an axle was twisted, the springs were broken, and the motor itself refused to work.

We came to the reluctant conclusion that we should have to go on afoot—although that meant a desperate journey of hardships almost unthinkable. After a last hopeless inspection of the wreck, we turned and attacked the climb from the crevice into which we had crashed.

In a few minutes we won the plain, which was already hot and dry, for the sun had been shining several hours there. Because of the heat, we had to leave the wonderful metal suits, without which life would have been impossible a few hours before.

We had covered hardly half the distance to Firecrest. We had two long days of travel before us, to make it afoot. And already we were exhausted from bouncing about in the machine, and from our feverish efforts to repair it. But we leapt on, driven by fear of a fleet that might be rushing to attack the city.

The red sun blazed down fearfully. We had no proper sun helmets; our heads were protected only with bandages of white rags. Indeed, we wore only the underclothing we had had on beneath the spacesuit. In a few hours my skin was cooked, and I saw that Jenkins was burning with fiery inflammation, though he did not complain. The worst of it was that we had no shoes—the foot-coverings of the spacesuit not being detachable. The cruel, sun-heated rocks cut through our socks with the first few leaps, and our blistered, bleeding feet left a mark of crimson for every leap.

That was a double terror. The pain of bare torn feet was all but unendurable. And it was almost certain that a band of the wild mooncalves would come across the trail of blood, and with their passion for animal food run us down.

Sometimes we stopped and bound our lacerated feet with the strips of cloth from our undershirts. But the wrappings were soon torn off, and the sun beat terribly upon our exposed shoulders. Two or three times we found a little unmelted snow lying in the black shadow of a cliff, and crammed handfuls of it into our mouths. But the intense cold of it seemed to sear one's tongue like hot ashes; and a few drops of water failed to slack a burning thirst.

Again and again I looked back over my shoulder, with a thrill of ungovernable terror. And at last my fears were realized. I saw four little black dots back of us, little dark specks that floated up into the air, and drifted back down to the rocky waste of the desert, always nearer.

I stopped, speechless, in a paralysis of fear. I could not speak, but I thrust out a trembling hand. Jenkins saw it, paused, with his red face blanching. From his dry, swollen slips grated a single word:

"Ka'Larbah!"

We hid and watched, cautiously—for Selenite eyes are incredibly keen. I think I screamed when I knew that they were mooncalves and that they were coming down our trail. Then we ran—wildly, madly. It was foolish, for nothing can outrun a Selenite. With desperate efforts I plunged into the air, flew forward, fell, and leapt again. It was a terrible death to face. The mooncalves have eaten many men, and the stories told of it are not good to think about.

My breath came in gasps, and my tongue felt vast and hard, like a great roll of dry leather in my mouth. My head felt splitting from the heat. I felt as if I ran over red-hot iron. Presently I found that I could leap no more. On hands and knees I crawled to an overhanging boulder, to wait for the end. Jenkins collapsed beside me, his whole body jerked with the heaving of his breast, and his eyes wild with terror.

The mooncalves were near now. I watched them in a vague apathy of terror. Four or five more hurtling leaps, and then...

Abruptly Jenkins sat up, sobbing with wild hysterical laughter. I stared at him in dull astonishment. A squat little man, he was, and incredibly grimy, his flesh cooked to a raw red. Brick-red tousled hair fell over his blistered face, and ragged bits of red woolen underclothing hung to his burned limbs. And he was doubled up with insane laughter.

Presently I saw that he was trying to speak. The racing mooncalves were almost upon us as he jerked out the words:

"Ka'Larbah! Like hell! It's M'Ob!"

I think I screamed when I knew that they were moon-calves, that they were coming down our trail. Then we ran—wildly, madly. It was foolish, for nothing can outrun a Selenite adapted by nature for fast travel on the rocky surface of the moon.

Illustrations by H. W. Wesso

"M'Ob?" I repeated, uncomprehending.

"M'Ob. My M'Ob. My mooncalf. He somehow got away. He followed us."

Indeed, I now recognized something familiar about the vast, red-armored beast, with its three huge green eyes, as it came to a crashing halt beside us. Jenkins ran down to it, with tears streaming down his red face, he embraced its long tentacular limb, while it fondled his sunburned body with evident affection.

In a few minutes we were mounted, and racing toward Firecrest at five times our former speed. As we sped, I kept an eager watch on the deep blue sky behind. Terrible hours went by, as we weltered and roasted in the increasing heat of the sun—but our relief was so great that we faced the new hardships without complaint.

Firecrest came at last into sight—a bright silver disk, close against a black crater wall. It was safe!

Then, looking behind, I saw six little spheres of polished silver, scudding toward us, swift and low. The fleet from New Boston!

It was evidently too late to get our ships out to meet the enemy.

I shouted my discovery to Jenkins. He urged our mounts to the limit of their speed, then leaned to me, and shouted:

"We'll go by the cave-mouth. You can drop off there, with the papers. I'll go on to the city, warn them. The beasts must not stop; it would show them where the cave is."

I shouted assent. On we flew. The white balls grew behind us. I saw the familiar boulders about the concealed cavern-entrance. Jenkins shouted and waved his arms to our mounts. They dropped beside the pit, where the great valve was yawning open. I slipped off my mount, with the dispatches belted about me. M'Ob thundered on across the monotonous waste of burned rock, with Jenkins upon him and the other monsters following. They would, I thought, have time to reach the city.

I ran for the valve, leapt down the stair to the engine-rooms, shouting the alarm. I found an idle watchman at the controls of the great sliding lid of the shaft, lounging indolently, in the act of taking a great pinch of wiz-wiz. He stared at me stupidly. In desperation, I seized the levers myself, despite his startled protest, sent the great door shut.

But it must have been too late to hide the shaft-mouth; or more likely, Benedict had revealed its exact location. Five minutes later, I heard the abrupt, shattering crash of an exploding atomic vortex, and the living rock trembled with the violence of a terrific detonation.

Soon the great cage had risen, was carrying me down into the hidden cavern. The fearful concussion of exploding vortexes were crashing continually about the top of the shaft. I was landed at the cavern floor, and sought Doane at once.

A tall man he was, of commanding aspect, with penetrating blue eyes. He listened calmly enough to my brief report of Benedict's treason and of the fall of Kurrukwarruk, and read the dispatches from Warrington. Then he informed me that the last adjustments on the ships had been made, and that he had only been awaiting my return with the final orders before leaving the cavern.

Now, with the fleet above, it was hopeless to attempt to get out.

In answer to my eager inquiries, Doane told me that father and mother, and Valence and her family, were all in the city by the crater—I had been hoping unreasonably that they would be in the safety of the cave.

"The city is fortified," Doane attempted to console me. "The fleet can be held off for a time, at least."

"But in the end, it will be like Kurrukwarruk—wiped out utterly," I said bitterly. "And we must sit here, idle. There is nothing we can do!"

"Nothing that I see," Doane agreed. "Though our twenty new ships could sweep them down in five minutes, if we could get at them. As it is, we'd better try to block up the shaft. If they find the valve and cut it out with their rays, there'll be hell coming down."

He hurried out, to give orders, and left me standing alone in his little office. I walked to the door, and looked out into the vast cavern. All about me was a modern industrial city, very new and rather ugly, with towering smokestacks, and huge naked machines, and long Iron sheds. Above was the white roof of glistening stalactites, bright with a million flashing ato-lights. To the west was a village of bright little cottages, with green gardens about them. And eastward lay the vast unknown regions of the cavern, cut off from us by the saffron screens of the fan-rays.

The sight gave me an idea. Once before I had been in that great cave, In need of an exit—when I had found the place, as child of twelve. I had but the vaguest idea of my terrified wanderings in the cavern. But I knew that I had come out in the bottom of a little crater, about fifteen miles due east of Firecrest. I was sure that I had gone through no passage too small for a war-flier.

Presently Doane came back.

"I'm having a great steel plate forged," he said, "the size of the shaft. We'll fasten it about midway up, and plant charges above to shatter the walls and bring them down upon it. We'll have something that will take days to cut through, anyhow."

"I think we can leave the cave," I said.

"If we came up that shaft," he objected, "we'd find their rays already focused on us, and no fan-rays to protect us. They would get us one at a time, easy as smashing bottles."

"I don't mean that. There's another way out of the

"Another way?"

"About fifteen miles east of here. We ought to be able to find it, with all our searchlights and navigation apparatus." He listened intently as I related my childhood adventure.

"We'll try," he said briefly.

The crews were already aboard the score of vast silver ships that lay in their cradles along the shore of the black lake. Doane called his orderlies and gave a hurried string of directions. Ten minutes later we were on his mighty flagship, the *Comet*.

We rose, with the rest of the immense vessels floating up behind us upon their misty atomic blasts. The yellow barriers of the fan-rays dropped before us, and we passed into the mysterious luminosity of the unexplored cavern.

Ours was indeed a fantastic cruise, through a weird hidden world. We sailed swiftly over luminous jungles for four or five miles down the main cavern, our searchlights flashing on glistening white vaults above us. Then the cyclopean cave divided before us like the arms of a Y. We followed first up the right arm. That brought us, beyond some miles of weird green jungle, to a great lake, filling the cavern for many miles. It was a-light, looking like a sea of red fire—there must have been luminous organisms of some kind in the water.

I knew that I had passed no such thing during my days of desperate and terrified wandering in the cavern as a boy. I had Doane return to the fork and try the other passage. The glistening crystal roof lowered upon us, and we swept low over an eldritch jungle of phosphorescent green and white and red—with the titanic silver spheres strung out in a long train behind us, alight with the blaze of searchlights and the weird flame of the atomic blast. The cavern fairly swarmed with gigantic black reptilian things, with wingspread of a hundred feet, their vast eyes burning, luminous, purple, malevolent.

A swarm of them surrounded our ship, which was somewhat in the lead. Scores of them circled close about, screaming with cries that rang dreadfully against the low roof and the narrowing walls of the cave. Their hooked claws seemed formidable enough to rip up metal plates. I became so excited that I eagerly importuned Doane to fire—he was standing with the other officers, searching the glittering roof above through the telescope of the bridge room.

His look, though smiling, reminded me that he was admiral and I a mere passenger. "Very good, Adams," was all he said. I returned to the window, and stared with bated breath at the immense winged things that were flying around us in their glistening armor of black scales.

A few moments later one of them plunged directly at the ship. Its purple eyes glazed terribly; it showed a long jaw filled with teeth that looked capable of chewing up steel ingots. Involuntarily I drew back from the window, tensing my muscles for catastrophe.

But a thin beam of rich golden light jetted suddenly from the D-ray port just below me. Instantly the black monster was outlined in brilliant incandescence. Then it was falling in burned and smoking death. I realized that Doane had given the ray men orders to bring down any of the things that came too near.

Hours more went by. We passed into higher regions—at one time we had been ten miles below the surface. We left luminous forest and winged monsters behind, and groped our way through midnight rifts where the searchlights pierced blackness that had not been broken for a million years. We felt a way through narrow winding passages.

But for our marvelous navigating instruments, we should have been utterly lost. As it was, Bris mapped the cavern as we went, and kept the position of each ship located on the map. The vessels were in radio communication, and each sent its discoveries to be recorded on the map. We wormed a way through endless caverns, frequently forced because of a narrow passage to turn and retrace a path, but always penetrating nearer to the spot that I had marked on a photographic view or map of the surface, as the crater with the opening in its bottom.

At last we reached a slanting upward shaft, and gazed up to see a patch of blue-black sky, with three bright stars gleaming in it. Doane sent out a call to the other vessels, and soon they were gathered in a long line of silver spheres behind us in the cavern.

We pushed forward steadily, but with caution, sometimes pausing to smooth a projecting ledge of rock with a D-ray, for the passage had become perilously narrow. We emerged at last in the bottom of a tiny, high-walled crater, shimmering in the glare of the white sun that blazed above the cruel and lofty peaks.

One by one the immense silver globes came out in flashing splendor to meet the day. In a few minutes our whole fleet was floating in close formation in the crater. As we waited for the other ships, Doane had been sunk in intense thought over the instrument board, carefully tracing a cabalistic design on the back of an old letter—he had an odd habit of drawing weird and meaningless diagrams while lost in concentration.

When the last ship drove up out of the crevice, he gave the order, and the fleet rose with the *Comet* in the lead. As we mounted above the cragged crater rims, I pressed my face toward the quartz port in the west, fearful that I would see Firecrest such a desolate smoking wreck as Kurrukwarruk had been.

But I saw that the city still held out. It gleamed in the sun like a bright disk of silver by the crater rim, with the scintillant D-ray still flashing up as if from living jewels set in it. Three of the enemy ships hung above the city, raining D-rays and atomic vortexes upon the sheltering saffron fan-rays. The other three ships were nearer, evidently bombarding the shaft.

We bore down upon the ships above the shaft at rocket speed. They must have quickly seen us, for the rain of flaming vortexes and the shifting shower of rays suddenly stopped. The three war-fliers lifted a little, and drew together, between us and the city. And the fliers bombarding that place redoubled their fire. Serious damage, I saw, had already been done to the glistening towers and domes of Firecrest.

Doane threw his fleet out to either side as we flew. The silver fliers took up a crescent formation; and when we closed in the horns of the crescent folded about the three enemy ships. They waited, hanging over the shaft, until Doane released his first broadside of atomic vortexes, followed by a glancing volley of rays.

Then they darted quickly upward, replying so heavily that they seemed veritable balls of flame, silver globes encrusted thick with scintillant gems that shot deadly rays. I can hardly explain their maneuver, unless they discounted our strength and expected to find our ships manned with raw recruits and an easy prey to their well-focused onslaught.

But Doane had seen that his men were thoroughly trained. The three Tellurian fliers found themselves helpless in the center of a deadly ring of fire. In a few seconds our dazzling rays were cutting through their screen. They made a desperate effort to break away, but too late. One of them was suddenly alight with vivid incandescence, and falling madly. Then the two others followed.

At that the three ships above the half-ruined city turned and raced away. Doane ordered instant pursuit. The weirdly rugged lunar wildness of jagged mountain and abysmal chasm and cragged circular crater was then flashing beneath us. The other vessels might have escaped if it had not been for the greater power of the new gold atomic blast generators that powered our fleet. As it was, we overhauled them before they had covered a hundred miles. Orange fan-rays spread behind the fleeing argent flyers, and hard, narrow rays burned viciously through in our direction. But soon the racing wings of our fleet were creeping up upon their flanks, and our vastly larger armament brought them down one by one. They fell in twisted masses of flowing ruin, to be smashed and torn beyond recognition as machines, when they crashed upon the cragged lunar mountains.

An hour later we dropped before the walls of Firecrest. The once trim glass armor was shattered, blackened, and crumbling from the bombardment. But busy crews were already repairing it. With a few of the officers who had had friends or relatives in the city, I hurried in through the airlock.

An eager crowd was waiting for us, clamorous with hysterical joy. Jenkins bustled out to greet me, strutting in a new red tunic, grinning and very glad to see me. I found father, with a weary look beneath his happy smile, with mother leaning on his arm. She was laughing with joy as I took her in my arms, but I saw the dry stain of tears upon her cheeks.

Before we left the ship we had received the order from Admiral Doane, "We start for Earth in four hours. Be aboard at 14:35."

CHAPTER TWENTY-ONE
Lafollette

THE hours seemed but moments until it was time to go aboard the *Comet* again. The whole population of the city, still in a frenzy of hysterical merriment, turned out in a clamoring throng to bid farewell to the fleet that had saved them. I saw, however, busy crews at work, repairing shattered walls and turrets; and another gang was busy with D-rays, opening the obstructed shaft to the great cavern.

Jenkins, though his equilibrium was a bit unstable as a result of his part in the celebration, was on hand to wish me a good voyage. He became eloquent, and even tearful, at our parting.

Valence and Tom Dowling were out to see me off, Tom a tall, tanned, clean young fellow, who looked rather odd with a soft pink baby on his lean, bronzed arm.

Father gripped my hand crushingly; then broke down his calm reserve so far as to throw his arms impulsively about my shoulders. Mother, as always in parting, was brave. She tried to hide her tears, to appear cheerful and smiling. Her last word was a happy little jest, though her voice broke with an involuntary sob.

I left them, hurried through the lines of soldiers that were guarding the vessels. An elevator whisked me up into the gigantic silvered bulk of our flagship, the *Comet*. A few minutes later I stood on the bridge, a licensed passenger, watching the bright silver circle that was Firecrest dwindle and vanish in the rugged gray panorama of crater and plain that was swiftly contracting to a huge mottled golden sphere behind us.

We rose at almost the limit of our power. Soon the moon was but a huge ball below us, with every sharp, jagged line of her mountains distinct in the merciless light of the sun that blazed upon her. And beside the dazzling whiteness of the moon, the sky was utterly black, and dusted with diamond stars.

I went to another window, and saw the Earth ahead of us, a pale soft sphere of misty green, with a crescent rim of white brilliancy, and its dark limb outlined in pale rosy light. First it seemed above me, and then my senses swung about oddly, and it appeared to be above, I thought of the girl who was waiting for me somewhere on that vast sphere ahead; and I left the bridge and went to my stateroom where I could play again the vocal record she had given me.

I heard her clear sweet words again, "I will be waiting... My radio-recorder will be tuned always on 5.678 meters. If you ever come, call that and tell me where I can come to you... You know that I love you—forever. Leroda."

Oddly, her words, with the ringing sincerity of their intonation, and the little catches in their utterance that revealed tragic despair, reduced me to the point of tears.

Our passage to Earth was made in record-breaking time. With the new projector, we were able to accelerate in a few hours to the limit of speed considered safe in the meteorite-scattered lanes. And with our greater braking power, and more responsive controls, the vessels could be checked or maneuvered more easily, to avoid meteoric collision, and we were able to exceed the usual speed. We started on May 5; and on the night of May 21, we entered the atmosphere of Earth.

I enjoyed my association with Paul Doane during the voyage. The mind behind his piercing blue eyes was as active as his tall and athletic body. As we sat at table I reveled in his cutting wit, and often he found time to join me for a game of chess, for an animated discussion of the latest drama from Earth, or of some principle of philosophy or even in a scientific speculation as to the future of the race—he was almost catholic in his breadth of understanding.

But he was not idle during the voyage. Besides the regular duties of Admiral, he took it upon himself to see that the D-ray crews had regular training; he spent a good deal of time writing a monograph on the complicated three-dimensional tactics of space warfare, and he spent long hours with me in working out the scheme for getting Lafollette and his supplies and men aboard the fleet.

At last we agreed that the main fleet should approach the Earth over the North Pole and land in north Greenland. The *Comet* would leave the fleet and descend just after dusk on the middle of Lake Michigan. Bris and I would be dropped, in a swift hydroplane, and the *Comet* would rejoin the fleet. Bris and I were to attempt to reach Chicago and get in touch with Lafollette. When we had made the arrangements with him, we were to communicate with Doane by radio, telling him when to return.

We entered the conic shadow of the Earth fifteen thousand miles above it, thereby escaping the danger that the glancing reflection of the sun upon our silvered vessels would be noticed by terrestrial observatories. At an altitude of five hundred miles we separated; the rest of the fleet vanished in the northward sky, and the *Comet* sank into the planet's murky atmosphere.

Bris and I were landed in our little speedboat without accident, though we were at first almost helpless under the powerful gravitational pull of Earth. We started the atomic engine, and soon were darting away from the colossal silver hull that rode so lightly upon the waves. In a moment it had risen behind us, vanishing in a pall of unfamiliar gray clouds that shut out the moonlight.

In half an hour the bright misty glow of a million lights was bursting through the haze before us. As we neared the shore a floating craft passed us. Her wide decks were ablaze with light, and we heard swift throbbing music from her. Other bright lights darted through the clouds above, but we were not molested.

Without accident, we reached the shore. We first approached a brilliantly lit garden, with jovial festal crowds moving through it, thronging amusement machines in a blinding glare of light, while harsh music glared and stentorian loudspeakers thundered out advertising slogans. We ran up the beach for half a dozen miles, to a quieter place, where there were dark, silent warehouses, and landed.

Bris opened the seacock in the little boat, and headed it out again into the lake, under power. We would not need it again.

In an hour we were lost in the merry, restless crowds of the amusement beach. We entered a colossal, glass-armored building that towered up in a blaze of electric fire, slender and tall as a lunar peak. We mounted an elevator to the flying stages above the roof, and there took a private plane to the Chicago offices of Tranco.

Lafollette, we soon learned, was in the great building—he had a suite of rooms there. At first the secretaries refused to call him up. By means of a generous bribe, I got in telephone communication with him. A word was enough. In a few minutes we were received as honored guests in his private rooms.

It was the first time I had met that great friend of the moon-people. He was only of medium height, but there was something of impressive dignity about him. Immaculately dressed, he looked the cultured aristocrat that he was. The quiet richness of his rooms revealed unostentatious good breeding.

He welcomed us most cordially, with a quiet sincerity. He inquired eagerly after Warrington and Gardiner, who were old friends of his. His eyes snapped with indignation when he heard of the destruction of Kurrukwarruk, gleamed with satisfaction when we told of the crushing of Masonby's fleet.

"And now the moon has a fleet, and she is ready to accept the aid I promised Gardiner?" he asked us frankly when our messages were delivered.

"She is," I said. "I am commissioned to be your secretary."

"Good," he smiled. "We can begin gathering my force in the morning. I'm sure your services will prove valuable, for I've never been to the moon; and I trust you'll find me an easy master."

It was late when we retired to the excellent rooms he provided, and by that time I felt much better acquainted with the polished gentleman who bore so sincere a friendship for the moon and for liberty.

The next day I arranged for the use of a long-range radio set that Lafollette had privately installed in the building—I could not use the public ethero-phone, of course. I sent two short messages, which were to mean nothing except to their proper recipients, and to which no answers were expected.

THE BIRTH OF A NEW REPUBLIC

The one to Doane ran simply:
"On the lake. May 26."
And on 5.678 meters I sent this call:
"Trance Building. Chicago. John Adams."

During that day, I fear, I was of little assistance to Lafollette in his secret collection of armed troops and supplies of war. I spent most of the time on the stage at the top of the building, scanning eagerly the faces of the endless lines of passengers that disembarked from the incoming aero-liners.

The sun went down, tawny and red in the saffron west, and dusk settled upon the stark buildings, lighted by the pale flood of silver moonlight, and by the dazzling gleam of man-made day upon the busy ways and amusement places. A few stars shone feebly through the hazy gray sky that is so strange to the visitors from the moon.

Until late in the night I waited on the platform, feeling new hope when each bright light glided down from the sky, and falling anew into the pit of despair, when each great liner rushed up and away without having landed the dear girl I awaited.

And she did not come.

The next day I was busy, and could not meet the liners. I spent the time in conferences with Lafollette's lieutenants, discussing conditions on the moon, the present state of political affairs, the military tactics which Warrington and Humbolt had found most effective, the supplies and equipment that an army would need for effective operations.

Lafollette was proving no mean ally. He was undertaking to collect and arm a force of forty thousand men, which was about as many as our fleet could carry. In addition to the equipment and supplies that his own troops would require, he was gathering immense amounts of certain chemical and raw materials badly needed on the moon, which could be obtained only by importations from the Earth—petroleum, rubber, etc. He had ready a hundred new D-ray tubes, of the latest design, which would prove a great asset for field operations, since they were mounted on light atomotored tanks.

That evening, Leroda had still not come. I broadcast both my brief messages again, on the chance that they had not been picked up. We had been on Earth two days, and it lacked but three of the time set to embark for the moon again.

Next day we were very busy. Supplies were coming in, being stored in warehouses along the lakeshore, many miles above the busy pleasure and commercial sections of the city. There it seemed that we had a fair chance to embark at night, without discovery. And if we were discovered, as Lafollette said, we could fight on Earth as well as on the moon.

The troops had been mostly collected, and were quartered in immense apartment buildings a few miles down the waterfront. We secured a number of motor boats for ferrying men and freight out to the fleet.

After our work was done on the third day, I went back to the landing stage on the roof, and met each liner that came in until long past midnight. A great dread was beginning to seize me. If Leroda had heard my first call, she had had time to come half way around the world to meet me. That night, after I had gone down to my room in Lafollette's palatial suite, I tossed sleepless with the fear that something had happened. She might have fallen victim to the implacable spies of Metals in the year since I had left Earth. Or she might have met some accident—I was the victim of a thousand gloomy speculations.

On the next day I sent the call again over the private radio. At the risk of inviting the attention of Metals agents, I made it a little more definite.

"Leroda, I am waiting. Tranco Building, Chicago. John Adams."

ON the fourth day I was busy with Lafollette and Bris, going over the lists of cargo, and planning the loading of it. That day, and the night, and the next day passed like an age to me—part of our preparations had to be made under cover of darkness, and we worked all night. But paradoxically, on the end of the last day, the yellow sun seemed to plunge with fatal speed toward the rim of the pale sky. It set. Dusk fell.

Lafollette, Bris and I, and some of the officers, ate a last hasty meal in the great dining hall in Tranco Building. Lafollette gave last instructions to the secretaries and vice-presidents who were to care for his interests while he was away. We took the elevator and were shot up to the roof stage, where the private flier waited to take us down to the old docks, where our force was gathered.

While the others were getting aboard, I ran to make a last inquiry, found that the through liner from San Francisco was due in five minutes. It was a last chance. With good-natured witticisms, Bris and Lafollette granted my eager request to wait for it. My heart drummed loud in my ears when at last I saw the bright lights of the ship cutting through the yellow haze of the westward evening sky. I think a guard held me by the arm to keep me off the platform until the long silver liner had come to rest.

Then my heart gave a glad leap, and I trembled with incredulous joy. For Leroda was the first to step out of the slender steel hull. Eagerly, she came running across to meet me. I leapt toward her, seized her arms, and scanned her dear familiar face. The lines on it showed fatigue and worry. But her dark eyes were alight with a great gladness.

Ignoring the noisy crowd and the busy attendants, I took her in my arms. Time passed in oblivion until Bris was by my side, suggesting that we come aboard the flier, so that we could be off.

"Sorry it took me so long," Leroda said. "I was in Hong Kong. I took the first aero-liner after I heard you. We ran into a frightful storm, a typhoon, out in mid-ocean. A freak wind, which had not been recorded by the Meteorological Service. Motors were overstrained in pulling out of it. They burned out, and we came down at sea. Had to wait hours for a slow surface boat to find us and tow us to Hawaii."

By that time we were seated side by side in the flier. I glided swiftly forward across the bright stage, and shot into the dusk. Northward we sped through the gathering darkness, with the splendid towers of fire that were gigantic buildings drifting past beneath us. As we went, the lights grew dim, scattered, gave way to a sheet of darkness.

Then we had landed by a dark lakeshore. Scores of men in uniform were bustling nervously about, and great piles of crates and boxes were stacked up above the water. By the old piers, which probably had not been used for a century, were long rows of boats, loaded and covered with white tarpaulins, with alert men waiting at wheels.

An hour went by, with men hurrying about, loading boxes and heavy sacks on trucks, and unloading them again. It all was confusion to me, and it was all in the vague twilight—a half-light that seems very strange to one from the moon, where it is always either blazing day or Stygian night. There was an undercurrent of strained suspense in the air.

What if Doane did not come?

He had not answered the message giving him the date, had not been expected to do so, for that might have betrayed his position. Nothing had been heard from him since he dropped Bris and me on the lake.

But that hour passed pleasantly enough for me. I sat with Leroda in the flier, listened to her vivacious account of how she had spent the last year, told her something of my recent adventures on the moon.

I was overjoyed to find her ready enough to go with me to the moon, in the face of all the perils of the journey, and in spite of the fact that life on the moon was a very uncertain proposition, until the war had ended favorably.

It had been dark an hour when one of the boats that had been out scouting on the lake returned with the welcome news that twenty vast globular ships were floating up toward the shore, upon the still water.

Then it fell to my lot to go out with a signal light, and establish communication with Doane. Leroda valiantly insisted upon going along in the motor boat instead of waiting on the shore, and I yielded. We were five or six miles out when my cautious signals were answered.

Five minutes later the massive bulk of the *Comet* was shutting off the pale stars before us. Guided by my flickering electric torch, the gigantic ship glided up before us, and I ran our little boat under the airlock. The elevator cage was let down in the gloom. I assisted Leroda to it, and scrambled on.

A few words to Doane, when we had been shot to the bridge, outlined the situation. He gave orders that sent the fleet drifting to within a thousand yards of the shore, to lie there with muffled riding lights until Lafollette's men and supplies could be carried aboard.

He received Leroda most chivalrously—then offered, with a grin, in his capacity as captain to marry us for nothing. But we had decided to let that wait until the end of the war.

Soon the long line of ships was in position, and the regular stream of men and supplies was coming across the black water from the old docks. Another three hours, and the work was done. Lafollette had come aboard, to be received as an honored guest; and the fleet was floating out, low over the dark lake.

Doane gave an order; signals flashed from flier to flier. The pale fire of the atomic blast jetted fiercely from the repulsion tubes, driving us out into space and toward the moon again.

CHAPTER TWENTY-TWO
When the Comet Fell

THE voyage back to the moon was a wonderful time to me. Never before, except for that too-brief period at New York, had I been much in the company of Leroda. Sometimes a space flier is a dull prison, of frightful monotony. But that wonderful girl transformed the *Comet* for me, into a paradise, a radiant garden of wonder.

We strolled the ray-tube decks together, hand in hand, and found secluded corners in the vessel where we could sit together for hours, unmolested. We spent endless periods in the bridge room, watching the ancient but never-aging wonders of the silver star-clouds, suspended in infinite space. We talked; we saw "stereo" pictures; we read poetry and romance. But the most precious moments were those rare ones, when we stood drinking in each other with the senses, almost one instead of two.

Leroda told me the story of her life. It was far from a happy one. Her father had been killed when she was a baby. Her mother had been hounded about the Earth for the secret that had led to her father's death. She had been spirited away when Leroda was twelve years old—to die in a secret prison. The girl had lived her life in terror.

But sorrow and fear had not spoiled a sunny, cheerful nature. Now we looked forward to a life that would bring her all the happiness she had missed. We dreamed together of the home we should have. Sometimes she sang to me, her marvelous low rich voice vibrating with measureless yearning, borne out of sorrow on golden wings of hope.

We were by no means to ourselves all the time. With Lafollette and his group of brilliant young officers from Earth aboard, things could hardly be dull—though some of them were not such experienced voyagers of space as Leroda and myself, and suffered considerably from space sickness. There were banquets and balls and amateur theatricals.

Of course the serious plans for the conduct of the war were going forward steadily. Every day I met with Lafollette and Doane and a few of the other officers for a conference that took several hours. Lafollette was full of suggestions, and by the time we reached the moon, a tentative plan of action was quite worked out.

We planned to divide Lafollette's men for the time being, sending about half of them to Colon and half to Theophilus, one contingent being placed under command of his associate, Langley.

We reached the moon without accident, after a passage of only fifteen days.

It was about noon of the lunar day when we landed. The sun fell in a white flood upon the jagged lunar wilderness. We came down at Firecrest. I had been a little afraid the city would be attacked in our absence; but the silver disk of it lay by the dark crater rim, bright as a new coin.

Doane brought the fleet down on the level plain just before the main airlocks. The men, who had been crowded in the transports for two long weeks, under rather unpleasant conditions, were now fitted out with sun helmets and white uniforms, and marched out of the ships for a bit of exercise and to become accustomed to lunar conditions of gravitation and barometric pressure. They were deployed about the burning desert for a bit, and then permitted to visit the city, where the inhabitants gave them an enthusiastic ovation. There had been, of course, many cases of space sickness; but the medical corps had cared for them efficiently, and the morale of the troops had been kept surprisingly fine.

THE BIRTH OF A NEW REPUBLIC

With Leroda at my side, I got off the *Comet* as soon as possible, and hurried through the airlock and up to father's office. Since she had lived on the moon before, the bright girl manifested no inconvenience from lunar conditions. And attired in neat white garments, with her dark locks drawn up under a snowy topi, she looked the very picture of exultant health and spirits.

We found father in the same spacious, bright room where I had spent years at work, with the familiar broad rich desks, and fine familiar rugs, the same curios on the walls—strange things from the far places of the moon—and the same atomic heater, contrived to imitate an old-fashioned fireplace of Earth, irradiating the great room with a ruddy glow.

Father stood by a broad window, looking out upon the vast bowl of the crater, with its scattered shaft-houses—now as neat and gleaming as ever, for hardly a trace of the bombardment was left about the whole city. A little stooped, my father was, with a wealth of silver hair. His face was a little more care-drawn than when I had last seen him; but his smile of joy, when his keen eyes perceived me, transfixed it with a luminosity of love.

He came to meet us—with the same quick step he had always had—and crushed my hand in his. I introduced Leroda, and the warm, genial sincerity of his welcome made the motherless girl feel at home at once.

Then we went to find mother, in the living rooms in the glass-armored tower above, overlooking the mines in the crater and all the country about—the same old rooms I knew so well.

My mother was sitting in the mellow flood of sunlight that streamed through the great windows, sewing, I think. A white-haired lady in lavender, slight and frail as always, but bright of eye and strong of spirit. She sprang up and embraced me with a glad little cry.

Then I presented Leroda. Mother looked at her keenly for the merest instant, then smiled and took her in her arms. As Leroda afterward told me, she found my parents "most delightful people."

Presently Valence came running in, a pretty young matron, with little Tommy with her. She gave me a warm and sincere embrace, and received Leroda with sisterly cordiality.

We had dinner in the same long, bright dining room—it was painful to me to see the walls had been newly decorated. Dinner from the same familiar beautiful dishes, with bluebirds on the rims—they had been used on festive occasion ever since I first remember.

Then I left Leroda with Valence and my mother, and went down to see about my duties. Jenkins had been waiting, with the usual "dispatches from Warrington, sir." I learned that Firecrest was the new capitol of the moon, since the destruction of Kurrukwarruk. At considerable cost in labor, a small tunnel had been sunk from the city to the end of the great cavern, to provide an avenue of underground escape, in case the city above the surface were to be beleaguered again. The Assembly had moved to Firecrest, and most of the executive officers of the new government were there. After our arrival, a series of conferences were held to further acquaint Lafollette and his officers with conditions on the moon, and to make definite plans for the coming campaigns.

After the troops had rested two days at Firecrest, they embarked again, upon nineteen of the vessels, which were divided into two fleets. Nine ships carried Langley and his men to Colon, the great city by the Appenines, where they could drill with Hall's forces. The ten other ships carried the remainder of the men and supplies to Warrington, at Theophilus.

Our flagship, the *Comet,* remained at Firecrest, in case of a surprise attack from space. The conference was still in session, and Lafollette, Doane, Greenville, and my father were deep in the new plans. Gardiner, who was still with Warrington at the crater city, was to return with Bris, who commanded the ships sent to Theophilus, to lend his support to the conference.

Plans were under way for "forging an iron ring about New Boston"—as one eloquent young speaker put it. Lafollette's and Warrington's forces were to close in upon Humbolt, while Doane met Van Thoren's fleet in a decisive engagement.

Leroda had a genius for getting into the thick of things. She attended the assembly meetings, and soon knew most of the delegates. She set out to devise a "seal" or flag for the moon. She made a model—the design was a white crescent, with "the old moon in its arms"—and had me present the idea to all the delegates I met.

Naturally, with so many young officers from Earth about, the social life of the little town was rather feverishly merry. Leroda and I were together at a good many affairs, and had more pleasure in staying away from others.

It was about that time that the "Eldorado Massacre" took place. It was not an important incident in itself, perhaps. But it had vast consequences in increasing the ardor of Lafollette's men, and in steeling the determination of all of us upon the moon. The near-catastrophe to so many important men, which came as a result of it, only impressed it more strongly upon the minds of the people.

The two fleets had been gone for some time, the *Comet* being the only war-flier left at Firecrest. The appeal came from Eldorado, a small mining settlement nearly two hundred miles east of the capitol. The call came by radio; and the interference of the sun's direct rays, which make radio communication impossible during the middle of the lunar days, made it almost incoherent, though the sun had now slanted far toward the west.

Since the moon has no "Heaviside layer" to keep the waves reflected back to the surface, the extreme range of a radio set on the moon is little over two hundred miles, under the best conditions.

"Ka'Larbah are..." it ran. "Ka'Larbah...million mooncalves... marching. West... D-rays...men with them...spacesuits...war-fliers above. Aid. For the sake of..."

It seemed incredible to Lafollette and his officers that Metals would descend to alliance with the wild mooncalves; but there had been stories since the beginning of the war of a pillaging, massacring band of the Ka'Larbah, officered by men in spacesuits, and aided by a few ships from Van Thoren's fleet. But until this time no important places had been attacked, and many even on the moon thought the force largely myth. But the disjointed call made it plain enough that such a dreadful army had fallen upon Eldorado.

Though there was but one ship available, and that had been left to defend the capitol, Lafollette demanded that we go to the rescue at once. Doane was not unwilling to set out. After Lafollette's fiery appeal, the Assembly voted permission for the *Comet* to go. In an hour after the call had come, we were aboard and rising.

Doane was in command, of course, and Lafollette and two or three of his officers, insisting that they were on the moon to learn the art of war as soon as possible, were aboard as passengers. I came as secretary to Lafollette.

Another half hour found us in sight of the ill-fated little city. It lay beyond the mountains, on a dark desert plain, like a bright square of silver foil. And all the plain about it was crimson with the glittering red forms of gigantic Selenites. Colossal red-scaled monsters leapt about like giant fleas, obviously obeying the silver-armored men mounted upon a few of their leaders. Many of the creatures carried long, slender D-ray tubes.

As we came in view a little group of men was making a desperate attempt to reach the city walls. Watching through a pair of binoculars, I saw the pitiful struggle of the poor fellows. There were only a dozen or so of them, in ragged working clothing; they must have been miners from some outlying prospect.

By way of arms they carried only a few hand D-ray drilling machines. They put up a brave defense against the milling horde of scarlet monsters that closed about them; a heroic battle, soon over.

I threw down the glasses in horror when I saw the colossal, crimson, green-eyed things snatching them up, rending them into quivering, bloody morsels, avidly crushed in terrible jaws. The savage beings fought even among themselves for the pitiful fragments of red flesh and bloody rag.

Lafollette and his fellow officers were amazed and horrified at the sight—after this "Remember Eldorado!" was a war cry among the men from Earth.

The Selenites had surrounded the bright-walled city, were taking it by storm even as we came in sight. And high above the scintillant roof hung three titanic silver globes, upheld upon the billowing, many-colored flame-mist of the atomic blast. Thin piercing rays of red and green and orange stabbed from them at the broken walls; and the vast flaming spheres of the disintegrating atomic vortexes, fireballs of white and purple and blue, rained down upon shattered roof and towers.

Eldorado had been pitifully unprepared. There had been one generator of the yellow fan-ray, and a single projector of the atomic vortexes. And the desperate inhabitants had hauled a dozen D-ray mining machines from their places, to serve as weapons. That was all the armament they had against the multiplied thousands of hellish, gigantic beings, and the three war-fliers.

One of the fliers darted toward us at once, while the other two kept up the bombardment of the little town. Our improved ray-projectors, with the precise skill with which our crew handled them, assured us a prompt victory. In five minutes the other ship fell in flames, a vast, luridly glaring meteor. It struck near the city; it must have crushed hundreds of the savage monsters to a hot death beneath it, but the frenzied attack went on regardless of the incident.

Both of the remaining ships came to take the place of the fallen one. Doane faced the situation with his usual coolness and skill. The Tellurian war-fliers were our equals in size and armament, though perhaps our crews were a little better trained. And certainly the increased power of the gold atomic blast was an advantage.

For some minutes we exchanged glancing rays and flaming vortexes, without visible result. The enemy fliers managed their fan-rays so cleverly that each screened the other, and no opening was left for us. Doane fought a furious battle, to win in time to save the city. The other ships were almost hidden in a terrific storm of flickering polychromatic flame.

Abruptly there was a shattering explosion below our flier, and it was plunging down in sickening flight. It seems that an exploding vortex had injured the atomic blast projectors which supplied our power. A few moments later it seemed that the trouble was repaired, for our fall was checked, and we were quickly back at our former level.

Meanwhile the innumerable leaping red hordes were closing in upon the city in defiance of the desperate defense. Ray tubes grasped in the ungainly tentacles of the Selenites swept the glass walls and towers, despite a fierce fire from window and turret.

The mooncalves must have found entrance through the holes torn by the explosive vortexes. Great leaps carried them like titanic leaping insects forward to the roof. For a time the darting, snake-like rays from the converted mining apparatus swept low upon them. One by one, those rays went out.

Eldorado was at the mercy of the Ka'Larbah, most terrible of the wild mooncalves.

At the same time we were desperately engaged with the two war-fliers. With a daring maneuver, Doane flashed in between them, caught one for a moment unguarded, as the fan-ray was shifted. He fired with a dazzling sheet of vari-colored rays that sent the Tellurian reeling moonward.

Below us, the Selenites were pouring steadily into the conquered city. Most of what happened we did not see; it is good for our peace of mind that we did not. Few sights that I have seen are more terrible than that. Glistening, scaly, crimson things, green eyes expressionless and unblinking, searched through the ruins for the bodies of dead and dying. Long, writhing, red tentacles dragged poor, shrieking wretches from their hiding. With avid greed, the monsters devoured living and dead, bodies crunching like red wax in their powerful teeth.

Suddenly the moonscape below us rocked with the force of a terrific detonation, and the bright glass city rose in a great mushroom of shattered debris of dust and flame. It spouted up, hung for a long moment in the air, and fell in a rain of ruin. Only a vast, burned crater was left.

Of the tens of thousands of attacking Ka'Larbah, only a few score escaped the desperate revenge of the conquered city. All the rest went up with the force of that mine. Perhaps it was set off by the last survivor—the world will never know.

The engineers were still having trouble with our injured generators. Once the *Comet* started falling wildly again. The lone remaining enemy flier hung over us, her flashing rays like the wings of an eagle of flame. Our desperate mechanics got the projectors to working again; we shot up and caught the other ship with the battery of a whole ray-deck as we passed inside her screening fan-ray. She was fairly fused as she hung there; glowing with vivid incandescence, she fell, slowly at first, but with gathering momentum, until she crashed like a plummet into the gaping chasm where Eldorado had been.

We set out for Firecrest at once, with the generators working most uncertainly. Despite the frenzied efforts of the engineers, the blast projectors failed to operate smoothly; and sometimes we fell alarmingly. At last, when not more than half the distance had been covered, we were forced to land.

The sun was not over twelve hours high, and we had made the alarming discovery that not a single spacesuit was aboard—we had embarked in the greatest haste. It was found, too, that the hull of the flier had been injured by the explosion, so that it would not hold air to last through the long lunar night.

After several hours of toil—Doane and I labored with the struggling engineers—we had the projectors functioning again. We rose easily, and covered seventy miles of the distance to Firecrest in as many minutes. Then the delicate tubes failed again, and we crushed down on the desert. This time the complicated mechanism was crushed beyond hope of repair.

Nothing remained except for someone to attempt to reach Firecrest on foot, to send back a relief party with spacesuits and with special welding equipment for repairing the leaking hull.

After some hesitation, I responded to Doane's call for volunteers. I thought that, of all the crew, I had had more experience in travel on foot over the lunar desert than any other. I selected two men to go with me—both young fellows, but of considerable experience as scouts in the lunar wilderness. One of them, named Payne, I think, had lived from about the age of three years in an outlying mining settlement; the other was a rugged young Australian, who had come to the moon as a stowaway when he was fourteen.

The two of them accepted my choice calmly, though it amounted almost to a sentence of death. A very few minutes saw us ready—every moment was precious. I shook hands with Lafollette, and with Doane, who whispered a brief word of encouragement. Then I was outside the air lock with tanned young Payne, and the red-faced, raw-boned Australian, Lieutenant Gerald.

The sun seemed hardly more than the breadth of its own disk above the black western crags. Like a sphere of white flame, it shone with a steady, dazzling brilliance; but all warmth seemed gone from its rays. I drew my light tunic close about my shoulders, and looked at my companions.

"Thirty miles." My lips moved to form the words, but little more than a rusty grating came.

"No backing out now," Gerald whispered grimly.

"Perhaps," Payne began. But we had leapt, and his other words were lost.

Leap…leap…leap. Each leap was a terrible age. Blocks of lava rattled beneath our feet. I heard the swift breath of my companions.

Hours passed, frantic, desperate hours. The immense silver ball of the flier soon dropped under the near horizon. The sun crept down, with relentless deliberation. We had covered the better part of the journey. I recognized the country southeast of Firecrest. Then, like the finger of doom, the slender spire of a western peak was drawn across the bright face of the sun.

Night fell swiftly. The sun darkened from a cold white sphere to a ball of writhing red, shrouded in a freezing mist of snow. White flakes danced about us in the frigid air, covering rocks and craters with a crystal layer that hid obstructions so that we often slipped and fell.

A high, bitter wind sprang up, piercing our scanty garments with a painful sword of cold. A thin, steel blue mist of ice flew upon it, biting our blue and trembling limbs. When we breathed, it seared our lungs with cold.

It was the utter cold of space, descending upon the moon. Cold that grasped and pierced and congealed. Cold that stopped all life. Cold that froze even the air to silver powder. Cold that was merciless, unthinkably intense.

Cold grasped at our limbs, hung about our waists, weighed on our shoulders, dragged us down. It cut into our bodies, gnawed at our hands, bit our faces like sharp edges of ice.

A frigid, leaden mist of fine snow and frozen air thickened gelidly all about. It hid the deep and bloody glare of the heatless, dying sun. It wrapped us close, leaving a silver crust of frost upon our bodies, hardening our garments to stiff, crackling, frozen armor.

Our breath froze before us, in clouds of tiny, glittering crystals.

Above, through the mist, the Earth was vaguely visible, a huge luminous ball, warm and green—but far, far away! I thought confusedly of my days upon it, of warm winds, warn blue seas rolling beneath soft azure skies in a flood of sun, of warm green gardens, where trilling bird-songs sounded through sweet-scented flowering shrubs; dreamed fleetingly of rooms lit with the ruddy glow of heaters, of tables loaded with steaming meals.

A thicker wisp of freezing mist hid the Earth, and we leapt on in growing darkness, and in utter silence—in the darkness and the silence of death. White rocks, hoary plains, fantastic frosted crags. A strange world of death—silent, ghostly white, unthinkably cold.

On we leapt, and ages fled. The flurries of falling snow grew thicker. Payne and Gerald became white ghosts, red-faced, puffing white steam. The air grew thin about us, exhausted by the freezing. I fought to breathe, while a cold flame seared my lungs.

The freezing mist grew thinner, as the nothingness of space crept down. Cold stars bit through it, danced mockingly before us. On we struggled. Every move was agony, every second an age of hell.

Through the darkness I saw the familiar rocks about the tavern entrance. They were near—yet I felt that I could not go on. To sleep, to relax, to die, seemed paradise. Every leap was a heart-breaking effort against that fatal lure.

As I leapt, a little refrain beat through my numbed brain. "Not for me... For Leroda... For father and mother... For the men on the *Comet*... For the moon."

I saw the metal rim of the great valve, gleaming in a frozen crust. And the pale lights of the city beyond danced upon the snow.

Gerald fell to the ground, sprawled in a little huddle in the snow.

"Come on," I tried to say. But a sudden fierce pain throbbed in my throat. Blood gushed out of my mouth, froze on my face. Payne bent futilely over the fallen man, feebly tried to lift him. Then he, too, fell in an attitude of weary abandon.

I left them, struggled on. On—through clinging curtains of cold. On—fighting intangible rivers of cold. On—while my body screamed with pain. On—for Leroda—for...

I reached the metal door, a thick cylinder of frosted marble in its crust of snow. I fell against it, hammering it with hands that had no feeling. A great dark cloud obscured my vision, and I collapsed in infinite lassitude.

The great valve slid open as I fell. Strange figures, grotesque and gleaming like men of metal in the silvered spacesuits, were clambering out. Quickly, tenderly, they picked up my fallen comrades and myself, carried us through the valve and down into the warm compartments at the top of the shaft.

Payne and Gerald were unconscious, nearly dead. I fought for my voice. The guards who had rescued us saw my struggle, poured powerful stimulants down my throat. I recovered enough strength to stammer out the story, to tell of the wrecked flier, with Doane and Lafollette in it, and to give directions for finding it without delay.

"Bris is back with his fliers," the guards told me. "He can go."

A great gladness came over me, like a welcome flood of warmth. We had won. Lafollette and Doane and the *Comet* were saved. I passed into a deep and undisturbed sleep.

When I woke again, I was in a small white bed, with Leroda sitting beside me. She was almost ridiculously attentive, but it was good to have her near. The exposure had been rather hard on me; I was in bed several days, with my beautiful fiancé, or my mother, or Valence with me most of the time.

Gardiner came twice, great, kindly man, with his cheerful jests and his news of Warrington.

Bris, with the fliers, had had no difficulty in locating the *Comet* from my description. The crew of the wrecked vessel had been transferred to another flier, and the *Comet* itself had been raised and brought back to the cavern, where it was now being repaired.

Lafollette and Doane came to my room to see me, with thanks for the dreadful trip through the night. They said they had seen my companions, Payne and Lieutenant Gerald, who were in the hospital, doing nicely.

My own condition improved rapidly; and when the fleet, a day before sunrise, left Firecrest for Theophilus, I was able to go along. A swift and uneventful voyage on the crowded ships left us at the great spaceport of that city, just as the white cone of the solar corona rose in the east.

We were greeted with a wild ovation. The whole populace of the city, it seemed, was waiting at the air lock to meet us with a loud welcome. Warrington's troops were passed in review through the streets, along with those men of Lafollette's which had been sent to Theophilus.

Lafollette, with his soldiers and supplies, had brought new encouragement and enthusiasm to the moon.

CHAPTER TWENTY-THREE
The New Plan

WARRINGTON met us as we entered the air lock, his shoulders still erect under the load of responsibility he bore, and his eyes still undimmed with care. He greeted us warmly, and we were taken at once to a banquet in honor of Lafollette. Following that was a conference, in which the plan that finally brought victory had its birth.

Warrington spoke to us, in his quiet, dignified manner.

"There is a plan that I have long had in mind," he said, "to turn against our opponents the natural elements and to let the dreadful night of the moon strike a blow for liberty. There are obstacles, however, that I have never overcome, though I have attempted the thing in our last two campaigns.

"Twice I have succeeded in enticing Humbolt out of New Boston. On each occasion, I was unable to hold him until it would be too late for him to return. Once the plan was to trap him in a crater—it was the one called Painted Pit, which can be entered only through a narrow defile. A hundred brave fellows had volunteered to stay and hold the pass, if Humbolt could be trapped inside, though the coming of the night would have meant death for all. Humbolt was to think that I had sought refuge in the crater, and a show was to be made of holding the pass, so that he would storm it and enter. It might have gone over, but Van Thoren's fliers saw my main force marching away beyond the crater, and that gave away the plan. Humbolt hurried back to New Boston.

"The idea is obviously impractical, while the enemy has a fleet. But the new fliers, under Doane's skillful command, might engage the fleet of Van Thoren while the action on the surface is carried out, or, at least, worry them enough to keep them from interfering with the operation."

The plan was thoroughly discussed, pro and con, but no definite action was taken upon it. In fact, it seemed that no one was able to suggest any practical means whereby it might be carried out.

Toward the end of the meeting Gardiner brought up another subject—that of a protective armor against the D-ray. It appeared that the old savant had been working on the problem for some time. He had the mathematics of it well worked out. On a blackboard set up on the rostrum, he illustrated his talk with drawings in colored chalk.

"You all know," he said, "that the destructive action of the D-ray depends upon the fluctuation of the several frequencies that compose it, in cycles incredibly rapid, so that the electronic vibration is enormously amplified in the substance under the ray, until it is literally shaken to the simpler atoms of the inert gases, when the frequency of the ray is adjusted in harmony with the natural period of vibration of the electrons." He proceeded with the lecture, saying the same thing in more scientific language. He sketched colored drawings of the atom according to the latest theory with a detailed discussion of the process by which the high frequency D-ray breaks it down, with the evolution of the inert gases of the helium group.

Finally he concluded, "As you know, any etheric vibration can be canceled by another wave of the same frequency and of opposite phase. That is the principle upon which the fan-ray is based. Now I have the idea for something new. It would be a paint of some kind, which would absorb part of the energy of the D-ray, and re-radiate it with such a wavelength as will cancel a vital part of the D-ray. Against such an armor the D-ray would be no more effective than, would be a beam of ultra-violet light. As I have demonstrated, the mathematical part is already worked out. There remains a good deal of research to be done, to find the exact chemical compound which will serve our need.

"If equipment and technical skill can be had, I am sure that it can be done."

The Assembly was enthusiastic in voting approval of Gardiner's plan. Funds for the work were put at his command, and he was urged to push the task with all possible speed.

When the meeting was over, I went to him and offered to undertake the laboratory work—the great Lunarian was so valuable as statesman and diplomat that he could ill be spared for months of isolated work.

With a grin, he informed me that he already had me in mind for the task. During the long lunar day at Theophilus I worked with him over the mathematical points involved, until I was sure that my understanding of the problem was as clear as his own. Then he helped me in selecting the needed equipment, designed one or two new devices for me, and suggested in detail the method of research to be followed. The Firecrest cavern seemed the logical place for the experiment work; and it was agreed that Doane would carry me there, with my books and equipment, during the next lunar night.

Meanwhile, Warrington went afield with Lafollette. The campaigns of the day were not important, amounting to mere skirmishing and guerilla warfare with Humbolt's forces in the neighborhood of New Boston. Our men were safely back at Theophilus long before sunset. The men from Earth were getting valuable training, of course, in lunar military tactics.

The sun set and Doane duly conveyed me and my new equipment back to Firecrest. I had a gloriously happy reunion with Leroda and father and mother, and fell to my work at once.

Leroda had finished her new seal, the crescent "with the old moon in its arms," surrounded with a ring of thirteen stars, to represent the thirteen incorporated cities. The seal had been unanimously adopted by the Assembly, as the emblem of the new free Moon Corporation. It adorned public buildings and documents of state, and as a flag with blue ground, it was carried at the head of the armies of the moon.

NEARLY a year went by. I worked as hard as I have ever done. I had a regular schedule; six hours sleep, two hours exercise—usually spent in a game of tennis or a hike with Leroda—

thirty minutes for meals, and the balance of the time in the laboratory. I had abundant equipment, and usually three or four assistants worked with me. Gardiner was frequently at Firecrest; he kept up with the work, and made many invaluable suggestions. Steadily I marched toward my goal.

The work was by no means without its element of excitement. After the mathematical details were complete, the experimentation consisted mostly in making a compound that satisfied the known requirements, painting a slab of rock or metal with it, and setting it up in front of a D-ray. Usually the object was merely fused, or vanished in a puff of vapor. But some of the substances we worked out seemed to act as catalysts to increase the violence of the disintegration.

On one occasion a boulder, which had been sprayed with a mixture of mercurous fluoride and calcium bromide, exploded with such deafening violence that our laboratory was wrecked almost completely. One of my assistants, a poor chap named Stanley, was killed. The heavy D-ray tube was smashed and the wreckage blown over on me. I suffered nothing worse, however, than a broken arm and a few minor contusions.

By the time I was able to be back at work, my fellow experimenters had moat of the equipment repaired or replaced, and we went on as before. That was only the most spectacular of a score of accidents and misfortunes. In spite of them, we moved steadily toward our object.

Meanwhile, Warrington and Lafollette and Gardiner were frequently at Firecrest, to meet with the Assembly. Military operations had not been important. But Lafollette's veterans were now used to lunar conditions. They had mastered the "mooncalf" technique of guerilla warfare; and the raw lunar recruits, training with them, had gained much in discipline and military spirit.

At this time the strength of the Tellurians was still concentrated in New Boston. Humbolt had nearly a hundred and fifty thousand men there. Opposed to him were Warrington's force of about sixty thousand men, Lafollette's forty thousand, and the army of almost twenty thousand under Hall at Colon.

Steadily, out of long hours of patient conference, grew the plan for the final campaign that ended the war.

THE BIRTH OF A NEW REPUBLIC

It was also about this time that Tom Dowling, something of a poet, composed the words and music to the lunar anthem, "To Ye Lunar Hills Ablaze." He had become an officer in the fleet, to the infinite anxiety and pride of Valence; he had been on a flier that rescued a little settlement attacked by a force from New Boston. Inspired by sight of the crude little fortification, defended by ragged miners with their drilling-rays, with the lunar flag that Leroda had designed waving over them, he had written a fervent, ringing lyric of patriotism. The song spread over the moon like a new wave of hope. It was sung in the streets, hummed in factories and mines, whistled in Warrington's ranks.

And Tom proved as able an officer as a poet. By the end of the year, he had won the captaincy of a war-flier and proved his spurs in victorious combat with a scouting cruiser from New Boston.

At last I was successful in my research. I found that the halide compounds of one of the isotopes of barium re-radiated a higher frequency of the D-ray in such a manner as to cancel it by interference, no matter how the ray was focused. Objects covered with an infinitesimally thin layer of this barium compound, and exposed to the D-ray, were not affected, save for a moderate heating effect.

The principal difficulty in the process had been to separate the isotopes of barium. Since the atomic weight of barium is 137.4, and since all atomic weights of simple substances, with the exception of hydrogen and a few others, are whole numbers, it is apparent readily enough that barium is composed of several isotopes, of different whole atomic weights, whose average is 187.4. But since the atomic number of each of these is 56, their chemical properties are identical, and it is quite impossible to separate them by purely chemical means.

A parallel case is that of chlorine. Its atomic weight is 35.46. But positive ray analysis shows that it is composed of two isotopes, of atomic weights exactly 85 and exactly 37.

My first experiments with barium had failed because of the presence of the other isotopes, which disintegrated under the ray, destroying the armor. But at last I devised a method of using the D-ray itself in removing these, leaving the pure isotope I required, of atomic weight 138.

Warrington, Gardiner, Doane, and Lafollette were at the time in Firecrest, still working on their plan of campaign. I called them down to the laboratory when the great discovery was completed, for a demonstration.

It was made simply enough.

I took the two metal bowls in which my simple breakfast of fruit and the liquid synthetic food combination had been brought me that morning. One of them I sprayed with a thin layer of barium bromide. I set them side by side on the ground in front of my D-ray projector and began focusing it.

Focusing the D-ray, which involves the synchronization of the several frequencies and their adjustment to the natural period of electronic vibration of the particular substance, to be disintegrated, is a rather slow and complicated process.

As I now worked over the tube, I spoke to Doane about the need of quick focusing in military operations. I had been much impressed by the fact that a few seconds of difference in the time required to focus the rays might turn the issue to victory or defeat in a contest of space fliers.

"Leave that to me," Doane said grinning. "But go ahead with your demonstration."

At last I got the ray focused. I closed the switch. The thin finger of intense red light flashed out and touched the two metal discs. The untreated one blew up, with a white flash of flame. The other was hurled a dozen feet by the explosion. But it had not been affected by the D-ray, save to be slightly warmed.

Doane gave vent to a wild yell of enthusiasm. Lafollette congratulated me, grasping my hand, while tears of joy stood in his eyes. Gardiner merely stood smiling at me, while Warrington began a volley of questions about the manufacture and use of the new compound.

"I knew you'd do it," he told me. "And we're ready to use it in the next campaign."

CHAPTER TWENTY-FOUR
Victory

BEFORE the conference was ended, plans had been completed for the final campaign. Before the lunar dawn, the repaired *Comet* carried Warrington and Lafollette and Gardiner back to Theophilus, to drill and equip their combined forces of nearly a hundred thousand men for the great attack on Humbolt at New Boston.

I stayed with Doane at Firecrest, where the fleet was being made ready for a decisive action. Acting under Warrington's orders, we were preparing immense quantities of the bromides and chlorides of barium, obtaining the metal by treating ores from a limitless deposit of barium sulphate in the Firecrest mines with the D-ray. The great machine shops in the cavern hurriedly turned out a large number of sprayers with which the protective compound could be rapidly and easily applied.

As part of the preparation for the coming battle, the war-fliers were thoroughly sprayed with the barium halides. That made them almost invulnerable to D-rays so long as the coating adhered, though the explosive atomic vortexes would be as destructive as ever, and it was feared that the violence of explosion would break the protective film, exposing the fliers to the rays.

Nearly a thousand steel drums of the barium halides were loaded on the fliers with three hundred of the compressed air sprays.

The luminous white cone of the solar corona was again in the east. Slowly the white blinding eye of the sun came up in a sky that was a pall of Cimmerian darkness, sparkling with a million crystal stars. The frost and solid air upon the desert once more rose in thick blue mist, rolling up in turbid clouds about the peaks, presently dissipating as the sun climbed into a dark blue sky.

Our preparation occupied us until well toward the lunar noon. Then old Jenkins, as odd and red and good-natured as ever, appeared, coming in flying leaps upon the scarlet elephantine M'Ob, with orders from headquarters.

Warrington had left Theophilus, was marching on New Boston with his and Lafollette's forces combined. Doane was to leave Firecrest as soon as possible, fly to Warrington's camp, and accompany him during the rest of the march. We were to find him in the vicinity of Smith's Crater, where one of the earlier engagements of the war had been fought.

The great war-fliers were brought up out of the cavern—having been taken, for refitting and repairs, back to the cradles in which they were built. I parted from father and mother—Valence, my sister, had gone aboard another flier, to take a final adieu from her devoted Captain Tom. During the long months at Firecrest, busy as I had been, I had had many happy moments with them all. Now, as I embraced my father's aging form, and kissed the smooth cheek of my mother, and held the lithe warm figure of Leroda in my arms once more, looking into dark eyes where tears were welling up, it was with a heavy and saddening sense of the perils that were before me. Valiantly I tried to shake off a gloomy foreboding that I would never return to the dear home of my childhood and to those waiting for me there.

Then the brass gong sounded, and I had to leave them with a last laughing word of unfelt cheer, and to run through the lines to the great silver ship. A few minutes more and we were drifting swiftly southward lover the towering mountains of the moon.

Six hours later we were in sight of Warrington's army, marching in long white columns down that road between Theophilus and New Boston that he had traversed so often in the progress of the war. Our fliers hung low upon the surface, and kept to the rear, in order that the enemy might know of them no sooner than necessary.

Forty-eight hours later we were in sight of New Boston, beyond the cragged summit of Meteor Hill. Walled and roofed with glass, it was like a thick slab of some white, shining crystal, lying in the dreary mountainous wilderness. It was mirthful with the forest of glistening towers and domes, with the bright pennons of Metals fluttering from them.

The buildings at the spaceport seemed largely deserted. The fleet of Van Thoren was not in evidence at the broad landing place below the city. Our own twenty vessels hung ready, low behind

Meteor Hill, while Warrington deployed his troops about the walls, and got his field D-ray units into position, as if he intended to storm the city.

The movement had not gone far, however, when our telescopes showed a little swarm of white dots in the indigo sky above, rapidly enlarging. Van Thoren had evidently been waiting out in space; now he was dropping to attack. Presently the men at the instruments announced that there were fifty-six of the silver spheres—they outnumbered us almost three to one.

Behind the ragged black mountain, Doane swiftly got his ships into position. He chose an odd formation—fourteen of the twenty vessels took places at the corners of a great imaginary cube, and at the center of each face. The remaining six vessels, including the *Comet,* were in the center of the cube, as a reserve. In this formation our protecting fan-ray screens would offer the maximum defense; and the fliers were far enough apart to interfere little with one another's fire.

The enemy fleet dropped for Warrington's ranks, without regard for us. I suppose that Van Thoren counted on little opposition from our few fliers, built on the moon and manned by simple miners, when pitted against his great vessels from the Pittsburgh shops, with their skilled officers and veteran crews. As the fleet descended, thin searching rays and gleaming atomic vortexes began to fall upon Warrington's lines about the city. Such fire from space fliers is, however, not very effective when the troops on the ground have fan-rays and are able to seek cover in the wild lunar hills.

Doane gave the order and our fleet rose from behind the mountain and came rapidly toward the Tellurians from below. No attention was paid to our advance until we were within some five miles of the enemy—below and a little to the side.

Then the fliers in the top of our mile-square cube, at Doane's order, fired a bristling salvo of rays and vortexes. Three of the Tellurians slipped moonward in incandescent ruin. The others paused in their descent upon Warrington, and began to assume battle formation.

We continued to rise swiftly, with eleven of our ships firing scintillant rays and flaming vortexes. The bright yellow curtains of the fan-ray were extended like broad amber curtains all about us. Two more of the Tellurians went down, having been caught in unfavorable positions where they became quick victims before Doane's well-trained crews.

The enemy fliers formed above us, in the shape of an immense inverted bowl, miles across. And the bowl dropped down upon us, until the fliers at its rim were at our own level. The Tellurians had been firing only spasmodically; but now a great burst of flaming rays fell upon us from above, and from all about the rim of the bowl. Red rays, and green, and dazzling fingers of white stabbed at us bewilderingly. And the vast fiery globes of the atomic vortexes—blue and purple and white, fell like hail upon the yellow wings of the screen-ray.

And there were dark, invisible metal projectiles, loaded with fearful atomic explosive—more dangerous to our armored ships than the flaming rays.

For defense we had the fan-rays, played from each vessel so as not only to shield it but several others. Smoky yellow walls of vibration, they cut off the D-rays, generally destroyed the atomic vortexes, and usually burst the explosive projectiles. But sometimes there were holes in the screens; and of course the other fliers had screen-rays of their own.

Steadily the great bowl, formed of silver ships, dropped lower about us, glistening in the sunlight and gleaming with the woven rays until it was like a jeweled mantle of doom. And the ships that formed the rim slowly drew together below us, so that we were soon completely inclosed in walls of wavering flame.

From all sides we received the fire of the enemy. Only our formation saved us. Had it been broken, our individual fliers would have gone down like falling leaves. As it was, we were almost invulnerable. Doane's study of three-dimensional tactics was paying a good return.

Little groups of Tellurian fliers suddenly began separating themselves from the main formation, making darting attacks, in an effort to break up our array. One of them, falling meteor-like from far above, came plunging through our screen rays into the very center of the cube. It was hurtling straight for the *Comet*. An atomic vortex left our flagship—an immense ball of blue flame—

like a splendid, blazing sapphire. I saw it strike the Tellurian globe. There was a terrific explosive blast of blue fire, angrily streaked with red. Then the ship was falling, a smoking mass of crumpled, twisted ruin.

At the same time a sudden flare of yellow light burst out against the side of the flier at the upper corner of our cube—a solid projectile must have passed its ray screen. With half its side caved in, it fell wildly, narrow rays still blazing from it.

The loss of the ship from the strategic position at the corner of the cube broke our armor of fan-rays. I anticipated quick disaster. I was quite unprepared for Doane's next move.

Abruptly the space all about us was filled with tiny bursting charges, swiftly growing into vast clouds of white mist. In a moment Doane had surrounded our whole force in the thick white clouds of the Ziker space cloud—composed of radioactive, electrically charged particles, similar to a comet's tail but of much denser material.

The dense swirling masses of smoky vapor hid the Tellurian fliers completely, though dazzling rays of ruby and emerald and topaz still burned through the ragged clouds. On the instant our ships were in swift motion. There was no delay; Doane must have planned the maneuver far ahead.

As the *Comet* emerged from the mists, an enemy ship was directly before us. There was a quick interchange of rays. The new D-ray armor—the halides of barium sprayed upon our ships—and the better training of our crews decided the encounter in our favor. The Tellurian sphere plunged downward, her hull cut half away, the bent plates and twisted girders of the wreck glowing with an infernal red.

Out beyond, we paused to build another vast cloud of dense, screening smoke. The sky was then dotted with those great masses of mist. Our ships darted back and forth between them, firing rays and vortexes at every opportunity. Doane's captains appeared to be well trained in the dangerous work, and seemed to synchronize the movements of their ships remarkably.

The maneuvers of the Tellurians were clumsy. Van Thoren was not used to this hide-and-seek method of fighting among the clouds of smoke. He was without doubt a courageous and able man, but he did not have Doane's genius, or Doane's years of experience in battle against fearful odds. Instead of the guerilla method of strike and run, his school taught fighting in the open, ship to ship, at close quarters.

His men must have become confused; must have blundered. He attempted to save the day by massing his fleet and plowing through the dense clouds of vapor, sweeping all before him. But Doane, with his usual brilliant foresight, evaded his charge, and fell upon him in the rear, as he emerged from the clouds.

Only some twenty-odd of Van Thoren's globes came out, to face the seventeen of Doane's that had survived the wild battle in the mist. Now Doane abandoned his Fabian policy and closed in, counting on our D-ray armor and the superior training of our crews. For hours, it seemed, we plunged through a weird storm of colored fire, a cyclone formed of flaming rays of emerald and crimson and yellow, darting and stabbing and striking like snakes; while the saffron wings of our fan rays were beaten with a hail of blazing, fearfully explosive globes of fire, the blue and purple vortexes. And again and again those dreadful curtains were cut with a blinding glare of flame, as a ship passed into incandescent ruin beneath our rays.

Van Thoren kept his dogged courage to the end. His flagship was the last of the Tellurians left—several times it had been saved only by the prompt sacrifice of another which had rushed in to shield it. He made no move to strike his colors. Instead, his immense flier came suddenly about, plunged madly at the *Comet*. He was attempting to ram us, to bring his conqueror down with him.

A hundred rays were fastened upon his ship, but he came on in spite of the fire. Even when it was a glowing mass of wreckage, when all on board must already have met a quick flaming death, it plunged on toward us. Its momentum was so great and its fall so cleverly planned that only Doane's amazing coolness and his quick brain saved us from fatal collision with the smoking wreck.

In a battle that had lasted seven hours, Doane had destroyed fifty-six of the greatest war-fliers ever built with twenty thousand men and more upon their decks. His own loss had been surprisingly light—only five ships destroyed and two more crippled. One ship had been struck by a solid projectile, as I had seen, one rammed, and two brought down by the combined effect of vortexes and D-rays. The fate of the fifth, the Uranus, has never been definitely known—it was lost during the fighting in the space clouds.

Never, perhaps, in all space history, had a fleet been so decisively defeated by a force numerically so much smaller, and at so light a cost.

Doane had broken the space power of Metals on the moon. Humbolt still had his immense force upon the ground; but Van Thoren's fleet would no longer support him or keep him supplied. And Warrington could now carry out his great plan, unhampered from space.

Tom Dowling, I might add, came through the battle with flying colors as captain of the Sirius. The Assembly subsequently awarded him a medal for a brave and resourceful maneuver which had saved one of our crippled ships from complete destruction.

Immediately after the battle, our fifteen remaining vessels put about in the direction of Firecrest, and set off at a high rate of speed. After we had gone a hundred miles or so, and the white walls of the city had dropped out of sight behind us, we came close to the surface and circled to the west, picking up Lafollette and his forty thousand men, who had been in camp near Smith's Crater. We approached New Boston again, landing about fifteen miles west of the city, where we were completely out of sight.

Evidently the whole maneuver had been planned beforehand. Warrington and Doane must have worked out even the smallest details long in advance. The annihilation of the Tellurian fleet had been but one item of the plan.

I did not see the next maneuver of Warrington. I can only give the reports that swept over the moon a few hours later. The general concentrated his forces just south of the city, as if planning for an assault. His D-ray batteries fired fitfully, without doing much harm to the walls.

Finally he provoked Humbolt to come out after him. Warrington had only sixty thousand men, to the hundred and fifty thousand Tellurians. Great pains had been taken to let Humbolt's spies inform him that Lafollette's forces were still far toward

Theophilus. And the Metals commander must have been forced by sheer desperation to make the campaign. He had seen his fleet defeated. He knew that his cause was lost unless he could win a decisive victory. He must have hoped that his vastly superior force could crush Warrington completely.

At any rate, he marched out of the airlocks, with 140,000 men, leaving less than 10,000 to defend the city. It would have been folly for Warrington to engage such a force. But it was no part of his plan to do so. After a short skirmish, our commander retired, with the appearance of much disorder—provision and D-ray tubes were purposely left to lead the Tellurians on.

The sun, by that time, was only forty-eight hours high. Humbolt knew that it was too late for Warrington to march back to Theophilus; he thought he had his old opponent trapped to die in the night. So great was his confidence that, when Warrington made a show of opposing him on the plain twenty miles south of the city, he sent an offer to receive our surrender, couched in such insulting terms that when the troops learned of it, Warrington was hard put to it to prevent a real charge upon the Tellurians, instead of a mere play at opposition.

Warrington affected to consider the offer. While Humbolt's advance was thus delayed, some forty thousand of Warrington's men retired beyond the mountains, and began a roundabout march back toward New Boston. When Humbolt became exasperated at the delay and advanced again, the remaining men beat a prompt retreat across the plain, and made a determined stand at the mountain rim.

Humbolt lost several thousand men in vain and reckless charges up the barren slopes, with his flanks exposed to D-rays from the ridge. Twelve hours later, when he had surrounded the hill at the cost of much effort, he found that its defenders had slipped away, leaving the heavy ray-tubes that had brought down so many Tellurians.

Now his scouts saw men making a great show of fortifying a hill a few miles farther on—white clouds of smoke and dust were rising from trench-digging machines. The scouts were fired upon as they attempted to approach.

But that last hill—though Humbolt did not know it—was defended by only about two hundred men, who had been equipped with spacesuits. Their orders were to make as much show as possible, and to keep the Tellurians in their pursuit at all costs. Warrington, with the rest of the troops, was already between Humbolt and New Boston.

Meanwhile, squat, red-faced Jenkins arrived at the hiding place of our fleet with the most important message of the war. He brought our orders from Warrington for the final part of the war-fliers in the great campaign. We rose and proceeded directly to the city—the two crippled vessels had been repaired while we were on the ground. We landed again, a mile or so from the walls, and disembarked Lafollette and his men. They were to cooperate with Warrington in the surface operations, while we bombarded the city from above.

But those of us who had anticipated a thrilling action were disappointed. Warrington's and Lafollette's forces, drawn up in an iron ring about the walls, had a most formidable aspect. And our war-fliers alone might soon have erased the city from the map. Everything was planned to make a show of force.

The officer left in command of the city refused Warrington's offer of honorable surrender. The rain of D-ray batteries about the metropolis shot a few holes in the walls, and the fliers dropped a few atomic vortexes, which are almost more spectacular and terrifying than dangerous. When the troops of Lafollette and Warrington, drawn up in endless lines of white, started forward on the double-quick, with keen rays flashing from their ranks, the courage of the defenders collapsed, and the flags above the glistening towers signaled surrender.

The officer chose to yield his arms to Lafollette, and soon our friend from Earth was in charge of the city. The air locks were opened at once, and the troops admitted and set to work to help the citizens repair the damage done to the walls and roof.

The drums of barium bromides and chlorides were landed from the fleet, and a crew of men was set to work with the compressed air sprays to cover the walls with a protective film of the D-ray armor. It was nearly twenty-four hours to sunset when the city yielded. Ten hours later the breaks in the walls were repaired, and the coat of armor complete.

The work was hardly finished when Humbolt appeared. It seems that even then he did not suspect the trick. He had given up the campaign and returned to the city to take up night quarters, confident that the cold would finish Warrington and his men, whom he imagined to be entrenched out south of the city.

His astonishment must have been great when he saw the flag of the Lunar Corporation floating above the spires of the city; greater still when Warrington sent him a courteous note offering to accept his weapons.

He proceeded, in turn, to demand the surrender of New Boston. When his offer met a grave refusal, he arrayed his teeming white-clad ranks in endless lines about the city, while his lumbering tractors and tanks pulled a thousand field D-rays into position along the summit of Meteor Hill, and upon other heights beyond the glass walls. Finally his troops rushed forward in a grand assault, while the ray-tubes vomited a storm of polychromatic splendor.

A thousand jeweled rays fell upon the walls—and nothing happened.

The new armor was a complete success. Humbolt's spectacular gesture came to naught almost ludicrously, when he discovered that neither his huge batteries nor the hand weapons of his men had any effect upon the city's walls. And he, of course, was completely at the mercy of the weapons mounted along the walls.

Still he held out, with a lot of bluster, until the sun was near the cragged summits in the west, and already reddening in the mists of the lunar evening. The quick chill of the air seemed to chill his own ardor.

He sent a deputation of his officers through the airlock to arrange the details of the surrender. It was to be performed with all the traditional details of military ceremony. Our fleet hung low over the scene, fifteen great globes of silver, so that I had a splendid view. The Tellurians stacked their arms, and left them at the camp, for our men to pick up.

The first part of the ceremony had a curious accompaniment. From the fifteen low-riding war-fliers ten thousand lusty voices bellowed out the stirring bars of the anthem, "To Ye Lunar Hills

Ablaze," which had been written by Captain Thomas Dowling, of the Sirius—I am sure the heart of Valence, my pretty sister, would fairly have burst with pride, if she had been there, to hear the patriotic song her husband had written falling in a swelling rain of sound upon the army he had helped so bravely to defeat.

The airlock was opened, and the sunburned, ragged, half-starved troops of Warrington and Lafollette marched out to form two mile-long lines from the gate toward Humbolt's camp. With colors flying, and martial music playing, the splendidly uniformed Tellurians came marching in perfect step down the lane formed by their shabby conquerors, Humbolt, in all the glory of red coat and medals and glittering braid, stalking in the lead.

At the end of the lines Warrington and Lafollette were waiting. When Humbolt arrived, Warrington received his haughtily tendered hand ray and extended it to Lafollette, who courteously gave it back to the conquered general.

Then, because of the increasing chill of the air, all parties made a hasty entrance into the city. The people, who had been chafing for years under the military autocracy of Humbolt, welcomed Warrington and Lafollette with wild jubilation.

We landed the fleet at the great spaceport, which we found in excellent repair, with admirable facilities for caring for the fliers and making such adjustments as were needed after our recent action. I was soon within the glass walls of the city; as a young officer, I took part in the innumerable balls and banquets given in honor of the victors. But my heart was seldom with them. I thought only of the dark-eyed girl who was waiting for me in the little city far across the frozen lunar wastes.

CHAPTER TWENTY-FIVE
Peace

WITH the surrender of Humbolt and the annihilation of Von Thoren's fleet, the war came practically to an end. For a few months more there was scattered fighting, as Warrington crushed, one by one, the smaller fortified posts that the Tellurians had established about New Boston, while Hall waged a campaign that brought the rebellious Ka'Larbah once more to terms. Doane carried his space operations to complete victory in the capture of a few convoyed supply ships from Earth, sweeping the fliers of Metals from the space-lanes.

After the news of their two great disasters had been carried back to Pittsburgh, the officials of Metals Corporation could have had no serious idea of carrying the war on further. They expressed an immediate willingness to consider terms of peace.

A few months later, Gardiner and Lafollette met in Chicago with representatives of the Metals Corporation to discuss terms of peace. After a session of nearly three weeks, the Treaty of Chicago was signed. Its most important provision was the recognition of the complete independence of the moon. It conferred upon the Lunar Corporation complete freedom of trade with Earth, and liberty to govern the satellite as it might choose. Lafollette secured trade rights for Tranco, thus breaking the old monopoly of Metals in interplanetary commerce.

Late in the year (2330) Doane's fleet carried Humbolt and his men back to Earth, and returned with the aged Gardiner, who was triumphant over having secured a loan which would enable the crippled industries of the satellite to re-establish themselves. In a year, too, Lafollette was back on the moon, as the ambassador from Tranco.

The organization of the new government proceeded rapidly. Based upon new ideas, which assured liberty of the people from the tyranny either of selfish minority or of ignorant majority, it placed authority in the hands of those peculiarly fitted for it, and guaranteed equality of opportunity to all.

Warrington was almost unanimously chosen as the first president. On January 1, 2331, in a stately ceremony at Firecrest, he relinquished his military authority and accepted the civil leadership of the Lunar Corporation. I remember the event very clearly. It took place before the long white-clad ranks of the army, drawn up in splendid array before the main airlock, with the imposing scintillant walls of the city on either hand, and the swarthy monotony of the cragged lunar desert stretching away under the rays of a slanting sun to a cragged horizon beyond.

With a few quiet, simple words the old general pledged his devotion to his new responsibilities. Tears glistened in his eyes as he bade farewell to the officers and men who had served him so long and so nobly.

Then someone started to sing the inspiring anthem, "To Ye Lunar Hills Ablaze." All those near joined in with heartfelt fervor; then the army took it up. All our emotion found expression in a noble pean of victory and thanksgiving that rolled over the desert, fairly shaking the same lunar hills it celebrated.

Two years later the capitol was moved from Firecrest to the new city, named Warrington in honor of the great commander, built on the former site of Kurrukwarruk, with its advantageous central location.

But during that time, all those things were not my chief concern. As soon as possible after Humbolt's surrender, I gave up my commission and hurried back to Firecrest. I was aboard the Sirius—by some wire pulling, Captain Tom had arranged to have his ship stationed there.

As the silver ring of the city's gleaming walls rose over the grim rugged wilderness ahead of our speeding flier, I vowed that I would never willingly leave it again. And though fifty years have passed since that time, I have in the main kept my vow pretty well.

Leroda, slender, and freckled a little from long days of sunshine, was waiting to meet me at the airlock. Hand in hand, happy and joyous as two children, we walked through the great metal valve and strolled together down warm bright streets with vivid, fragrant plants. It was a long time until we came to the central tower building, where Mother and Father were waiting.

Valence, with her sunburned, brown-haired Tom Junior, had been waiting to take possession of the eager Captain Dowling.

On January 1, the same day that Warrington was inaugurated into the duties of president, Leroda and I were married. The ceremony was quiet and simple, with only a few friends present. It was just after the inauguration, and Warrington and Gardiner had been able to come up, to offer their wishes for our happiness.

A few days later—we had spent our honeymoon simply at Firecrest, both feeling that we had enjoyed enough of travel—Gardiner pressed me into service again as a laboratory assistant. He was still working on his old dream of ether communication with Earth. Despite his age and failing strength, he devoted himself to the problem with remarkable energy. Two years later he had designed a short-wave transmitter that successfully penetrated the Heaviside layer. By the time of the old scientist's death, several years later, he had brought Earth and moon together with the bond of perfected radio-television communication.

DURING the past fifty years, intercourse has progressed marvelously in a score of ways. To Gardiner's radio-television was soon added Hamlin's new atomic attractor, which quickly antiquated the old atomic blast. Now great liners make the trip from Earth to moon in four days, with a comfort and safety to the passengers that seems wonderful in comparison with the hardship and danger of flight on the slow and clumsy ships of my youth.

Better communication has done much to foster cordial relations with the Earth. The moon has been freely admitted to the brotherhood of corporations, and her citizens are received with respect and friendship in every city of the Earth.

Good feeling with Earth has done much to build up the moon. The tide of immigration was soon flowing again. Our world has increased vastly in population, in industry, in commerce. The number of incorporated cities has increased from thirteen to forty—Firecrest was admitted to the Lunar Corporation as a sovereign city in 2321. Now, in addition to the broad roads that bind those cities together, they are united by the new vacuum tubeways.

The exploration and development of the moon have gone on by leaps and bounds. Now most of her farther side is well known, and miners and farmers are steadily pushing civilization forward, against the vanishing race of Selenites. It is thirty years now, since chubby, red Jenkins visited me last at Firecrest. In vain I tried to persuade the old scout to settle down there and spend his last days in peace. He showed me a few grains of radium in a leaden tube, whispered to me of a great strike rumored far beyond the Hercynian Mountains on the borders of the moon. He left me, with a last grip of his sunburned hand—which was not so firm as it once had been. Upon scarlet old M'Ob, he went leaping away, into the unknown wilderness beyond "the rim."

He never came back.

THE BIRTH OF A NEW REPUBLIC

During these last forty years, the exploration of the other planets has gone forward swiftly. In 2340 an expedition from Earth visited the cloudy world of Venus. Three years later, Paul Doane led a fleet of three new fliers from Firecrest on a voyage of discovery to the red planet Mars—what he found there is no part of my tale.

Mercury, several of the larger asteroids, and Jupiter were soon reached, and each has been partially explored for minerals. In the past twenty years colonies have been established on Pallas, and on Callisto, one of Jupiter's moons. And the fleets of wandering ships that frequent the planetoid belt, mining those tiny rocky worlds of their precious minerals, have been the crescendo of all adventurous youth for the last quarter of a century.

In the year that I write, an expedition is setting out for ringed Saturn, upon which no man has yet set foot. It is a source of pride, as well as of anxiety, to me that my grandson, another John Adams, who is as fine a young man as I know, is to command one of the four ships.

I am an old man now—there is no escaping that. Leroda and I have lived together for fifty happy years. The Firecrest mines are now among the greatest on the moon, but I have relinquished the management of them to my son. Now, from the eminence of a long life that has been for the most part peaceful and happy, I can foresee for my children a glorious United Solar System.

THE END

If you've enjoyed this book, you will not want to miss these terrific titles…

ARMCHAIR SCI-FI & HORROR DOUBLE NOVELS, $12.95 each

- **D-251** **THE BEAST WITH SEVEN TAILS** Robert Silverberg & Randall Garrett
  THE WRECK OF THE ASTEROID by Laurence Manning

- **D-252** **THE RED DEATH** by David H. Keller, M.D.
  LUNARCHIA by Emerson B. Hartman

- **D-253** **LORD OF THE LAMIA** by Otis Adelbert Kline
  THE WAR OF THE UNIVERSE by Clinton Constantinescu

- **D-254** **DARK INVASION** by Frederic A. Kummer, Jr.
  MYSTERY MOON by Edmond Hamilton

- **D-255** **BEYOND THE STRATOSPHERE** by William Lemkin
  CRYPT-CITY OF THE DEATHLESS ONE by Henry Kuttner

- **D-256** **TOMORROW** by John Taine
  MARTIAN AND TROGLODITE by Neil R. Jones

- **D-257** **A MAN NAMED MARS** by Rog Phillips
  MISSION TO MARAKEE by Bryan Berry

- **D-258** **VOYAGE INTO THE LIGHTNING** by Robert Moore Williams
  THE COLORS OF SPACE By Marion Zimmer bradley

- **D-259** **THE BAT-MEN OF MARS** by Wood Jackson
  HE WHO SHRANK by Henry Hasse

- **D-260** **THE WAR-NYMPHS OF VENUS** by Ray Cummings
  SPACE PRISON by Tom Godwin

ARMCHAIR SCIENCE FICTION CLASSICS, $12.95 each

- **C-87** **THUS FAR**
  by J. C. Snaith

- **C-88** **BIRTH OF A NEW REPUBLIC**
  by Jack Williamson & Miles J. Breuer

- **C-89** **THE RADIO BEASTS**
  by Ralph Milne farley

ARMCHAIR SCI-FI & HORROR GEMS SERIES, $12.95 each

- **G-35** **SCIENCE FICTION GEMS, Vol. Eighteen**
  Frank Belknap Long and others

- **G-36** **HORROR GEMS, Vol. Eighteen**
  Paul Ernst and others

If you've enjoyed this book, you will not want to miss these terrific titles…

ARMCHAIR SCI-FI & HORROR DOUBLE NOVELS, $12.95 each

D-231   **THE TRANSPOSED MAN** by Dwight V. Swain
PLANET OF DOOMED MEN by Robert Moore Williams

D-232   **NEWSHOUND, 2103 A. D.** by Milton Lesser
ZERO, A. D. by Robert Wade

D-233   **SPACE-ROCKET MURDERS** by Edmond Hamilton
D-99 by H. B. Fyfe

D-234   **EXPLORERS INTO INFINITY** by Ray Cummings
DESIGN FOR DOOMSDAY by Bryce Walton

D-235   **LAST CALL FROM SECTOR 9G** by Leigh Brackett
TIME CRIME by H. Beam Piper

D-236   **SCYLLA'S DAUGHTER** by Fritz Leiber
TERRORS OF ARELLI by Aladra Septama

D-237   **FURLOUGH FROM ETERNITY** by David Wright O'Brien
INVASION OF THE PLANT MEN by Berkeley Livingston

D-238   **THE SUN-SMITHS** by Richard S. Shaver
THE OPPOSITE FACTOR by Chester S. Geier

D-239   **THE EXILE OF THE SKIES** by Richard Vaughan
ABDUCTION by Steve Frazee

D-240   **BEYOND THE WALLS OF SPACE** by S.M. Tenneshaw
SECRET OF THE NINTH PLANET by Donald A. Wollheim

ARMCHAIR MASTERS OF SCIENCE FICTION SERIES, $16.95 each

MS-13   **MASTERS OF SCIENCE FICTION, Vol. Thirteen**
Robert Silverberg, The Ace Years, Part Three

MS-14   **MASTERS OF SCIENCE FICTION, Vol. Fourteen**
H.G. Wells, The Amazing Stories Collection, Ultimate Illustrated Edition

ARMCHAIR MYSTERY-CRIME DOUBLE NOVELS, $12.95 each

B-45   **NIGHTSHADE** by John N. Macriss
ONCE IS ENOUGH by David Wright O'Brien

B-46   **NAKED FURY** by Day Keene
MURDER IN BARACOA by Paul E. Walsh

B-47   **FRENZY** by James O. Causey
IN THIS CORNER—DEATH! by Emile C. Tepperman

If you've enjoyed this book, you will not want to miss these terrific titles…

ARMCHAIR LOST WORLD-LOST RACE CLASSICS, $12.95 each

B-48   **THE DRUMS OF TAPAJOS, Illustrated Edition**
by S. P. Meek

B-49   **THE TEMPLE OF FIRE, Illustrated Edition**
by Fred Ashley

B-50   **THE FACE IN THE ABYSS, and other Fantastic Tales, Illus. Ed.**
by A. Merritt

B-51   **INLAND DEEP, Illustrated Edition**
by Richard Tooker

B-52   **THE SILVER GOD OF THE ORANG HUTAN, Illustrated Edition**
by David Douglas

B-53   **THE KING OF THE DEAD**
by Frank Aubrey

B-54   **THE BOATS OF THE GLEN CARRIG, Illustrated Edition**
by William Hope Hodgson

B-55   **THE SECRET OF THE EARTH**
by Charles Willing Beale

B-56   **THE WORLD OF THE GIANT ANTS, Illustrated Edition**
by A. Hyatt Verrill

B-57   **PHALANXES OF ATLANS, Illustrated Edition**
by F. Van Wyck Mason

ARMCHAIR CLASSICS OF SCIENCE FICTION SERIES, $12.95 each

C-80   **OPERATION: OUTER SPACE**
by Murray Leinster

C-81   **THE FIRE PEOPLE, Special Illustrated Edition**
by Ray Cummings

C-82   **THE BLACK STAR PASSES, Special Illustrated Edition**
by John W. Campbell

ARMCHAIR SCI-FI & HORROR GEMS SERIES, $12.95 each

G-29   **SCIENCE FICTION GEMS, Vol. Fifteen**
Milton Lesser and others

G-30   **HORROR GEMS, Vol. Fifteen**
Henry Kuttner and others

If you've enjoyed this book, you will not want to miss these terrific titles...

ARMCHAIR SEXPLOITATION CLASSICS, $9.95 each

- **SC-1**   **SHE TRIED TO BE GOOD**
  by Florence Stonebraker

- **SC-2**   **RENO TRAMP**
  by Florence Stonebraker

- **SC-3**   **THREE MEN AND A MISTRESS**
  by Florence Stonebraker

- **SC-4**   **FLESH IS WEAK**
  by Florence Stonebraker

- **SC-5**   **LOCAL TALENT**
  by Florence Stonebraker

ARMCHAIR MAMMOTH MYSTERY DOUBLE NOVELS, $16.95 each

Mammoth Mystery Doubles are all illustrated editions with over 440 pages,

- **MM-1**   **THE WINDOW AT THE WHITE CAT** by Mary Roberts Rinehart
  THE MAN IN LOWER TEN by Mary Roberts Rinehart

- **MM-2**   **THE GREEN RUST** by Edgar Wallace
  THE CLUE OF THE TWISTED CANDLE by Edgar Wallace

- **MM-3**   **THE BLACK GANG** by H. C. "Sapper" McNeile
  ALIAS THE LONE WOLF by Louis Joseph Vance

- **MM-4**   **THE VOICE FROM THE VOID** by William Le Queux
  THE MIDDLE TEMPLE MURDER by J. S. Fletcher

- **MM-5**   **THE MYSTERIOUS AFFAIR AT STYLES** by Agatha Christie
  THE SECRET ADVERSARY by Agatha Christie

ARMCHAIR SCI-FI & HORROR GEMS SERIES, $12.95 each

- **G-32**   **HORROR GEMS, Vol. Sixteen**
  The Best of Weird Tales, 1923, Pt. One

- **G-34**   **HORROR GEMS, Vol. Seventeen**
  The Best of Weird Tales, 1923, Pt. Two

If you've enjoyed this book, you will not want to miss these terrific titles...

ARMCHAIR SCI-FI & HORROR DOUBLE NOVELS, $12.95 each

- **D-241**   **THE LAKE OF LIFE** by Edmond Hamilton
  MARTIAN ADVENTURE by Robert Moore Williams
- **D-242**   **THE BATTERY OF HATE** by John W. Campbell
  TREASURE OF THE GOLDEN GOD by A. Hyatt Verrill
- **D-243**   **BIDDY AND THE SILVER MAN** by E. K. Jarvis
  FOUR-DAY PLANET by H. Beam Piper
- **D-244**   **THE POWER PLANET** by Murray Leinster
  SWORDSMAN OF SARVON, THE by Charles Cloukey
- **D-245**   **THE SCARLET SAINT** by Manly Banister
  THE MAN FROM SATURN by Harriet Frank
- **D-246**   **THE COLOSSUS CONCLUSION** by S. J. Byrne
  THE MENTAL ASSASSINS by Rog Phillips
- **D-247**   **RULERS OF THE FUTURE** by Paul Ernst
  PURSUIT by Lester del Rey
- **D-248**   **WORLD WITHOUT MEN** by Charles Eric Maine
  THE SYNTHETIC MEN by Ed Earl Repp
- **D-249**   **CITADEL OF THE GREEN DEATH** by Emmett McDowell
  DRUMMERS OF DAUGAVO by Dwight V. Swain
- **D-250**   **ACT OF GOD** by Richard Ashby
  THE CHEMICALLY PURE WARRIORS by Allen Kim Lang

ARMCHAIR SCI-FI & HORROR GEMS SERIES, $12.95 each

- **G-31**   **SCIENCE FICTION GEMS, Volume Sixteen**
  L. Sprague de Camp and others
- **G-33**   **SCIENCE FICTION GEMS, Volume Seventeen**
  Raymond Z. Gallun and others

ARMCHAIR MYSTERY-CRIME DOUBLE NOVELS, $12.95 each

- **B-58**   **FIND EILEEN HARDIN—ALIVE!** by Stephen Marlowe
  MURDER ON THE MAKE by Robert Martin
- **B-59**   **SOMEBODY WANTS YOU DEAD** by Robert Moore Williams
  THE BLACK KEY by M. Scott Michel
- **B-60**   **SCREAM STREET** by Mike Brett
  MURDER MAKES THE CORPSE by Sean Gregory
- **B-61**   **MY FLESH IS SWEET** by Day Keene
  THE MORTGAGE LOAN MURDERS by Francis M. Deegan

If you've enjoyed this book, you will not want to miss these terrific titles…

ARMCHAIR LOST WORLD-LOST RACE CLASSICS, $12.95 each

B-74 **THE LAND OF THE LOST, Illustrated Edition**
by Roy Norton

B-75 **THE GREAT STONE OF SARDIS**
By Frank R. Stockton

B-76 **TROYANA, Illustrated Edition**
By S. P. Meek

B-77 **THE GOLDEN FETICH**
by Eden Phillpotts

B-78 **THE GLYPHS**
by Roy Norton

B-79 **THE DEVIL-TREE OF EL DORADO, Illustrated Edition**
By Frank Aubrey

ARMCHAIR MASTERS OF HORROR SERIES, $16.95 each

MS-11 **MASTERS OF HORROR Vol. One**
Allison V. Harding: The Forgotten Queen of Horror

MS-12 **MASTERS OF SCIENCE FICTION, Vol. Twelve**
H. P. Lovecraft: The Ultimate Illustrated *Weird Tales* Collection, Pt. 1

ARMCHAIR SCIENCE FICTION CLASSICS, $12.95 each

C-83 **THE SHAVER MYSTERY, Book Eight**
by Richard S. Shaver

C-84 **VENUS LIBERATED**
by Harl Vincent

C-85 **RECLAIMERS OF THE ICE**
by Stanton A. Coblentz

C-86 **FIRST HE DIED (aka TIME QUARRY)**
by Clifford D. Simak

ARMCHAIR SCI-FI & HORROR GEMS SERIES, $12.95 each

G-35 **SCIENCE FICTION GEMS, Vol. Eighteen**
Henry Slesar and others

G-36 **HORROR GEMS, Vol. Eighteen**
Paul Ernst and others

If you've enjoyed this book, you will not want to miss these terrific titles…

ARMCHAIR MYSTERY-CRIME CLASSICS, $12.95 each

- **B-62**   **MURDER HAS MANY FACES**
  by William O'Farrell

- **B-63**   **A TIME FOR MURDER**
  by Milton Ozaki

- **B-64**   **MURDER CLEAR, TRACK FAST**
  by Judson Philips

- **B-65**   **MURDER'S END**
  by Robert Kelston

- **B-66**   **THE CROOKED CIRCLE**
  by Manning Lee Stokes

- **B-67**   **MAN BAIT**
  by Jack Liston

- **B-68**   **BODY FOR SALE**
  by Richard Deming

- **B-69**   **THE DECOY**
  by Edward Ronns

- **B-70**   **TOO HOT TO HANDLE**
  by Frank G. Presnell

- **B-71**   **EMPIRE OF EVIL**
  by Sterling Noel

- **B-72**   **THE JUDAS HOUR**
  by E. Howard Hunt

- **B-73**   **THE CROOKED CITY**
  by Robert Kyle

ARMCHAIR SCIENCE FICTION CLASSICS, $12.95 each

- **C-83**   **THE SHAVER MYSTERY, Book Eight**
  by Richard S. Shaver

- **C-84**   **VENUS LIBERATED**
  by Harl Vincent

- **C-85**   **RECLAIMERS OF THE ICE**
  by Stanton A. Coblentz

- **C-86**   **TIME QUARRY**
  by Clifford D. Simak